ACCLAIM FOR CHANTAL V. JOHNSON'S
POST-TRAUMATIC

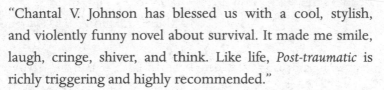

"Chantal V. Johnson has blessed us with a cool, stylish, and violently funny novel about survival. It made me smile, laugh, cringe, shiver, and think. Like life, *Post-traumatic* is richly triggering and highly recommended."

—Myriam Gurba, author of *Mean*

"This sharp psychological novel tracks the obsessive ruminations of an attorney at a New York City psychiatric hospital named Vivian, who is 'the only upwardly mobile person' in her black Puerto Rican family...As Vivian's behavior increasingly contradicts her own intellectual convictions, a series of minor disasters prompts her to reconsider her need for control."

—*The New Yorker*

"Stunning and riotous, *Post-traumatic* took me right under and then revived me, like only the best fiction can do. Johnson's delicious, meticulous prose delivers such intimacy and hilarity on the page, I laughed and cried all the way through. This is a raw, brilliant, and unforgettable debut. I love everything about it!"

—Deesha Philyaw, author of the National Book Award finalist *The Secret Lives of Church Ladies*

"*Post-traumatic* is the deepest literary dive yet into the psychology of the messy black girl, and perhaps the most complex due to its granular representation of the somatic effects of trauma…The power of Johnson's novel is the way in which it makes the reader complicit in Vivian's fantasies, even when they cause destruction within and around her…*Post-traumatic* has opened up a space for error and ugliness that black women are seldom afforded in real life, and the book beguiles the reader into loving her in spite of her mess."

—Marina Magloire, *The Nation*

"*Post-traumatic* is swift, caustic, charismatic, beautiful, terrifying, and so incredibly funny. It learns and unlearns itself continually, propelled by a restless main character whose gaze withers the world, the reader, and more achingly, herself. Johnson composes such precise, pathologically consumable prose that I couldn't stop reading, even if it was the way I'd watch a scary movie: through my fingers."

—Tommy Pico, author of *IRL* and *Junk*

"*Post-traumatic*'s Vivian is one of the most fascinating characters I've read in contemporary fiction: self-aware and lost, cutting and wounded, resilient and vulnerable—all those misfit bits that add up to the whole of a real human being. And Chantal V. Johnson writes her with a startling intimacy that makes reading feel like an illicit thrill."

—Dawnie Walton, author of *The Final Revival of Opal & Nev*

"Original and darkly hilarious. Johnson taps into the psyche of the modern trauma and enlightens readers via one of the most memorable characters of the year."

—Adam Vitcavage, *Debutiful*

"Chantal V. Johnson is a brilliant documentarian of the unstable. She writes with a forensic and unsentimental sense of justice, in sentences that spark with life."

—Vanessa Veselka, author of *The Great Offshore Grounds*

"*Post-traumatic* is astonishingly funny, intimately neurotic, and so honest and necessary that I can't stop thinking about it. From the first sentence, we are thrust into the hyperawareness of a character whose boundless vigilance makes us feel like both observer and observed. Johnson's attention to detail is so salient that it's simultaneously shocking and familiar. This book is a mirror I couldn't put down."

—Jill Louise Busby, author of *Unfollow Me*

"With searing intelligence, wicked humor, and an utterly captivating heroine, this brilliant debut shows us what it means to live with, and beyond, trauma. I felt such kinship with Vivian that I sometimes felt like Johnson was reading my mind."

—Jessamine Chan, author of *The School for Good Mothers*

"The deep anxieties that permeate *Post-traumatic* are the other side of the class ascendency that many millennials of color navigate as we square our routinely chaotic lives with memories of go-go '80s and '90s years that instilled in us implausible fantasies of 'the good life.'"

—*Vulture* (Most Anticipated Books of Spring)

"A brutally funny and poignant debut...Dark humor is another coping mechanism for Vivian, which Johnson deploys with tremendous skill...Throughout, Vivian's confrontational interactions feel achingly true to life. This is revelatory and powerful." —*Publishers Weekly* (starred review)

"A sardonic, searching novel...Her singular musings—on dieting, dating, and self-medication—entertain and enlighten." —*Oprah Daily*

"I stayed up until 7 a.m. reading this book, and I feel as though the top of my head has been taken off, in a good way. *Post-traumatic* is a wildly perceptive, sharp, often very funny novel about trauma and surviving." —R. O. Kwon, author of *The Incendiaries*

"Highly readable...*Post-traumatic* reveals sociopolitical rot by way of one woman's crack-up. We are living in a moment of cultural backlash—against feminist politics, against Me Too and other indictments of rape culture. In writing a character and a novel with such careful nuance, Johnson makes it clear that these issues have never been cut-and-dried. 'Ambiguity,' muses Vivian, 'was horrifying in real life.' Yet it is ambiguity that gives *Post-traumatic* its power." —Jamie Hood, *Vulture*

POST-TRAUMATIC

A Novel

Chantal V. Johnson

BACK BAY BOOKS

Little, Brown and Company

New York Boston London

Back Bay Books / Little, Brown and Company
Hachette Book Group
1290 Avenue of the Americas, New York, NY 10104
littlebrown.com

Originally published in hardcover by Little, Brown and Company, April 2022
First Back Bay paperback edition, March 2023

Back Bay Books is an imprint of Little, Brown and Company, a division of Hachette Book Group, Inc. The Back Bay Books name and logo are trademarks of Hachette Book Group, Inc.

The publisher is not responsible for websites (or their content) that are not owned by the publisher.

The Hachette Speakers Bureau provides a wide range of authors for speaking events. To find out more, go to hachettespeakersbureau.com or email HachetteSpeakers@hbgusa.com.

ISBN 9780316264235 (hc) / 9780316264334 (pb)
Library of Congress Control Number: 2021945961

Printing 2, 2023

LSC-C

Printed in the United States of America

POST-TRAUMATIC

THE KNIFE

IT WAS THE new nurse's fault. She brought a butcher knife onto the children's ward to cut up watermelon for the kids as a treat. She set it down for a couple of seconds to hand Nicole a plate and before you knew it, Melissa was threatening the other girls with it. The new nurse wanted to prove herself, so instead of getting a more experienced de-escalator involved she scolded Melissa, demanding that she "give back the knife," while holding out her hand to take it. It was basically an invitation. Melissa accepted, slashing the nurse's open palm. As the nurse looked down in shock, Melissa ran to her room, where, after slamming the door shut, she proceeded to slice open both of the mattresses while screaming with rage at the pain of having been born.

Vivian was in the dayroom down the hall speaking to her new client, Anthony, when she heard the screams. It was just past eleven a.m. and, as usual, she hadn't slept well the night before. She had a joke about it. "I haven't slept well in twenty-five years." The person she was speaking to would laugh in the moment. Later they'd wonder what had happened twenty-five years ago.

Anthony was a tall, lanky black kid, no more than fifteen. The cops had brought him to the hospital after he'd flashed a couple of women in the park. It seemed he lived on the streets but didn't want to talk about his family or give any identifying information other than his name. Vivian was giving him her spiel about his rights in the hospital. She was his state-appointed attorney, it was her job to try and get him out, and everything he told her was confidential. Anthony scanned the dayroom as she spoke and fixated on another male patient who was watching TV.

"You all right?" Vivian asked.

"That dude, man, he keeps looking at me, man. I think he might be gay or something."

Vivian suggested that they move into the hallway. It didn't work. Now Anthony alternated between intensely looking at Vivian, absentmindedly touching his crotch, and scanning the hall, eyeing every passing boy suspiciously. He was telling Vivian that he didn't want to take any meds when the screams started. She recognized Melissa's voice immediately. Anthony laughed.

"This place is crazy, man," he said.

Vivian turned and jogged toward the noise, passed the empty nurses' station, and arrived at a small crowd of nurses, psych techs, and mental health patients ranging in age from seven to fifteen gathered outside the closed door to Melissa's room. The human survival instinct was no match for morbid curiosity.

Carl, the towering head psych tech, told Vivian what had happened and advised her to stand back as he moved into position outside the door. From here, Carl and some other techs would rush in, tackle the ninety-pound girl and inject her with haloperidol before putting her into four-point restraints in the seclusion room.

"Newbies always underestimate the risk of violence on the children's ward," Vivian said with a laugh.

Carl laughed back. He liked Vivian, he'd told her weeks before, because she didn't walk around all scared like most of the other lawyers. That, and she resembled his favorite aunt. She prepared to use this to her advantage as she stepped up next to him and listened by the door. She raised her index finger, calling for patience and quiet. The breathing and rustling suggested Melissa was on the opposite end of the room, near the window.

Before Carl could object, Vivian opened the door a crack and slipped through, gently closing it while stooping reflexively to pick up a pillow that had been spared Melissa's wrath. Vivian stood up quickly, holding it in front of her abdomen for protection.

"Melissa," she said softly.

Melissa spun around with the knife in her hand, sweaty and crazed. She was only ten feet away, a distance she could close quickly if provoked.

"Carl," Vivian said to the door while maintaining eye contact with Melissa. "I'm in here with Melissa. She's not a danger to anyone and she's going to do the right thing."

Relief flashed in Melissa's brown eyes. She was a small dark-skinned girl wearing a bone-straight jet-black weave with a middle part. Sharp cheekbones. She wore street clothes—black jeans and a white tank top that showed off her muscular arms. Beautiful and tough.

It was clear that Melissa's mind was clicking. The consequences of her irrational act were sinking in but she tried not to break, twisting her face to look menacing. She took two steps toward Vivian with the knife and called her a "Legal Aid bitch."

Vivian didn't flinch. She looked at Melissa calmly, as if she were sitting by a lake in summer. Melissa took another step. Vivian continued her patient stare. Seconds later, Melissa's aggression dissolved. Behind it, fear. The hand that held the knife was shaking now. Without breaking eye contact, Vivian walked over, reached out, and took the knife, bloody and matted with the cheap cotton insides of the mattresses. Melissa did not resist. Vivian turned her back to Melissa and walked out of the room sure that there would be no further violence. She handed the knife to Carl without changing her face.

Then, as she walked down the hall, through the locked set of double doors marked in bold with the words ELOPEMENT RISK, she lost the ability to detect individual sounds. Her body began to send out distress signals. With every step, sharp spasms traveled from the right side of her back all the way down her leg.

She had a sensation that she was being filmed. The camera recorded two selves: a self that was limping and wearing a face of cheerless efficiency, and an identical self, defensively crouched and shaking against the wall, watching the other struggle to walk. Whether the quaking entity was from the past or the future Vivian couldn't say. She knew only that the entity was terrified, huddled up against the wall, looking up at her with her own face. The form remained there, a witnessing presence, until Vivian was safely in her office with the door closed. She realized she was shaking. Her nipples were erect. Removing her pointy-toed flats, she saw that her feet were pale and her toes had turned blue. It was as if she had been barefoot in the snow.

"I don't fuck with carbs," the man on the street said with a laugh, when a well-meaning white woman had expected him to devour a half-eaten bagel with frantic appreciation.

Vivian smiled. *Whoever said beggars can't be choosers has never experienced the glorious recalcitrance of the New York City homeless*, she thought.

She wondered whether that was the kind of joke she could successfully tell on a date. The date would have to know the meaning of *recalcitrance*. She wouldn't want to say *obstinacy*, and *stubbornness* didn't sound right.

It was early September but still sticky in the city. She had just left the hospital for the weekend. Her headache indicated that she had only an hour before she would faint from not eating, so she walked toward CVS to buy something to eat on the way to Jane's.

While walking, Vivian caught her reflection wherever she could. She was smaller now than she'd been in a year, but not as small as she was last spring, when her doctor, treating her for muscle spasms, had joked that her body mass index of nineteen was almost worrisome.

"Eighteen point five is an eating disorder, all right?" he'd said, laughing to establish rapport.

"Oh, don't worry. I'm too addicted to control to be addicted to anything else," she'd responded, laughing back, "including diet and exercise." She'd rehearsed the rhythmically interesting one-liner before the appointment. Her doctor was visibly uncomfortable, as many people were when she spoke to them directly.

Now it was happening again: her breasts weren't filling

out her bra completely. When Vivian was alone at night, she lifted her tank top and looked at them, extending her bottom lip like a kid peering down at something, pleased with the growing gap between breast and bra. Her nipples seemed to be pointing forward, as they should be, for the first time in a long time.

Vivian walked past a beautiful thin woman, *Persian-looking*, she thought, and cringed at this microsecond of mental laziness that made her feel like a white person. The woman's ethnicity was in fact indeterminate, and she had the same sandy brown complexion as Vivian. She wore heavy black eyeliner and a soft matte lipstick in mauve. No fat could be seen through her cream-colored bodycon dress and Vivian suspected shapewear. She was talking on the phone and held a black bag in the crook of her arm with her wrist limp. Whether a woman did this while looking annoyed, bored, or harried, it made Vivian smile. She appreciated it as a canonical gesture.

The woman scanned Vivian up and down, assessing her brown legs. She did not smile back. Her gaze was almost accusatory, *as if*, Vivian thought, *I were a lesbian. As if*, Vivian corrected herself, *I were eroticizing her. As if*, Vivian corrected herself again, *she had caught me desiring her.* Yes. That was the purest articulation of what had just occurred.

(Vivian grew up in a house where it was important not to say the wrong thing and she'd been editing her thoughts for precision ever since she was a child. Finding the right way to phrase something was as soothing to her then as a stuffed animal was to others, and in fact the closest thing she'd had to a transitional object was a copy of *The Must Words*, described as "a collection of 6,000 essential words to help you enrich your vocabulary.")

After the woman in the bodycon dress passed, Vivian felt a chill and thought again of Paula, a psychologist she'd met last year at a conference. They'd been on a panel together ("On The Uses And Abuses of Psychiatry") and Vivian returned to their encounter with embarrassing regularity.

Paula had delivered an intellectually unadventurous talk on rates of adverse childhood experiences in the acute care setting, while Vivian had electrified the conference room (if she said so herself) with her paper on "sanism"—an implicit bias against people with mental illnesses based on false assumptions (that they are dangerous; that their conditions are immutable; that they are incapable of self-governance). During the Q&A, all the questions were for Vivian, and she noticed Paula shifting in her seat, stealing glances at Vivian's body as she spoke.

After the event, over drinks at a nearby bar, Paula kept commenting on Vivian's appearance and that of every woman in the bar, doling out awards for smallness and symmetry. When Vivian finally objected, playfully referring to Paula as a human panopticon, Paula countered with her retrograde theory that judging other women was "biological."

According to Paula, women were evolutionarily designed to calculate their relative value to secure a mate. "We all compare and compete with each other! It's natural and harmless."

It was an infuriating explanation. It made Vivian feel like a dumb animal, defenseless and prerational. And so Vivian responded with a lecture, arguing that whenever women evaluated each other's appearance—whether "her ashy elbows," or "her perfect bikini body"—they were committing moral crimes, participating in the disciplinary project of controlling women's bodies. These comments, though seemingly harmless in themselves, were corrosive to womankind in the aggregate, as they contributed to women equating their social value with their bodies, leading them to confuse a smooth, toned, dimpleless exterior with inner perfection, purity, or worthiness of love. But this was a fallacy, ergo, by making these comments, whether positive or negative, one was committing the most unethical, unfeminist act possible: reducing women back to their bodies, increasing their pain, and making them stupid.

"And they do it to me every day!" Vivian had said. On the subway, a woman's eyes would bounce around the packed car as if following the jerky flight pattern of a moth, until finally settling on Vivian's body. In the entrance to her gynecologist's office, an administrative assistant would inspect her between sips of her morning coffee, using Vivian's body shape and clothing choices to figure out what kind of black person she was while she struggled to close a cheap umbrella. When, in a comic mood, Vivian performed an impression that required exaggerated gestures, another woman's gaze was there, dragging her back into self-consciousness. Regularly she caught them staring at the smudge of dirt on her white Keds or her intentionally unwaxed mustache or her emerging gray hairs, as if their judgment mattered at all, as if it were remotely interesting or correct.

"Competition among women," Vivian concluded, with a haughty air, "is a dangerous waste of our time. We should opt out of it entirely."

It was a masterful argument—very Julia Sugarbaker; very

Norma Rae. But Paula was unmoved. In fact, she'd taken Vivian's monologue as an opportunity to free her hair from the elaborate bun she'd worn for the panel, painstakingly searching out and placing a dozen bobby pins down on the table in front of them to reveal irritatingly long brown locks which instantly transformed her from a decidedly plain-looking person to a moderately alluring one, and she seemed to know this, running her fingers through the endless hair now almost mockingly.

"You're talking about what women should do," Paula said. "I'm talking about what women actually do. It's just not clear to me that women can opt out, like you say. For example, you aren't opting out. I noticed you looking at my body earlier, while I walked onto the stage."

It was true. Vivian had done that. She'd studied Paula's body and felt better about herself for being smaller, by about ten pounds, she guessed, with a more attractive silhouette. To have been caught in this surreptitious comparison was embarrassing.

Then, Paula had taken her by the shoulders. "I hate to break it to you, girl," she said, "but you're one of us." And she laughed and went to the bar to get another drink, leaving Vivian standing there, unable to respond.

Now, as she reached the corner, Vivian turned around and scrutinized the woman in the bodycon dress like Paula had known she would. The order of events was always the same: first, the up-and-down eye flicker, assessing overall shape and sense of style. Next, a consideration of whether the woman's breasts sat higher than her own (they did), and whether she had the workout-resistant lower-abdomen pouch that greets women at the threshold of midlife (not yet). The bulk of

Vivian's attention, however, was on the woman's bottom half. Vivian had the broad, lumpy backside of a childbearer while this woman had a perfect one, *like an upside-down heart,* Vivian thought. She tuned back into the sensory world just in time to avoid stepping into a pothole and she put her hand on her rapidly beating heart and laughed.

Years of heavy traffic combined with ordinary wear and tear had cratered the streets of New York, and a decade ago the city had added bike lanes. A pedestrian had to be on alert for threats from every direction. Would a left-turning car hit her, or would it be a zippy delivery bike racing to fulfill an online order? Traveling through a city soundscape made up of horns of varying intensities and durations, engines, whistles, and voices, she made it to Fourteenth Street. She watched a couple walk in sync until they no longer walked in sync, feeling a vague unvocalizable pain as she headed into CVS.

<hr />

There was no longer any pleasure in eating; it was merely something she did to survive. When shopping for food, as in other areas of life, it was important not to make a mistake. So she took her time, picking up food products and turning them over, scanning the nutrition facts. Gluten-free popcorn contained fifty calories for every two cups; one large rice cake: sixty calories. Did she want portion control? If so, there were almonds, crackers, and "cookie crisps" sold in individual one-hundred-calorie packs, or she could get a Cheerios cereal cup. How about something sweet with high water content? Grapes, maybe, or a banana. No, she remembered—too many carbs. She crouched wearily by a row of protein bars, irritated by the sugar count. When she stood up, no closer to being able to decide, she was dizzy and nauseated and her breathing was shallow.

Suddenly an affable-looking black guy shelving cat food inserted himself into her life, saying she looked like a model. The only things more oppressive than the eyes of an insecure woman were the eyes of an undesired man. She smiled through malice, thinking she had an ugly face and would have to be at least ten pounds lighter for it to be even remotely true that she looked like a model.

"Ha. Yeah right."

"You okay, though, sis?"

"I'm fine," she snapped.

"I never seen anyone take thirty minutes to pick a snack, though," he said, laughing lightheartedly.

Had it been thirty minutes?

Embarrassed, she quickly grabbed a bag of roasted reduced-salt cashews, a low-carb high-protein venison bar, a twenty-ounce bottle of lemonade-flavored Vitaminwater Zero, and an unsweetened iced green tea containing epigallo-catechin gallate (an antioxidant associated with weight loss) and got in the line, which snaked back toward the photo center and was not moving.

There was a problem with one of the credit card machines that required managerial assistance. To her left, an obnoxious row of Thanksgiving décor: decorative plastic gourds, fake cornstalks, paper plates covered in turkeys and fall foliage. Her throat tightened as she remembered an unanswered text from her brother, so she tried to focus on the song playing distantly over the sound system: "If This Is It" by Huey Lewis and the News.

There had been other times in Vivian's life when she had reluctantly walked into a drugstore to buy toilet paper after days of not leaving the house and wiping herself carefully with paper towels, days lost, days where it was as if her attention had been picked up by malevolent fingers and dropped somewhere she didn't want it to be, days where she was unable to stay in the room she was in, unable to focus on the task at hand, either having dark thoughts—the darkest thoughts in the history of humankind—or replaying, in minute detail, certain past events that were sources of intense irritation, anger, sadness, or general pain, and then she found herself wandering through the aisles listening to a yacht rock song, its relentless vacuity spotlighting her own. There was something about shallow clichéd lyrics combined with a sweeping sonic landscape in the sterile setting of a CVS, Duane Reade, or Rite Aid that always moved her in a Don DeLillo way.

As Vivian listened, she empathized with the singer's entreaty, vaguely recalling her own attempts to get a man to end a relationship honestly rather than slowly fade away or gaslight her into thinking her insecurities were unfounded.

Ambiguity, though central to aesthetic greatness, was horrifying in real life. When a man inflicted it upon you in a romantic context, it highlighted his cowardice and your abjection. They did it casually, like flinging a toddler into a body of water and walking away, insisting calmly that it will swim. Huey Lewis was right, man—if loss of interest is inevitable, just get it over with and leave me, already.

A couple of years ago, when she'd become newly single, Vivian had been excited about using her goal-oriented mindset to find a super-hot creative soul mate. Dating would be strenuous, dopaminergic. It would give her an excuse to strive and to be appraised.

But she soon learned that dating as a black woman in your thirties was like running a marathon through a swamp wearing steel-toed boots. It was the topic of a dozen think pieces: *Black Women Are the Least Desirable*. While her white peers complained about dating app message overflow, Vivian got a trickle of lazy openers (*Hey, what's up*), unsolicited inductions into the monarchy (*Hello my queen*), and food-related adjectives describing her skin tone.

And the ones she actually went out with? The cinematographer ghosted her after a solid first date. The lit professor claimed to be separated, but when she asked to go back to his place, he admitted to still living with his wife. The painter told her, after a night of passionate sex, that there was "no spark." Veering away from men in the arts, she dated a tax analyst, thinking his rationality would predispose him to see her as a great catch and to treat her well. He had a panic attack while he was inside her and began muttering about his ex-girlfriend, who had recently reappeared in his life and with whom, he said, he was more simpatico, "because she wants kids, you know," unlike Vivian, who had cheekily announced her intention to remain child-free on their first date.

She inched forward in line and tried to ignore the paper turkey's beady stare. Not even the fact that she had a date the next day with Matthew, a musician she had met online, could soothe her now. The sense of doom she felt, the sense that she would Never Be Loved Again, spread out to envelop the entire human condition as manifested by all of the customers and employees in the store. Vivian's eyes lost focus and she swayed back and forth to the song, feeling a sort of staged emotion which, though exaggerated, was founded on a real bit of sadness. By the time the cashier finally rang up her purchase, she had brought tears to her own eyes again, with her maudlin thinking.

Back outside there was a brilliant sun and a cloudless sky. Vivian crossed her arms and waited at the intersection for the light to change. To her immediate right, a man straddled his parked motorcycle, breathing heavily into his phone. She took two steps back and reached into her tote bag, gripping her phone as if it were a weapon.

"You fuckin' bitch!" he yelled into the phone but also beyond it, louder and angrier than an agitated client at the hospital. He revved his engine loudly then, the gray exhaust blowing in Vivian's direction, and for a millisecond she believed the smoke to be the physical manifestation of the man's rage, that it was spreading out, like her sadness had in the store, that she was going to be enveloped by it. When the light changed, she quickly jogged across the street.

On her way to the train, her attention shifted. Now she looked over her left shoulder every half a block. She used store windows also, to see who was behind her. It seemed that almost every man eyed her now, deciding on the purpose she would serve. The bolder ones said things.

"Sexy."

"Beautiful."

"Princess."

On good days, these encounters could be shrugged off as the cost of living in the city. But most days were not good.

It was unfair, what they were doing. They made you feel simultaneously alone and not by yourself.

Vivian eyeballed a tall white man striding toward her who gave off bad vibes. He had on a dirty gray tank top and gray fleece sweatpants—heavy and out of season. When Vivian looked at him she believed he said, "You have a nice body but you need to work on your face," before walking quickly toward someone on the other side of the street. Eventually, Vivian's eyes focused and saw that he had singled out an Asian tourist and was now following her, yelling incomprehensible things at her. Vivian gripped her phone and imagined the man spontaneously combusting. The tourist looked around for help. No one else reacted or even slowed down. After a minute the man stopped yelling and walked away, aiming his frustration at the ground. Vivian exhaled, released her phone, and put on her sunglasses.

Underground, Vivian kept the sunglasses on to avoid eye contact, to hide her strabismus, and so that no one could see her microexpressions. She was anxious as she watched a piece of aluminum foil get picked up and tossed by the arriving train. She entered the train harried, scanning the car instinctively for lovers from the recent past until, not seeing any, she opened her bag. She stood in front of the doors in the middle of the train car so that she could scan the space around her, assess the makeup of the car, and reconstitute herself.

Slowly, Vivian reached for her earbuds, unwinding and then untangling them, also slowly, while intermittently looking up to see if she was being watched, before finding the piece of music that matched her current state of sad pensiveness, Bach's "E-Flat Minor Prelude" from *The Well-Tempered Clavier*, as performed by Friedrich Gulda.

It took a couple of stops for Vivian to notice the bank of empty seats in the middle of the subway car. She chose the seat closest to the railing on the left and regretted it immediately (for though it would allow her a quick exit it would also encourage hovering nearby) but she didn't have the energy to move.

At the next stop, a man got on and stood directly in front of her and started to bang—violently and arrhythmically— on the handrail above her. It became impossible to concentrate on Bach, and she felt the need to be aware of her surroundings, so she muted her earbuds but kept them in to maintain the appearance of listening. Vivian so resented men in these moments, lacking in spatial empathy, never having had to learn to lessen themselves, like the male commuters who would hover over you while holding an open tumbler full of coffee on the one day you weren't wearing black, having decided to "step out of your comfort zone" with a pale pink sheath dress from Club Monaco.

A young black mom and her two daughters boarded. The mom was short, weighed about 150 pounds, and her thighs were spilling out of the top, back, and sides of her shorts. Though the fat made Vivian uncomfortable, there was something beautiful in the mom's shamelessness. She wore fake pearl earrings, and her toenails were painted bright pink. She had a gap between her front teeth. Her hair was short and relaxed and her sideswept bangs marvelously flattered her face.

The older daughter, about eight years old, was chubby like her mom. She wore her hair in a high bun. Her nails were painted the same bright pink as her mom's. The younger daughter's hair was in an adorable teeny-weeny Afro. She was bouncing, smiling, laughing.

Soon, the mom got angry with the older girl, who for some reason had been put in charge of directing their commute and had confused the express train with the local. Realizing this, the mom exploded, and began to berate her daughter, calling her stupid loudly enough for everyone to hear. Vivian twitched, reflexively raising her hand to her neck, scratching it.

She studied the dejected older girl, who, out of embarrassment or to hide her tears or both, looked out of the subway car into the darkness. Vivian knew there was nothing to see out there. Then, after a few minutes, the older girl dug around her sister's stroller while looking back at her mom to see if she'd be scolded. She took out a handheld video game and looked intently down on it before starting to play. The little sister then stood up and bopped from her mom's lap to the empty seat next to her sister and started tapping playfully, repeatedly, on her sister's shoulder. Vivian's breath quickened. She knew this wasn't going to end well.

Sure enough, the big sister grew irritated. Unable to express her feelings to her mom, she began hitting at the little one's hands, telling her to stop. Mom, who had been absorbed in her phone, refocused on her daughters now, and sharply told the older girl that she was the one who needed to stop, looking at her with scorn before smiling lovingly at the younger one.

Aside from a brief Black Nationalist phase when she'd considered populating the black middle class to be a political issue, Vivian had never really wanted kids. But they were vulnerable humans, to be protected from harm, and rescued if they were in trouble. So Vivian kept looking over there, smiling at the older girl whenever she could, trying to provide an affective counterpoint. But this only made things worse, for whenever the mother saw Vivian looking at her daughters, she would cast the older girl a censorious look or grab hold of the young one, trying to control her random squirming.

Eventually the big sister took the little one onto her lap and started bouncing her around roughly. Again, Vivian felt a sense of foreboding that was incongruous with the innocent behavior being displayed; the little girl liked it. But Vivian never could tolerate roughhousing. She always anticipated broken bones or lost teeth. Her stomach muscles clenched, she reminded herself that these people were not her family.

A teenage junk food vendor roamed through the car now, offering sweet and salty carbohydrates. The mother purchased two bags of Cheez-Its from the teenager and silently handed one to the older daughter, a wordless apology. Disappearing into their snacks, they looked almost happy now, which helped ease Vivian's rising cortisol levels.

Still, she frowned, worrying about each of them, including the mother, though she noted that it is easier to have compassion for people when you aren't the one subject to their volatility. Vivian saw how over time the older girl would internalize her mother's contempt, treating herself with brutality whenever any needs surfaced. But by then, the memory of her mother's loathing having receded, she would be unable to locate its source. It would just seem as if she were "like that." The fate of the younger daughter, meanwhile, was unclear. She might remain the favorite, leading to a rivalry between the two girls, or the mother could turn on the little one once she evolved into more than a prop and began to have her own personality and desires. Perhaps then the sisters would develop a trauma bond that would enable them to gain perspective on their mother and disrupt their warped dynamic.

As the trio left the subway car, Vivian thought of the second thing that Paula, the psychologist from the panel, had done that night.

By the end of the evening, Paula could barely stand, but she didn't want to leave the bar. Vivian had insisted they head out together ("Too many dudes here") and they'd shared a cigarette while waiting outside for their respective cars.

"I don't want to go back there tomorrow," Paula said. She worked at another public hospital in the city. "Every day it's the same. Poor, neglected, abused; poor, neglected, abused." She looked at Vivian as if weighing the risk of what she wanted to say. "You know what? Sometimes I wish I had at least one of those 'adverse childhood experiences.'"

This is why you can't hang out with white women, Vivian thought. She liked to bait them, though. "Why would you want that?"

Paula took her final drag, tossed it, and said, "For the story."

It was the kind of comment that could make Vivian hate someone for all of eternity.

As Vivian recalled the incident, she dwelled on the remark. It seemed emblematic of white opportunism and theft. *They even want to colonize our experiences!* she thought. But before she could map the contours of Paula's offense to her satisfaction, she was jolted back to the present by the feeling of eyes on her. It was the handrail-tapping man.

She made eye contact with him and decided he had been looking at her all along, and with sexual intent. She opened her mouth and grimaced a little; then, feeling disappointed in herself for reacting at all, she looked around blithely to show the man how insignificant he was. It was comforting to see so many commuters reading books on this car, scattered among all the people scrolling up and down and swiping left and right on their phones.

A man across from Vivian was reading the book where an older man sleeps with a young woman, it is unclear who seduced whom, and there are lots of puns. The teenage girl in the corner, meanwhile, read the chatty book of poetry that seemed as if it had been composed by the internet. The older, cerebral-looking bird-woman held the book where a woman's mysterious illness is never cured, though her presence does have a curative effect on others. An inarticulable desire surged within Vivian. She clamped it down.

At the next stop, a faceless man got on and as he walked through the train, Vivian imagined him slitting her throat and then casually continuing on through the car while she gasped and writhed on the floor, spraying the rest of the passengers with her blood. Vivian would likely dominate any argument about the feminist ethics of care and yet, in the next moment, she felt herself refuse to give up her seat to the old woman with severe spinal curvature who had just entered the train because she couldn't bear to do anything that would attract attention right now, so that it was the young white woman whose meticulous French braid was almost certainly the product of a YouTube tutorial who immediately got up and offered the woman her seat.

Vivian looked up at the handrail-tapping man again. He

finally sat down in a seat directly across from her. She wasn't sure, but she thought she could still feel him looking at her from over there. She pulled a book out of her bag, deciding to use it to cover her face. Vivian had all kinds of feints like this. When she was standing up on the subway, for instance, she liked to position her handrail-holding arm directly in front of her face to hide from a creep sitting below. But her book was not helping now. The sense of being watched made reading difficult and Vivian's eyes crossed, glazed over. She felt like she was about to be disemboweled. *Stop fucking looking at me.* She wanted to say it through her teeth.

The demeanor of men who objectified her often dictated her response. Some men looked like they were capable of swift and brutal aggression. Vivian would never sneer at a man like that. She'd read a news story about a woman who had re-buffed an antisocial man's advances; he had attacked her with an axe. Not only was the violence surprising, but so was the mechanism, because who walks around with an axe in urban life? With these men, Vivian tended toward obsequiousness. If they said things to her she would sweetly thank them.

Leering men were often unattractive. She hadn't quite grasped the psychology of it. Maybe being ugly meant they had nothing to lose. Or maybe the ugly man compensates for his ugliness by being a brute, a counterphobic reaction. In any case, such lewd behavior offended Vivian not only as a feminist but also as a shallow person who believed that although she was no model, she was at least more attractive than the man in question. How dare he address her at all?

Now another man, a man with a hat, was sitting next to the handrail-tapping man.

Suddenly the man with the hat pulled out his right earbud.

He touched the arm of the handrail-tapping man, to get his attention.

Quickly the outlines of a predatory conspiracy formed in a corner of Vivian's mind.

They would isolate and trap her. It would be brutal.

Vivian looked down at her book again, heat radiating over her back, shoulders, trapezius, and neck. Red splotches bloomed up out of her V-neck dress toward her face. The cramps in her abdomen worsened, and it was unclear whether they were of gastrointestinal or uterine origin. She read the same line over and over for two minutes before she realized she was reading the same line over and over.

Once, a man had exposed himself to Vivian on the subway, in a crowded car at rush hour. She had been thinking about how *American Idol* singers overuse melisma when it happened. He stood in front of her, in hospital-scrub-type pants with a slit in the front, his semihard penis poking out, inches away from her face. Vivian froze like a cat that has just heard a loud and unfamiliar sound. She looked to the women around, expecting help from them, as if she were in a nineties movie where women band together in response to intimate terror, vanquishing an abuser and creating an alternative family where they are safe and can become their best selves.

It was then that she saw the horrific sophistication of the man's plan.

He had chosen this car *because* there were so many women in it. He knew the women of real life, not those of Vivian's fantasy, and predicted that they would do nothing. Two white women in particular kept looking at Vivian, making big sympathetic eyes and pouts that conveyed just how bad they felt for her because she was in the worst position, face-to-face with the penis, but neither of them said anything. The women seemed relieved that she was suffering through it in their place. They were maybe even a little thrilled to watch her look at the penis, then away, then back at the penis, then away. Her humiliation was becoming an anecdote for these white bitches to tell at happy hour. She hated everyone on the damned train.

It had seemed that it was up to Vivian alone to do something but she did not. She didn't confront the man angrily. She didn't play it cool and say, "Excuse me, did you know that your penis is exposed?" She didn't interrupt the bystander effect by calling attention to a particular woman. She didn't even stand up and move. She just sat there, besieged by animal fear, until the man got off the subway.

Despite understanding that she had been violated and so should not feel that the flashing incident was in any way her fault, Vivian continued to experience her incapacity in this moment as one of her major failures in life. The flashing also stood as evidence that she should never expect assistance. Because some people are selfish, and others are afraid to embarrass themselves, and it's more likely than not that no one will help you if you are in trouble.

So she was alone again now being watched, trapped in a society that hadn't come around to her view of these situations. There's no law against leering or impure thoughts, and most Americans don't even consider it a violation of the social contract. And the field of psychology, whose more damning assumptions about mentally ill people Vivian fought against every day, had determined that her reaction wasn't rational. It wasn't appropriate, psychologists said. It was out of proportion to the threat.

Vivian seethed with a *Firestarter*-level rage. Her rage was operatic, her rage wanted victims. She would look at them both, directly in the eyes, call them out and publicly shame them. *THIS OBJECT HAS BECOME A SUBJECT,* she would say. *CONTEMPORARY LIFE IS A WOMAN TRYING TO THINK AND BEING INTERRUPTED,* she would say. They would see, then, that she didn't belong to them, and that you can't go around watching people.

Vivian gathered her courage.

She looked up.

But the situation had changed.

The man with the hat was asking the handrail-tapping man where he got his shoes. They seemed oblivious to Vivian. There was nothing to declare.

Vivian noticed that her shoulders were up around her neck and her back was arched away from the subway seat. Her right leg was tightly wrapped around her left leg, so that her right foot clutched the calf of her left leg. *There is an iconic photo of Anne Sexton in this pose,* she thought. But Vivian was not a poet, and her left foot was on tiptoe, the muscles in her calf painfully flexed. Her head was pitched forward. Her lips were dry. She twirled a strand of her kinky hair nervously.

Dropping further into conscious awareness, Vivian looked around the subway car.

She heard the noise of the car rolling on the track.

It whistled as it slowed.

The air-conditioning rumbled.

Slowly she uncrossed her legs, rotated her shoulders back, settled into her seat, and breathed.

When Vivian walked through the city, sometimes she

would imagine that she was winding through a zombie apocalypse as one of the sole survivors, speaking into a camera. All around her lay the wreckage of what had once been a dense metropolis, and it remained unclear whether the human species could regenerate in the face of an unrelenting enemy. But on this occasion, on her way to Jane's to smoke weed and sweep a searchlight across her defects while staring ahead at a big screen, Vivian realized that the zombies were just regular human males and females, persisting in their age-old quest to keep her from leaving the house. "Join me," she said to her imaginary viewers, "as I attempt to take up space."

Vivian caught her reflection in every store window, pinching and poking the stubborn fat of her middle, ignoring another string of texts from her brother.

JANE AND MARY JANE

SOMEHOW VIVIAN HAD arrived at Jane's apartment, a junior one-bedroom in Crown Heights, where Jane was already drinking wine. Vivian needed coffee first. She was depleted from the subway ride and had been too shaken to eat any of the carefully chosen snacks.

"I like my coffee how I like my men. Weak and sweet. But not too sweet, because that's disgusting," she called to Jane from the kitchen. It was no longer true that she liked her coffee sweet, but Jane wasn't the type to fact-check a joke.

Jane said, "I like my women how I like my wine. Cold and white."

Vivian laughed, spilling coffee onto her fingers on her way back to the living room. Licking them, she told Jane what a good one that was. Vivian tucked herself into the chaise of Jane's navy-blue sectional and covered her bare legs with a nearby throw.

"I'm so cozy out here!" she yelled to Jane, who had gone into her bedroom. "It feels like HGTV."

The apartment had been converted from a studio by a greedy landlord, so although Jane had a separate bedroom, it was the size of a closet. But she had an exposed-brick wall! There were plants everywhere, and Jane had named them all after black divas. The pothos plant climbing the wall was Aretha. There was a snake plant named Nina and a money plant named Beyoncé. The ZZ plant had been christened as Erykah, and the spider plant was called Patti. A vinyl LP of Sade's *Promise* decoratively leaned against the north wall on a console. Jane had African statues dotted throughout, and a painting of little black girls holding hands and running. It didn't feel like race performance so much as turning blackness into a cohesive design aesthetic. Framed pictures of Jane's family gathered dust but retained their place: here she was as a toddler, playing with her sister, Corinthia, in the bathtub; here she was enveloped by Corinthia and her parents at her college graduation. There was an altar lining the south wall with Santeria candles, incense, palo santo, yellow crystals, and several stacks of tarot cards.

Vivian loved to look at the large framed photograph on the brick wall above the TV. In it, two brown girls with kinky, reddish-brown curls embraced each other in a forest, blowing smoke in each other's faces. The girls were the same size and they both wore light pink polos. The smoke obscured their faces so you couldn't tell if they were platonically experimenting with a cigarette or about to kiss. Jane's girlfriend, Collier, had taken the photo. Collier was a successful visual artist who had used her gallery sales to buy a farmhouse upstate, which she'd turned into a cooperative living space for a dozen women. Vivian hardly ever saw Jane now, because she and her troupe were upstate every weekend "making community" (Jane's words). The weekends, which involved a big group of women hanging out, getting together and fucking and breaking up and fucking, cooking and watching movies and playing sports and having sometimes-heated arguments and then sleeping all together in piles throughout the house, seemed to Vivian, depending on her mood, either the ultimate embodiment of women's liberation or a nightmare of intimacy.

Jane returned from her bedroom, smiling and holding an engraved wooden box. Inside, rolling papers and a baggie with a skull and crossbones sticker on it.

"Don't get me wrong, I love my vapes, but I'm feeling nostalgic today."

Vivian laughed and finally made sustained eye contact with her good friend, who was wearing her hair natural today. The picked-out kinks looked great with her nose ring.

"Why the sticker?" Vivian asked.

Jane grinned and flipped the baggie around. On the other side, the name of the strain: Comfort Killer. "This shit is lethal."

Jane didn't have any filters but was of the opinion that a little coughing never hurt anyone. Vivian said she was too old for that and insisted on making one. She dug through the wooden coffee table's shelf and pulled out a *New Yorker* magazine insert with a *voilà* gesture. Jane opened her legs wide and hunched over the coffee table, which was now their workstation. She removed three flowers from the baggie and held one out for Vivian to smell, which Vivian did, enthusiastically, as she ripped up the insert to the size of her thumb and carefully folded it at one end: once forward, then once backward, then back again.

"If you're really feeling nostalgic," Vivian said, "we should watch an old abduction episode of *Unsolved Mysteries*."

Jane put the weed into a grinder and then, once it was fine and clear of all stems, began distributing it onto the rolling paper.

Vivian weighed the relevant factors out loud while tightly rolling the other end of the insert.

"On the one hand, it would be nice to scare ourselves in an environment free of consequences. On the other hand, we'll be high and paranoid out of our minds."

Vivian did a test suck. "Not bad," she said, handing it to Jane, who arranged it on the left edge of the rolling paper and went back to carefully rolling and tucking. Jane said she was always in the mood to plug into her fears of abduction. "Never gets old." Then she licked and sealed the joint, smelled it, and admired it before lighting up.

After a couple of hits, Vivian felt her lips peeling. She groped for her bag and out fell an overhyped book from several years ago with the best title ever that she had unsuccessfully tried to read on the way over.

"No shade...," Jane said, picking it up.

Vivian waited for the shade.

"But white people love this book." They laughed. It was an ongoing bit. Though they each had their share of white touchstones, the charge of something being culturally white could be strategically deployed to playfully call into question the other's identity.

"How is it?"

As Jane flipped through the book, Vivian said, "Well, I was kind of into parts of it but then the narrator said something like 'The worst thing about child abuse is empathizing with your abuser' and I got annoyed."

"Um."

"I'm like, no. The worst thing about child abuse is being the only girl in your kindergarten class with HPV."

Jane doubled over with laughter. "That's like when girls who hadn't been molested were freaking out over their virginity."

"And you're like 'I haven't had a virginity since I was five!'"

They were officially high.

"Stop it. I'm dead," Jane said. "I was more like, ashamed of not having The Virginity."

"No, we had it, though. You get to define your virginity, I think."

"Right, like, it wasn't the first time I had sex, but it was the first time I wanted to have sex. Who's going to be the great abuse survivor comic of our time?"

Vivian became ecstatic. "I think Margaret Cho's been doing it, and Roseanne kind of did it years ago, before she was an Ambien-tweeting conspiracist. There's that one episode that takes place mostly in the bathroom and her and Jackie just talk about hiding from their dad between beatings for ten minutes. Not even vaguely pandering to the majority audience who must've been like, 'Is this really happening? Because this is the nineties and we aren't talking about child abuse as a society.' So good."

Jane got up to light some palo santo. "Ugh I love that episode so much. How did they even get away with that?"

"'Those network executives got played," Vivian said, as the room filled with a lemony scent.

"It was so nice to just see the saddest realest shit but like, such levity too."

"Yesss! Also there should be more TV and movie scenes

of women in bathrooms. I have so many memories of my mother dragging me into the bathroom when she was drunk, apologizing to me. But yeah, child abuse comedy. Are we ready yet as a society?"

"I'm ready to bring this voice to the people, man," Jane said. She stood up, joint in hand, turning her living room into a stage. Vivian nodded, smiling approvingly at her friend's performative impulse. Jane hopped in place and shook her arms like a boxer in the ring. Her gold hoops bounced around.

"I must have been a really cute kid," she said between puffs, "because I was molested by two *different* people. Wish I could 'me too' them, but they're both dead."

It was the funniest thing Vivian had ever heard. Unrepeatable, though.

They were high enough to be real, so Vivian could describe what happened earlier. "I got so paranoid on the train over here. I thought these random guys were going to, like, attack me or whatever. They were just talking, though."

"I mean, they're men. They've probably attacked *someone*."

"Ha, ha, just not together. It turned out the one guy was just asking the other where he got his shoes!" Jane howled and Vivian leaned into it. "They didn't even *know* each other. That was the fucked-up part."

"Yeah, you imagined a rape cabal. And you weren't high? Okay, that's a little cuckoo. But I got insanely high the other night (off this right here), and I ended up spending an entire night researching *dogs that look like wolves*. That's funny, right? I thought so too, until I learned there's an epidemic of people killing these dogs because they think they're wolves. I was getting really worked up about it, and, like, maybe *too* worked up about it? Like, I was theorizing it. Stop laughing. I can monetize these thoughts."

Vivian and Jane met at a dorm room party in their first year of law school, the year *Let England Shake* came out. (Only war album Vivian ever liked.) Law school parties were weird because law school was weird. There were Christians and virgins and Christian virgins, aggressive men, and closeted people. But there were also principled leftists and the smartest, most ambitious women she'd ever known. It was a lot to handle.

On this particular night she was having an okay time until she noticed this guy follow one of her profoundly drunk female classmates to the bathroom and it felt like predation so she followed them, watching. When the woman came out the guy was there, waiting. He rubbed against her and tried to force a kiss. In reponse, she laughed, pushing past him as if he were just an innocent commuter on a subway platform, and Vivian was horrified that this woman who should feel threatened... didn't. After all, sexualizing someone out of the blue showed a fundamental lack of respect for women, the bounds of which were unknown.

She couldn't enjoy the party after that so she started following the guy around and eavesdropping on his conversations, which were, not surprisingly, decorated with gender slurs. At a certain point after he said some bullshit she just stared at him and he noticed and thought it was weird, but he also clearly found her attractive as he took in her baby-doll dress and her small frame, and his mind couldn't deal with the incongruity so he quickly looked away, and she'd found it all pleasurable, almost erotic.

He was in this cluster of people and Vivian said, loudly

in the direction of the cluster, "Has anyone ever told you that you have the psychological profile of a misogynist from the 1980s?" Vivian laughed as she said it, aware that she was abruptly changing the tone of their conversation and liking it. This was a law school party filled with people and social codes she knew, not a crowded subway where she was all alone.

Contempt flashed across the guy's face as she spoke. His nostrils quickly flared in rejection of a "bad" or "weird" woman. She kept smiling, buzzed on adrenaline.

"I've been listening to your stories. Your ex is a 'crazy stalker' and your boss is 'such a bitch,' right? I didn't even know they made people like you anymore. You sound like a woman-hater from one of those made-for-TV movies about rape."

He gave this look that was like, *If there weren't other people around,* but there were, so he'd have to modulate his brutishness. "You're fucking crazy," he said, bumping into her with his shoulder, glaring and walking with purpose toward the kitchen, where Vivian imagined him "pounding" a beer and setting it down on the counter.

The women that eighties-TV-movie guy had been speaking to were still standing there. Vivian turned to them now hopefully.

"He's the literal definition of a red flag, right?" she said. And then: "Where's my rape whistle?"

"I don't know," said one of them. "That was a bit much." The women made quick and furtive eye contact with one another and walked away.

You had to feel bad for women like that. Decades of competition with other women—*social,* not biological—combined with a desire to maintain, always, a veneer of friendliness toward men, made them perceive Vivian as the enemy. Or maybe it wasn't jealousy at all, just the resentment bred by a woman who reminds you that you could be raped, or that you have been.

As Vivian smiled in awkward triumph, a diminutive black woman with a short Afro and a nose ring laughed from the corner of the room, kindly breaking the silence that Vivian had created. Jane was grinning uncontrollably. "That was just the kind of entertainment I needed at this shit show. Do you smoke weed?"

As they passed a spliff back and forth on the fire escape, Jane analyzed Vivian's "feminist prank," calling it an "intervention."

"You're a killjoy," Jane said, inhaling to take a beat, like all the great stoner sages do. "But it's political. The 'joy' is misogyny."

Jane's words felt like a benediction, offering an excuse, a reason, and a plan all in one, some kind of loophole against embarrassment, shame, and self-recrimination, after which she'd be forever changed. By the time they finished the joint, Vivian was hooked on Jane and they'd been friends ever since.

Over drinks in a dark bar soon after they met, Jane said she'd known she was gay since she was a kid, but her parents were in the church, devoted to sexual conformity. When her mom refused to let her get her hair buzzed into a fade, Jane did it herself. Afterward, her mom beat her.

Jane had frequent lung infections growing up. Her mom would blame her for them, or excoriate her for being weak, or claim that she was faking, and refuse to take her to the hospital until Jane's condition reached a crisis point. As she got older, the beatings stopped, but she became the scapegoat of the family, the repository of all their failures and regrets. Jane knew what it was like to start dreading Thanksgiving in September.

Vivian had softened toward Jane as she spoke, reciprocating with a bulleted account of her own history: all manner of violence by one of her mother's boyfriends, hitting and verbal humiliation, she wasn't allowed to eat when she'd done something bad, and that was just the stuff he did in front of other people. Death threats if she revealed *that*, and she'd even been abducted, briefly, and thought she was going to die. This was all decades ago, though. She'd recovered, she told Jane.

"Nothing to see here," she said. "Except for these burn scars!"

She laughed provocatively then, and didn't break eye contact with Jane, who looked in the direction of Vivian's limbs.

"I have no clue how they got there."

"Maybe a curling iron or something," Jane said, examining her hand in a way no one had ever done before, dispassionately, as if she were just noticing a mysterious smudge on the wall.

The women shared more details of their childhoods in a detached, clinical tone. There were no tears. Vivian was proud to have survived, took it as a measure of her strength, insisted she was over it. Jane's affect was minimal no matter what she was talking about, and in fact she became more animated about the general injustices experienced by women and queer people than about anything that had ever happened to her.

Vivian and Jane found their militancy reflected in each

other, and it was glorious to be affirmed. They felt united together against everyone else, and considered themselves The Only People Talking About Rape, the Only People Brave Enough to Mention Rape Indiscriminately Whether in a Classroom or at Parties, in a Crowded Café or Your Grandmother's Living Room, While Everyone Else in the World Is Completely Useless in this Area. And though, back then, it was not done, and though they did it alone, their bond allowed them to cast off the shame of being The Only People Talking About Rape, because it wasn't their shame, it was the shame of the world.

They talked about sexual violence in all contexts, all across the world. Girls were being raped in Syria, in the Jehovah's Witnesses, in the STEM fields, and women janitors were raped at night. Sometimes little girls were abducted by strangers and then strangled, raped, and dumped. Sometimes they were abducted, raped, and forced to breed like purebred dogs, and Elizabeth Smart and Jaycee Dugard were heroes. But mostly? Mostly they were raped by supposed protectors: by their fathers, their grandfathers, their brothers and cousins, babysitters, coaches, teachers and preachers. Indigenous women were twice as likely to be raped as other women and the Violence Against Women Act was poorly implemented on reservations. Black women were the least likely to report, due to the legacy of lynching and a desire to protect black men from the carceral state. It was only in the 1970s that various states outlawed marital rape, which, under English law, had been considered an oxymoron.

But they differed from each other in how they behaved in public. In law school, Vivian was just as much of a fighter as she was in their private talks. She'd call a classmate out for an offensive comment, she'd send long, critical emails to their libertarian contracts professor about the unequal bargaining power of indigent people, and would go down swinging against the two-party system when an elite Democratic political strategist visited their campus and tried to make his party look like the ultimate solution.

But Jane didn't say anything in class. She'd either sit way in the back so she could see everyone without anyone seeing her, or she'd plop down next to a huge obstruction, like a column, so that she'd be shielded from the eyes of others. Sometimes in the midst of whatever confrontation Vivian had gotten herself into, she would crane her neck to look over at Jane, hoping for backup, but Jane was gone. She'd either physically left the room, having to go to the bathroom at the very moment Vivian had popped off, or she was tucked into her laptop or phone, disappearing into some communiqué bearing the utmost urgency. Days later, though, when processing The Incident over drinks, Jane would deliver a brilliant analysis of everything that she'd witnessed but hadn't participated in.

Their second year, Jane abruptly dropped out of law school and moved back in with her parents in New Jersey. Vivian couldn't really tell you why, because Jane was guarded about it, as if to protect herself from some perceived failure. Also, Vivian had an uneven memory.

After dropping out, Jane isolated for a while. Months passed and they didn't speak. Finally Vivian got her to agree to a movie night. This was back when Vivian was obsessed with Katharine Hepburn, the most dynamic of the Old Hollywood actresses. During *Bringing Up Baby,* Jane went along with the delightful screwball universe, in thrall to Hepburn's vitality.

She later told Vivian that when Cary Grant violently stomps on Hepburn's bare foot out of nowhere because her character has just done something annoying, something snapped. The gag left Jane upset for weeks, as she reckoned with the history of the world she lived in. She decided to write about it.

Now Jane was working toward her doctorate in American Studies, and her parents were so relieved that they were paying half of her rent, which explained how she was able to live alone in a cool neighborhood, while Vivian, a full-time lawyer who had supported herself financially since she turned eighteen, was relegated to Kensington, a subway desert a mile south of the park. Jane was currently writing a dissertation on violence against women in popular culture. She recited misogynistic scenes the way men in the mid-aughts quoted *Anchorman.* So now when Jane and Vivian got together and talked about abuse it wasn't pathological, no, it wasn't ruminative at all. They did it for Jane. It was research.

"But dude," Jane was saying now, from the kitchen, where she was arranging a charcuterie board, "I was thinking about progress the other day. Most of the time I think everything is fucked but, like, sometimes I'll be with these eighteen-year-old kids and, like, they've been absorbing lefty-politics stuff online and it's really affecting them."

Vivian got up from the couch to join her and open a new bottle of wine.

"Interesting—what kind of stuff?" she said.

"Well, one of my female students brought up the Weinstein thing and this guy was like, 'My problem is there's no evidence,' and then another male student was like, 'There's never any evidence for rape!' and I was like, 'This is so cool.'"

Vivian poured them each a generous glass of Malbec, and after they clinked glasses and took their inaugural shared sip, Jane continued.

"And last semester in a small seminar I was teaching, one kid said, 'You know, fat people who can't fit into a single seat on an airplane *should* have to pay for two seats,' and before I could even craft a response, these three other students just really got on him about it, saying you shouldn't use the term 'fat' and that everything he was saying was fat-phobic and I didn't even have to do anything! And I was just like, 'This is awesome, these are basically kids.'"

"That's...interesting," Vivian said, opening a box of raisin and fig crackers, inhaling their fruity aroma and worrying about the carb count. While Jane laid out Genoa salami and a complicated argument about fat oppression under late capitalism, Vivian snuck a peek at the nutrition facts: a moderate amount of carbs. She snakily arranged a handful on the large wooden cheese board.

As they walked back into the living room, Vivian swiped a cracker and said, through her crunching, "But don't they want to be called fat now? Aren't fat people like, owning it, and reclaiming the label?"

"But the kid wasn't saying it in a reclaiming way," Jane said, making a salami-and-cheese roll-up. "He was using it like an epithet."

Vivian was quiet for a moment, thinking of how to respond. She craved another cracker but wouldn't let herself have it. Instead, she settled for a slice of unadorned Gouda.

Finally, she said, "I feel distinctly not critical and actually optimistic about younger people being able to talk about things in new ways. If I'm optimistic about anything, it's that. I wonder, wow, what if we had had that?"

"We had to either find it, or infer it, or live without it," Jane said, and then quickly downed several raisin-cracker-and-cheese sandwiches in succession.

Vivian said, "I think that at least around sexual orientation I was able to be that ally in the classroom as a teen. I didn't feel imperiled around sexual orientation in the same way I felt imperiled about other things, so it was easier for me to 'defend gay rights' or whatever 'cause I had the privilege to do so. But nobody chimed in." She circled her nearly empty wineglass with her finger, looking down at the remaining puddle. "And then I would just cry," she said, finishing off the glass. "I'd lash out at people in debate class and cry."

"I lashed out at people and cried in college, not in high school. In high school I just cried."

Vivian laughed.

"Remember Trevor, that kid I tutored who revealed in an essay that he'd been abused? He got into Wesleyan!"

"Aw, that's a great place to go if you were abused."

Jane's laughter warmed up the room as Vivian refilled their glasses, thinking *they* were the great child abuse comics of their time, only no one knew about them. They shared the dark humor of traumatized people, a humor that made most people so uncomfortable (either because they had been abused and never told, because they had witnessed someone's abuse, because they had heard of the abuse of someone close to them, because they were in denial about abuse occurring, generally, or, more rarely, because no kind of abuse had ever happened to them) that they only revealed it in its full splendor when they were alone with each other, or, in Jane's case, in therapy.

Vivian didn't need therapy. For one, she didn't adhere to the biomedical model of mental illness and didn't want to be diagnosed, labeled, and quantified like her clients. And she didn't want to hear any overdetermined theories about how she'd been programmed by her dangerous upbringing, either. *I am completely sui generis,* she thought. Third, she knew the names of all her problems already and believed she could read her way out of them. Also, she had all the jokes. Isn't the final stage of recovery when you can tell jokes about it? Lastly, she didn't need to pay someone to make her feel less crazy. Anytime she needed someone to contextualize or affirm her reality, she went to Jane.

"Hey, how's your sister doing?"

"Corinthia? She's super busy planning the wedding."

"You going to be in it?"

"Who knows? Last time I talked to her and my mom, my mom was like, 'So, maybe, I just thought, it might be better if you... didn't bring Collier.'"

"Why?"

"Why do you think?"

They exchanged a look.

"Our families are beyond fucked up," Vivian said, and they both laughed. "Just stuck with them, I guess."

Jane looked thoughtful. "Did you know that there are debates in moral philosophy about what an adult child owes their parents?"

Vivian didn't know this. If she'd been with anyone else, she'd grab her phone and look into it, quickly digesting the information necessary to participate in the conversation as an equal. But she was with Jane, so she just asked, "What are the terms of the debate?"

"The prevailing theory is that we owe our parents a debt because they raised us, clothed us, kept us housed, et cetera."

"What if they didn't? Like, what if they were too poor?"

"Now, you know poverty isn't accounted for in these hypotheticals. I mean, it's moral philosophy."

They laughed.

"But the basic idea is that the parent-child relationship is like a creditor-debtor relationship. A child has incurred a debt for the parent's resource investment. Like, they expended their time, money, and energy on raising the child and as a result they have less resources. So then when the child grows up—"

"The child has to repay the debt, I get it. But the metaphor doesn't totally track, right?" Vivian sat up, to help marshal her critical faculties. "Like, if I borrow money from a bank, I'm choosing to do so, and the obligations are laid out from the beginning (fine print aside). But children don't choose to enter into relationships with their parents or caregivers."

"It's true, we didn't choose to be born. So the metaphor isn't perfect. Can you think of a better one?"

It got quiet for a while. Vivian picked at stray fibers on the couch while Jane went around checking on her plants.

"It appears I am too stoned to find a better metaphor, so we'll stick with this for now. But I'm still hung up on the quality of the resource investment. Doesn't it matter, what kind of care we got? In terms of defining our corresponding obligation?"

"Well, the theories don't offer a justification for shirking the obligation. They're just attempts to describe *why* children are obligated to their parents."

"So even the field of philosophy, which purports to criticize everything, takes it for granted that we *are* all obligated to our parents."

"Exactly. You know the family keeps this society function-ing, honey."

"Ah yes, what is a child but a future worker?"

"Future homeowner, et cetera. But I think the idea is that if you incurred a debt, you have to repay it, no matter whether the company treats you fairly or whatever."

"There's an upper limit to that, though, even with a contract. The law permits rescission in certain circumstances. Like, with our backgrounds, we could maybe argue that the contract is void as against public policy."

"Ha, ha."

"Okay, so you've incurred this debt. How do you pay it back?"

"The responses range from an obligation to support the parents financially if they need it, to caretaking responsibili-ties, and some say the child is just obligated to show gratitude and respect, and to maintain the relationship."

Vivian flinched. "Do you buy this? You're really less moral if you don't want to support people who didn't support you?"

"But lack of support might not be the parents' fault, right? Like, some parents *been* set up to fail. Generational poverty, generational trauma. Take migrant families escaping political persecution or gang violence, or like the black families who came up here during the Great Migration. If you follow debt theory through, then black and brown Gen-Xers and millen-nials might have a highly specific and extra moral obligation to the generation before us, because of the immense social and historical strain that generation survived, that we all benefit from."

Vivian normally loved listening to Jane pontificate. There was nothing more beautiful than a black woman making a point. Still, she felt unsure of Jane's arguments, obscurely unnerved by them, and not sober enough to really engage with them just yet.

"Well," Vivian said. "My mom certainly thinks I owe her. You know, *family is everything. Blood is thicker than water.* The fuck does that even mean?"

"I think it means that even if you're an ocean away, they'll find your ass."

"Hahahahaha."

They'd talked enough and it was time to watch a movie. Jane picked *A Nightmare on Elm Street 3: Dream Warriors* and Vivian agreed, too high to think of an alternative. As the opening scene played, Jane moved onto the floor, sitting right in front of the screen with her knees pulled up. She told Vivian that *Dream Warriors,* like Stephen King's *It,* was a survivor's revenge story. It imagined a world where traumatized young people united to kill a monster on their own, their caregivers having abandoned, mistreated, or just failed to prioritize them. The fantasy of coming together with other survivors and fighting back, Jane said, was profoundly therapeutic.

Vivian interrupted to ask if Jane was writing a paper on this. Jane didn't answer; she didn't even turn to acknowledge that a question had been asked. In *Nightmare on Elm Street,* she continued, there's a double horror: the threat of the otherworldly monster and the violence of the human world. It is almost as if the humans have *produced* the monstrosity.

After all, Freddy Krueger is the product of a gang rape, the so-called bastard son of a hundred maniacs. It makes sense then, that he would visit teenagers in their bedrooms, a clear allusion to familial rape, and the cycle of abuse.

"It *sounds* like a paper," Vivian said, laughing to herself. And then, wistfully, "I wrote papers once." She relit the joint and then inhaled too much, too fast. The smoke scalded her throat.

"You good?" Jane asked. "I haven't heard coughing like that since Reggae Fest 2010."

Tears in her eyes, Vivian made her way to the kitchen, downed a glass of water and a spoonful of honey, then popped back in to flash a thumbs-up.

Vivian wanted to enjoy Jane's dynamic theories, but she'd smoked so much that she lost the surrounding environment and found herself revisiting violent events. In particular, she thought of the day the violent man carried her, on his shoulders, to a secluded part of their blighted city. She remembered the underside of her right leg being scratched by the wrench in his back pocket, and she remembered holding on tight. That was it, she thought, grabbing her phone to tap out a rejoinder.

> The worst part of child abuse is not empathizing with your abuser, it's holding on tight to him while he carries you to a secluded area for the first time and then wondering, while he engages in a routine act, whether he has planned some particular form of violence against you with, say, that wrench, or whether he is just going to a job later, whether he intends to kill you via blunt-force trauma to the head or whether he's, like, a mechanic, and then, decades

*later, not knowing whether the fear you believe you recall
was justified, or whether it's just a tragic gloss that you
are putting on it now, a way to manufacture self-pity.*

After writing that, Vivian felt that she was being contaminated by toxins, or as if a deranged tormentor were pouring warm, dark sludge over her body, or as if she were being entombed.

What the hell did I smoke? she thought, clicking back into her body. Her throat burned, her lips were chapped, she'd never drink enough water, and she was on the verge of complete annihilation in the face of a looming creature, but she was still self-conscious enough, still prideful enough, to know that it was best to hide everything she was feeling from Jane, because she couldn't bear to look weak in front of her, so she tried to marshal her cognitive faculties in the direction of the television. *Look at the Toshiba,* she said to herself.

"The state itself is a site of violence," she heard Jane say. "The kids are being involuntarily detained at Westin Hills Psychiatric Hospital, and threats abound. Kincaid (a black teen) astutely calls out the racism of the institution, so he's labeled 'aggressive' and sent to the quiet room. A male orderly objectifies and threatens Taryn, whom he views as disposable, a 'junkie whore.' Hospital staff try to force Kristen to sleep through sedation, causing her to violently lash out..."

Vivian thought of Melissa as Kristen sobbed with a scalpel in hand, singing the Freddy Krueger nursery rhyme. In walks Nancy, the survivor from the original *Nightmare on Elm Street,* now a grad student in psychology specializing in pattern nightmares. She completes the last line of the nursery rhyme,

"Never sleep again," and walks toward Kristen, who allows Nancy to take the scalpel from her, sensing that she is safe. Vivian's abdomen tensed and tears silently fell out of her eyes.

Night was coming again in the film and Phillip was about to die. Vivian continued to cry in the dark room on the sectional, biting her knuckles while the teenagers watched Phillip fall to his death and then discovered their powers in a group hypnosis session, but the story lost steam as more characters died absurd deaths. Vivian grew bored, smoked more, and went to the bathroom to be alone with her phone.

Jane's bathroom felt like a bad neighborhood. There was hair all over and grime on every surface. The sink was covered in encrusted toothpaste and caked on globs of hair care products and soap. When she sat on the toilet, the broken seat slid to the side and unholy smells from the past bloomed up from the bowl. Vivian didn't care, though. Jane's was a life of the mind.

Sitting there, Vivian thought about her date tomorrow. She checked Matthew's online dating profile and public social media accounts. He'd last been online a couple of hours ago.

She had a thing for hot and kind of dense guys, despite or perhaps because of her braininess. Matthew was tall and white with chin-length brown hair that curled at the ends when it was wet. From the messages they had exchanged in the week prior, he seemed to measure high on extroversion and low on neurosis, which excited and worried her.

Despite being from Boston, Matthew loved black people and black culture, and his social media was curated to demonstrate this affinity. Here he was demonstrating his support of the movement for black lives and Saying Her Name; here he was sitting in and playing saxophone at a black R&B club; here he was leading an all-black middle school band in Harlem. She arched an eyebrow, for sure, but as she swiped through his photos and scrolled through their messages, she felt *desirable,* quite different from how she normally felt. Anything was possible!

She came out just as the ending credits began to roll, then asked Jane to read her tarot so she could sober up before going home. She wanted to be told that unconditional love was in her future, but the results were inconclusive.

—•—

Once she was home, Reginald, her gray tiger-striped domestic shorthair, greeted her with food-frenzied howls. She'd gotten him a decade ago. His marvelous eyes were crisply lined in white and he had a perfectly symmetrical face. He was beautiful and aloof, a combination of traits that guaranteed Vivian's everlasting devotion. He did figure eights around her legs now while she shucked off her bag and keys. She crouched down to pat the white tufts that hung off his fat belly like sheep's wool, cooing at him about his desire to be fed. She liked to feed him slowly, in several installments of wet food, so that she could extend the window of his affections.

Afterward, she drifted from the antics of the *Designing Women* to those of the *Golden Girls* without interest. The Comfort Killer was still in her system, and demented thoughts pinballed in the background of her consciousness. While wiping off her lipstick and brushing her teeth in the bathroom, she caught sight of her face in the mirror and got pulled in a bleak direction, recalling the words from the man on the street before. "You have a nice body but you need to work on your face."

It was true that Vivian wasn't as attractive as she wanted to be. In public, she made up for this as best she could, wearing bright-colored lipstick, narrowing her eyes to slits and holding a remarkable amount of tension in her face. But when she was alone, without makeup, stoned and crying in the mirror as she was just now, she felt acutely hideous. And then, after, she wanted to revel in that hideousness. So she relaxed her face completely, indulging in the misalignment of her eyes. She placed her fingertips on her under-eye circles, irremediable due to decades of chronic pattern nightmares, and tugged down on the delicate skin there. Her profile was compromised by a receding jaw, which she inspected now by turning to the side.

(Vivian's attitude toward her own face, premised as it was upon ugliness, might one day be redescribed as internalized racism à la *The Bluest Eye* and then dispensed with or, better yet, replaced with pro-black confidence, but she was unable to embrace this view now, seeing as she was in the shadow of the thing, convinced that people in her life were ruminating about her ugly face when she wasn't around. Surely her ugliness was something everyone was secretly thinking about whenever she left a room, so why not take back control by listing her deficiencies?)

Suddenly Vivian had an idea for a book.

An ugly woman manages to conceal her ugliness by elabo-rately tensing the muscles in her face. Her labored beauty attracts a man whose beauty is naturally occurring and the two of them marry and enjoy a happy life together for years until one day, after an accident and due to being heavily medicated, the woman is left temporarily unable to tense the muscles in her face at all, let alone elaborately, and so her husband realizes that she is ugly and is faced with the question of whether he will stay with her or leave. The book, which had until now centered on the woman's experience of "secret ugliness," would switch to the husband's perspective for a hundred pages as he pursues various lines of inquiry regarding the nature of ugliness, inquiry that causes the reader to develop real affection for him, where before, the reader had thought he was merely a beautiful man with no interior life. The irony of the story would be that after the hundred pages, just when the husband decides that, out of equal parts romantic love and ethics, he will stay with the ugly woman and in doing so will reject the social conventions of normatively attractive people, the expectations of his family, and even the basic principle that "like attracts like," so that his wife will finally be able to relax her face in someone else's presence—after he decides this, the ugly woman will reject the husband for someone whom she deems to be "much hotter" than him, someone that she has to even more elaborately tense and clench and flex her face for.

It was a cool idea, but writing felt useless. One had to help people, thus her decision to become a lawyer in a psychiatric hospital, working to free people from forced institutionalization by the state.

Still, she allowed herself to imagine the book from beginning to end. She even came up with a title. Crawling into bed, she wrote three lines in the Notes app before becoming distracted imagining how successful the book would be and how she would frame the writing process in the endless interviews that would glorify her despite all her detractors. One day she'd be interviewed by an attractive British journalist and when he asked her why she wrote she would coyly smile and say, "I have always wanted to be in a position where attractive men would ask me questions about myself, in the public sphere." They would then proceed to talk about various cultural objects and when Vivian referred to Kate Bush as her favorite musician the journalist would perk up, asking her, in a very male way, to name the top five best Kate Bush songs. She would respond, in a very Vivian way, that she was not a fan of superlatives in cultural criticism and that she preferred to speak in terms of personal preferences and also that rather than ranking Kate's songs she clustered them into songs that she could sing and songs that she could not, and that through songs in the latter category she experienced the distinct pleasure of being shown her limitations. By and large, she would tell the journalist, she could emulate white pop singers because they tend to sing in a very controlled way—Madonna is the epitome of this. Black singers were often beyond her ability to emulate (at least the ones that grew up singing in gospel choirs, which Vivian did not, as she wasn't close to her southern relatives) because of all the melismatic singing, which she thought about a lot, perhaps because she was unable to do it well. In melismatic singing (also found in opera) the voice was at once unbridled and severely controlled, as you had to both master the ability to do quick vocal runs, which takes incredible technical skill, and also have the confidence *to be loud,* and to expand your chest and diaphragm, which Vivian could not do, because that would constitute exposure, or surrender. But anyway Kate was an exception to her racial rules about voices, at least on *The Dreaming,* where she abandons the meek head voice of the earlier albums and gets quite out of control, and that's the point of the album, isn't it? Breaking free from her brothers, producing herself, eschewing fuckability in favor of hee-hawing like a donkey and producing odd, guttural, discordant music? In the end rather than answer his question she would suggest that the journalist accompany her to a karaoke bar, where she would sing the entire Kate catalogue in alphabetical order. In the article the journalist would write that he fell in love with her somewhere around "Cloudbusting" but didn't make a move until "Wow."

Vivian noticed, suddenly, that in her fantasy state, the feelings of ugliness and contamination had eased. This seemed important somehow. She should make a note in her phone, a note saying that she had *successfully, and somewhat automatically, gotten myself out of the feeling of ugliness* by imagining a performance that would make someone fall in love with her. But she was too tired, her body was heavy and warm. She closed her eyes, hoping she'd remember.

A LITTLE BIT IN LOVE

THE NEXT MORNING, Saturday, Vivian woke up panicked from dark, predatory dreams. Her dreams were clichés, of course, but terrifying clichés. There were the ones where she was chased by a hidden figure and the ones where she was felt up by someone she knew. Then there were the ones where she arrived at the single-family home which she understood to be hers but she couldn't open the door, for various reasons: keys lost in bag, keys dropped on ground, trembling hands, or numb hands. She would find the keys at last and get inside, but there was never any safety in the house. If there were stairs, then once she made it inside she'd hear a radio turn on upstairs, and she'd look up the stairs and know she should run, but she could only move in slow motion. If she managed to reach an exit somehow, a faceless man would appear. *No. You aren't going anywhere.* Or, if she managed to unlock the door and walk outside, he'd grab her arm and she'd wake up. She was never actually attacked in these dreams; the scariest part was becoming aware of the threat.

Somehow she came to remember where she was in time, and that she was a woman who had a date later in the evening.

She shuffled through the apartment in a daze and made a cup of coffee, drinking it standing up in the kitchen. Her bachelor's fridge was filled with cans of seltzer, old bottles of cider from a failed brunch, Ziploc bags of semisoft cheeses, half-eaten paleo meat bars, and expired half-and-half. The shelves were encrusted with egg yolks and the debris from various spills—coffee, takeout leaks—that she never cleaned up. She waded through tumbleweeds of cat hair, stray bobby pins and paper clips, and the seemingly endless piles of lassoing cords that defined her life until she found a crumpled sports bra on the couch and greasy no-show socks that didn't smell too bad. A morning run would shake off the adrenaline from the nightmare.

On her way out of the building she encountered her elderly neighbor, Roseydi, dragging in a shopping cart, anxiously rifling through the multiple bags of different shapes and sizes that hung off her shoulders and arms. Her oversized glasses sat perilously on the edge of her nose, her auburn-colored wig had shifted to the side, and her cherry-red lipstick was a sloppy ring of color outside her natural lip line.

"Hola, señora," Vivian said, touching Roseydi gently on the shoulder. Roseydi came up to Vivian's chest.

"Hi, mama," Roseydi responded warmly.

"Necesita ayuda?"

Roseydi was afraid to ride the elevator alone after having been trapped inside years ago, so Vivian took her up to their floor. During the ride, Roseydi showed Vivian pictures from the Foodtown weekly circular, telling Vivian about the current sale in a mix of Spanish and English, seeming always to sense the limits of Vivian's fluency. Roseydi licked her thumb before turning each page, and as Vivian's eyes went over the familiar brand names—Mrs. Dash, Wish-Bone, Tropicana, Bounty, Ronzoni—she thought of her mother's well-stocked kitchen cabinets and felt her throat constricting.

"Cuidate," Vivian said, dropping Roseydi off on the third floor.

"Igualmente—and don't forget about the pork chops, mama—a dollar ninety-nine a pound until Monday," Roseydi said as the elevator doors closed.

Outside, Vivian ran, avoiding a stray thought about her mother and trying to focus instead on the diverse architecture around her. A single block contained so much: brick row houses; detached two-family Victorian homes; two-toned Craftsmans with large, inviting porches; multiunit condos and huge brick rent-stabilized apartment buildings like her own. It was a car-dominated area. There were few pedestrians aside from the group of men who drank, slept, and used the sidewalks as bathrooms in the neighborhood, so she could never relax. During the day she had to be careful not to be hit by a speeding car. At night, the absence of people was terrifying.

She tried to remember the information she'd gleaned from backstalking Matthew online to prepare the self that would greet him on their date. The self would originate in her; it wasn't a total fabrication. She would merely come into their interactions armed with knowledge that she could use to gain advantage. Recalling his love of Kendrick Lamar and Nirvana, for instance, she listened to them both on a loop for material, satisfied when she landed on an argument about the philosophical complexity of "How Much a Dollar Cost" (wealthy black narrator encounters a homeless man in South Africa and describes, in granular detail, the moral struggle that arises as he is asked for money, dramatizing the larger question of diasporic duty) and "All Apologies" (everyone *is* gay).

She'd also studied videos he'd posted of himself playing the tenor saxophone, the piano, and the drums. When she saw that he was teaching himself how to play movements from Bach's *The Well-Tempered Clavier,* she broke into a wide, dreamy smile and her mind sped up, thinking of all the things she could say about Bach.

Vivian had always wanted to play an instrument but, due to poverty and caretakers who didn't understand the value of a musical education, she'd been deprived of lessons. So she wouldn't be able to discuss Bach in a music theory-ish way, but she knew he had created a complex composition containing a range of musical styles and that it was subject to seemingly endless interpretation. Friedrich Gulda tended to take an extraordinarily slow tempo, his long legato lines bringing out the drama and sensuousness of the composition. Glenn Gould, by contrast, seemed to dash through the pieces, ignoring dynamics, playing undemarcated notes staccato, and inserting himself into the music at every turn. He even hummed along!

Vivian's smile had vanished, though, when she'd noticed a particular woman who Liked all of Matthew's videos. After quickly clicking and scrolling, Vivian learned that she was Matthew's ex-girlfriend.

Though her Facebook was private, Elana's public Instagram vaguely identified her as a "designer" running a "creative studio," and featured hyperstylized photos of the "environments" she curated. Vivian felt a wave of superiority and then a sudden need to see the woman's body, to study it. Luckily since Elana was manically building her brand there were also ample photos of her in fashion-forward outfits striking the poses of the day (leg in front, sidewalk squat, mirror selfie) so that Vivian could see, to her horror, that Elana had the super-thin, strangely desexed body of an Eastern European teen model. As she scrolled through the photos and read the accompanying text extolling the virtues of being a well-hydrated vegan (the latest ethical cover for an eating disorder), Vivian was overcome by impertinent, size-related thoughts. In the span of seconds Elana went from being an object of mockery to a slender superior, a harbinger of inevitable rejection.

Convinced that Matthew would not want to date anyone over 110 pounds, Vivian had mechanically gone on a keto-genic diet in the week leading up to their first date. In the mornings before work she'd eat a hard-boiled egg smeared with mustard, then reduced-salt cashews as a midmorning snack. For lunch and dinner, a salad with salmon or chicken. The diet, combined with lifting or running every day, caused her to lose four pounds (water weight) in a week. Though Vivian was not aware of this possibility at the time, she saw now that this was why she'd been revisiting the conversation with the psychologist at the bar. She really was, as Paula had said, "one of them."

She'd made it to the park. The sun was blazing in a clear sky and her running mix was turned up to the highest volume. Vivian wasn't fast, but she had the fortitude of a long-distance runner, perfect form, and energy to burn. When she reached the hill, she met a caravan of women dance-walking while lis-tening to headphones. A woman with long curly hair and the body of a swimmer shimmied like a 1920s flapper. A pregnant dark-skinned woman wearing a head-to-toe purple tracksuit silently rapped while softly tapping her belly. Women without rhythm didn't care and there were a lot of jazz hands. Vivian smiled at the spectacle as she wove through them and briefly snapped in time to the Dawn Richard anthem blowing out her eardrum. She picked up her cadence and angled toward the incline, pumping her arms and hoping to feel like a champion when she reached the top.

While running she thought about what Jane had said yesterday. She appreciated Jane's perspective on filial obligations and respected the logic, as well as its desired end of generational uplift. She recognized herself in it, as this very line of thinking had led her to become a lawyer. Certainly she felt an obligation to her people, those who had survived brutal upbringings. And we couldn't all be feckless. Someone had to make sure that the most vulnerable members of our society weren't completely abandoned.

But Vivian wasn't sure what she owed her family. She thought of a conversation she'd had last week with her brother Michael. He'd fallen out with their mother again and was considering not coming to the family reunion. Vivian called to mediate. This was partially selfish, because she worried that if Michael wasn't there she wouldn't have anyone to talk to. When she called, he was drinking in a park near Vivian's high school, a park where Vivian used to drink too, and get high, and a park where their dead brother used to cruise, if you could call it cruising when it was an adult with, like, teenagers. When, after some chitchat, Vivian brought up the reunion, Michael went into an angry ramble and Vivian put the phone on speaker while she swept. When drinking Michael tended to ruminate about everything bad that had ever happened to him and blame it on their mother, whether she was the proximate cause or not. As he went on about their mother's failure to supervise his homework or keep him focused on basketball and how that related to his juvenile delinquency it started to feel as though he was ruminating *at* Vivian, wanting her to collude with him in his rancor toward their mother, and Vivian felt this most acutely when Michael said he knew she must feel some kind of way after what she, their mother, had allowed to happen to her, Vivian. Vivian didn't want to talk about that and she resented being baited, so she evaded as best she could but he wouldn't let it go and finally he'd said something that had briefly stopped her cleaning, which was "You know, Mom had a *lot* of boyfriends." Before Vivian was born, he meant. And then he said there were things that had happened that he just tried to put out of his mind, and there were things that had happened to her dead brother, too. That was how he put it. Things that had happened.

Vivian hadn't been able to respond to the disclosure in the moment other than to apologize and it didn't seem like Michael wanted to unpack it either, so they both just returned to the original subject of the phone call, Vivian insisting *It's not going to be so bad* and *We'll be there together, I need you there,* and eventually he agreed to come and he finished his six-pack and they said they loved each other and he insisted he was sober enough to drive home and she finished cleaning her apartment and she didn't really think about it again after.

Mom had a lot of boyfriends. The phrase kept appearing in her mind, becoming over time a devastating euphemism not so easily contextualized by those well-worn liberal concepts— generational poverty and generational trauma and power and control—she'd used for so long as a bulwark against maternal recrimination. Jane relied on those overarching concepts too; Vivian thought of the regular excuses Jane trotted out for her own mother—"It's how she was raised," "She thought hitting me was protecting me," and so on. It all seemed weak now, nothing more than motivated reasoning, at least in Vivian's case. Because this new information revealed that what had happened to Vivian wasn't the result of an isolated mistake made in the context of limited choices, but was instead part of a larger pattern of *a spectacular inability to protect children from harm,* she could say if she felt charitable, or a pattern of *collaboration in exploitation,* if she didn't. Did filial obligation extend to a relationship so degraded?

Vivian was by now a couple of minutes away from the end of the park loop. She wasn't sure she could make it, but the woman in front of her wouldn't stop. She had a swift gait and pink running shoes. Vivian blotted out the rest of life and focused only on the woman's pink shoes, how her feet confidently hit the ground and then sprang back quickly after contact. Vivian matched her step for step, quietly muttering. Pink shoes. Pink shoes. Pink shoes. Finally, she reached the bottom of the hill and sat on a bench watching the geese sun themselves and call out. The lake rippled on endlessly.

Her next task was visiting the Dominican salon down the street from her apartment to spend three hours having her hair straightened in a room full of brown women speaking to one another familiarly and in Spanish. They spoke too fast for Vivian to understand, so she felt powerless and excluded but also invisible in a way she liked.

Today Vivian's hairdresser was Marisol, a young woman with perfectly blown-out jet-black hair. She had a delicate face and she never once yanked Vivian's head while combing her hair. Instead, she proceeded with care, slowly dragging the wide-toothed comb through methodically parted sections, stopping occasionally to ask if anything hurt. Marisol had a big ass that she wasn't ashamed of, and she danced around the shop and sang along with the bachata music that formed the soundtrack of the morning. Vivian had never liked bachata, maybe because it was mindless and repetitive, or maybe because Vivian was Puerto Rican and had a cultural preference for salsa, which was also repetitive, but more intricate musically. She enjoyed Marisol's personality so much, though, that she nearly caught her enthusiasm for the genre.

When she was growing up in the Midwest, surrounded by white Christian girls with messy top buns and swinging ponytails, Vivian's coarse curls were an aberration. She had not yet gained the ability to turn her difference into a strength, so she internalized the judgment of others and felt ashamed. While starving herself and jogging around the HUD-subsidized projects she lived in, she imagined how desirable she'd be, and how socially at ease, if her hair flowed effortlessly over her shoulders like theirs.

Vivian's mother, Anita, was Puerto Rican with fine curls, so she didn't understand the specific challenges of straightening Vivian's hair. (She was also impatient and intolerant of any hassle, such that learning how to manage her daughter's hair was unfathomable.) They'd outsource the labor to salons but none of them were run by black people, and something would always go wrong. The stylist would use a too-mild relaxer before blowing her hair out with insufficient heat and it would wind up big and wavy. Once Vivian got a perfect blowout but then ruined it with water because she didn't understand hair science and no one told her otherwise. Now that she was in New York, though, she had access to the best blowout artists in the world and could go back and forth between textures as often as she liked.

"Tu cabello es hermoso, pero muy seco," Marisol said.

Vivian laughed.

"You understand?"

Vivian nodded.

"You're just a wash-and-go girl, right?"

"Yeah."

"I can tell," Marisol said with a laugh. "But every once in a while you have to deep-condition, okay? Especially when you're losing pigment—you have these grays here," she said, grabbing a handful of Vivian's hair in the front.

Vivian wanted to say she didn't have any time for deep conditioning and couldn't care less about gray hair, but she didn't.

"Anyway, it's not too bad, not much breakage," Marisol said, as if to acknowledge that she'd been a little harsh before.

Occasionally, while Marisol was blow-drying and then flat-ironing her hair, one of the hairdressers would playfully yell at a coworker across the room in Spanish, and Vivian shrank back, flashing to being yelled at, nonplayfully, by a family member, as a child, and she'd get a contaminated feeling that she'd have to shake off. But after just three hours of flickering, vestigial sensations, Vivian left the salon with heat-damaged but bone-straight hair looking like a completely different, ethnically ambiguous person. Every block or so, she ran her fingers through her hair or shifted her head just so, hiding her side profile with her hair.

At home, she listened to "Right" by David Bowie, featuring

Luther Vandross, which always made her feel sexy, and changed into her first-date floral tennis skirt (the keto diet had eliminated her lower-belly pooch) and white Keds. On her way to the Williamsburg rooftop bar where she was meeting Matthew, she could see her reflection in empty store windows, and the reflection was good. You couldn't see any cellulite in the sun. While walking the mile-long stretch of Bedford Avenue between McCarren Park and the bridge, Vivian thought about the long history of white artists bringing black singers into the recording studio to prop up their weak voices and then about how the neighborhood had changed since she'd moved to New York. There used to be graffiti here, independent restaurants and shops, a robust Latino community. Now there were an Apple Store and a Whole Foods and everyone spoke French.

She was alarmed to hear a child crying behind her. She turned to see a toddler having a temper tantrum while a woman (mother? babysitter?) coolly recorded him with her phone. Vivian tried to make sense of the fact that the woman didn't engage with the boy in any way. She didn't yell at him or express embarrassment to the other adults, like the subway mother would have, like her own mother would have. Nor did she move to comfort him through his big emotions, like the ideal mother would have. She just filmed him, as if he were some safari animal, a potential source of internet fame.

Vivian arrived at the hotel rooftop bar five minutes early and quickly surveyed the room, evaluating the attractiveness of the women she saw there. Matthew hadn't arrived yet, so she started a conversation with a very fit woman waiting to order a drink at the bar, so that when he arrived he would see her as gregarious and unafraid to talk to strangers. The woman's name was Ally, or something. Ally, she learned, had "finally reached that point" in her life where she could "be bicoastal." Vivian joked that she would probably get even thinner in LA because of the social contagion of eating disorders, and for that reason alone she'd love to move there, and Ally laughed and relaxed and offered her a stool.

After a bit of back-and-forth, Ally went into a monologue about how ("You'll appreciate this") she grew up in Atlanta "during the 1980s child murders" and how, due to her mother's hysteria, she was raised to be afraid of being kidnapped and asphyxiated. Vivian did appreciate this, and leaned in conspiratorially to say, "Tell me more."

In childhood Ally's mother had been super-protective, going as far as buying a bullmastiff to protect her daughters. With age Ally developed a neurosis around being attacked, and, now tipsy, she speculated that maybe that was why she "got a huge boyfriend in high school," whom she was now engaged to, though despite having him around she had still been a fearful teen, and had, for example, attacked a handyman with a cast-iron pan one day when, assuming familiarity, he had opened the unlocked front door unannounced. He didn't press charges.

Vivian noted to herself that the victims of the Atlanta child murders had all been black, according to the Wikipedia page, which she had surreptitiously looked at while Ally was talking. Ally was white, which meant her neurosis was mistaken, a version of unnecessary suffering that made Vivian laugh, thinking of it as a kind of *psychological reparations,* she wrote in her Notes app, only to be interrupted by a text from Matthew, who had arrived.

He tapped her on the shoulder and when she saw him, sweet terror. He had a boyish face that looked like the person behind it hadn't experienced anything bad or, if he had, he had metabolized it quickly, and his smile broadcast "carefree" and "love of life." He was the most enticing thing in the world. They hugged each other hello, and as he said, "I wasn't expecting you to have straight hair," she frowned into his shoulder.

"Disappointed?"

"Not at all. Though I do love natural hair," he said playfully.

As they walked up a dark flight of stairs to the second bar, on the roof, Vivian chided herself for the blowout. And why did men insist on having the woman walk up the stairs first all the time?

Matthew said he chose the bar so they could see the sunset, that he loved "chasing sunsets." He said he'd just returned from a week at his brother's place in a tiny town butted up against the Sierra Nevada, and that he'd gotten used to the peaceful feeling of hiking up and watching the sky until dusk.

Channeling nineties black humor, Vivian deadpanned, "White people *love* hiking," and Matthew sort of cringed. To save it, she softened, saying it actually sounded amazing. "Nature's theater," she said, and he smiled, opening toward her.

They talked about where they were from, with Vivian delivering her line, years recycled, "I don't have a sense of geographical identity," which had the desired effect of shutting down any inquiry into her family or childhood.

Matthew said he grew up in Massachusetts, near Boston, among other biographical information that Vivian already knew about him. He continued, though, with details that weren't available online. In high school, a shoulder injury led to a surgery that was perhaps premature and the wrong move (that his parents had chosen surgery instead of physical therapy seemed still to bother him), which led to him giving up playing sports at the college level and focusing all his efforts on the saxophone.

Vivian joked that his life sounded like a story arc on *Friday Night Lights*, which she loved despite it being about football, and he laughed, while she mentally constructed a narrative of their essential compatibility as highly musical and creative people, although her creativity had lapsed since college. A relationship with Matthew would allow her greater access to it.

They hit their stride in the conversation when she mentioned meditation, which she knew he'd been practicing for years. "I love the quiet superiority of the Buddhist attitude," she said, scoring another laugh. Meditation was slow going, though, because whenever her thoughts wandered, she felt like she was making a mistake.

Matthew winced. "No, it's not like that, you need to get rid of the concept of 'mistake' entirely, the whole philosophy is about experiencing your thoughts and not judging them or yourself for having them, so there aren't any mistakes. Self-criticism actually takes you away from the whole purpose of meditating."

The irony of being scolded for a fear of making mistakes was not lost on her, but she eroticized it so it stung less, and with deliberately reverent curiosity, she asked how meditation had changed him. It had made him less judgmental, he said, more aware of his body and emotions, and he experienced moments of pure joy.

Starting to become attached, Vivian said that there was now a backlash against meditation in the culture ("which is stupid, because it's like having a backlash against the sun"), and that anti-meditation jokes were appearing in popular comedic programming. "And it's like," she said, "I'm not better than other people because I meditate." She paused. "I'm better than other people because I meditate, I run twelve miles a week, I represent patients in a psychiatric hospital, and I'm writing a novel about representing patients in a psychiatric hospital." Vivian laughed to let him know that she was performing narcissism. Matthew laughed back with his entire body.

He asked what kinds of stories she had about her job, so she gave him what she thought he wanted: a well-paced thriller that would demonstrate her heroism in the face of danger. She narrated taking the knife from Melissa yesterday, how she expertly covered her vital organs, how her connection with the girl was instantaneous and strange, as she'd never really been interested in teens, how protective she felt toward her, how she'd felt no fear in the moment.

While speaking she scanned Matthew's face for romantic interest or at the very least fascination. His eyes were enlarged but she wasn't sure. It might just be respect.

After, he made a bad joke that her story was "insane."

"How did you think to protect yourself with the pillow?"

"I go on weird research binges at night," she said. She also knew how to escape from the trunk of a car, get out of handcuffs, and survive being buried alive. But that wasn't first-date conversation.

Matthew asked if she was comfortable where she was standing. She said she didn't know, which made her ashamed.

"I guess I haven't been meditating enough to know what my body is feeling," she said, laughing. As he laughed very hard in response, she realized that no, she wasn't comfortable. Her lower back was vaguely throbbing, actually. How long had that been going on?

Still, Vivian felt a small sense of victory, and excused herself to go to the bathroom. She didn't have to pee, she was just tired of being looked at. She walked through the bar, projecting sociability until she stepped into the single-occupancy bathroom, where an obscure emotion dragged her face down. She pulled down her skirt and black cotton underwear with lace trim, smelling herself, trying to eliminate water and alcohol, recalling the softness of Matthew's T-shirt, which she had gently gripped when they hugged, and that phrase of his, "pure joy." That was not a state she knew anything about.

In truth, she wasn't meditating as much as she implied, but she needed him to feel like they were simpatico. What she hadn't told Matthew—because she didn't want to make him feel uncomfortable—was that to her the appeal of meditation was the tantalizing possibility of perceptual transformation. It promised that a bleak world view could be challenged, changed even, if you worked hard enough. Hard work was comforting.

After flushing, Vivian squatted in front of the bathroom's long mirror in a chair pose, looking for indentations in her legs, noting that they were simultaneously thin and full of fat. She stood then, flexing her right arm, admiring the muscles that were slowly starting to form there.

She hoped her arm would always appear so thin.

She feared it wouldn't.

She popped a travel Tylenol and returned from the

bathroom to find that Matthew had settled the bill. He was rejecting her. The date was over. Dreading the loss, she was protectively blithe.

"You paid! Thanks."

They walked through the crowded bar in silence. Each second of their not speaking felt like a condemnation. In the elevator, Vivian crossed her arms and tried not to reveal how unstable she felt. If Matthew ended the date now, it would be unmanageable. She said it was very quiet in the elevator and made another mindfulness joke, instructing Matthew to "Feel the soles of your feet on the floor" in her best meditation-instructor voice, and he said she was pretty funny, that she made him laugh out loud but also sometimes in his head.

Vivian said, "Is that sarcasm?"

Matthew smiled but didn't answer.

"Because I think I'm sarcasm-blind."

He laughed again but didn't say anything.

Vivian reflexively pinched her belly fat as they walked out into the night. She couldn't read him, couldn't tell how she was doing.

"So," Matthew started. "What's your schedule like tonight? Can you hang out more?" She felt a wave of relief; she had passed the first hurdle.

As they walked to their second destination, which Matthew kept a secret, Vivian talked with renewed, if exaggerated, vigor. She went on about how she had been a raver as a teen ("Always house and drum and bass, never happy hardcore, sometimes yes to drugs, sometimes no to drugs, always dancing, wearing candy and a crop top, my girlfriend wore fairy wings and my boyfriend had a pacifier!") and when she was playing him "If You Believe" by Chantay Savage on her phone, explaining that it was emblematic of deep house, and that she had always wanted to be one of the "soulful, a synonym for black" singers on a house track, Matthew laughed, took her hand, and stopped walking. She turned to face him.

"You're so funny," he said again softly.

She looked away while he stroked her hand.

"Humor is my favorite defense mechanism."

"That was funny too."

"Well, I'm really scared right now."

He kissed her. Vivian was slow to open her mouth at first but when she did, he pulled her close to him.

"That was, like, on cue," Vivian said.

The venue turned out to be a restaurant and bar that featured unobtrusive live music. They arrived in time to get a pretty choice seat, best in the house, with a full view of the pianist, the drummer, and the small horn ensemble.

Matthew said of the horns tuning before playing, "Often this is the best part," which she had actually thought before, and believed that the fact that he said it demonstrated that they were made for each other.

They sat side by side in the curved booth and he put his arm around her, gently stroking her neck and shoulder. She hadn't been touched by someone so great in a while, and she liked it very much. Still, a vague fear was present at the edge of her consciousness. As the music played, Matthew stomped his feet and bit his lower lip in a way that Vivian thought was both lame and adorable and she alternated between watching the musicians and looking at him. She was assessing, barely listening.

Matthew took the lead in ordering for them and Vivian allowed it, sitting up tall in a posture of automatic obedience.

He first ordered the mushroom crostini, which she resented because she didn't like mushrooms and didn't want to eat bread. But then, seeming to suddenly remember that she was there, that she was a person who might have her own desires, he asked her what she wanted. It was nice to watch him recalibrate.

Vivian wanted mussels (she always wanted mussels, she told him, because they were a nutrient-rich food and because it was very involved to eat them, which gave you something to do with your hands when you were nervous, but also they were easily manipulated, so you could eat them on a date while still posing and looking beautiful. Also, they weren't messy), so they got mussels and a salad, no fries because, she said, "I try to keep a low-carb diet."

Matthew made a slight, nearly imperceptible shrinking movement, as if he was resisting this statement.

When the food came, Matthew had the idea of feeding the mussels to Vivian, which played into one of her fantasies where she was serviced by someone and didn't have to do anything. He broke open one of the shells, separating the half with the meat in it. He dunked the half-shell into the rich, buttery sauce and then put it into Vivian's mouth, as if it were a spoon. Then, when some of the sauce dribbled onto her cheek, he kissed her there. She was so overwhelmed that she had to run to the bathroom to hide her feelings. Her joy felt so childish, so over-the-top.

"Make sure you come back," he said with a smile.

Vivian confronted herself in the mirror again. She practiced smiling and slowly danced to the music she could hear through the walls. With every twist and turn she appraised her face and body, examining herself from different angles.

Afterward, she stood at the doorway to the performance space. The music was pleasant, graceful and consistently medium-tempo. She could see Matthew but he couldn't see her. He was completely absorbed in the music now, stomping his right foot harder than before, bopping his head, grinning, not self-conscious. The look on his face resembled hers when she listened to something good. His body moved like hers. No matter where she was, at the supermarket, in a work meeting, on the subway, deep on a ward visiting a psychotic client, if a good song came on, she broke character. Her body reacted, rocking and responding, her eyes gleaming. Despite Vivian's little pretenses, this aspect of their connection was genuine.

The song ended and it was time to return to the table.

"I was listening from over there," she said, and Matthew leaned toward her, nuzzling her cheek. "It's like a supper-club set," she said. His kisses felt like acceptance.

"What do you know about supper-club sets," he whispered into her ear.

Was that some kind of dig because of my gender, Vivian thought, but before she could pick a fight, Matthew placed her hand on the crotch of his pants.

"No wonder you are so confident," Vivian said, squeezing him there.

Matthew sounded kind of stupid when he responded, "You seem confident too," and Vivian wanted to be demonstrably turned off again, but he was so good-looking and big that she kept kissing him.

Matthew kissed off her lipstick and remarked that she looked "like a completely different person," to which she responded, "Isn't that what men want? The feeling of dating different people?"

The art of conversation-in-between-kissing was another one of Vivian's specialties. It came naturally to her and she liked to turn it into an aesthetic act. Matthew meanwhile wore a dumb expression and kissed her again.

They left the restaurant. While waiting for her car they kissed a lot; they kissed intensely. He framed her face with his hands like they did in the movies. He squeezed out the world; he was the world. And though he hadn't asked for a second date, he said, into her ear, after a particularly deep kiss, "I think I fell a little bit in love with you tonight."

Vivian spent the night rolling around in her bed and touching herself. If he chose her, it could change her life.

SNAKE PIT

NO MATTER HOW happy you are, Mondays have a way of making you want to end it all. It comforted Vivian to imagine that rather than starting another workweek at Wellhaven, a hospital with one of the largest psychiatric units in the country, she was on a sound stage starring in a comedic legal procedural. Each week adoring fans rooted for her to win the big case, armed with a little legal knowledge and a lot of moxie. Based solely on the courage of her convictions, this underdog would get every client released from the hospital, cracking jokes and learning valuable lessons along the way.

But before she could save the day, someone would have to let her into the psych unit.

After arriving on the nineteenth floor Vivian rang a buzzer and waved her ID badge in front of the window. An older black nurse of considerable heft, Nurse Jackson, spied Vivian through the glass. When they made eye contact, she looked down at her clipboard, made a face like she'd just remembered an urgent task, and walked away from the door. It wasn't an isolated incident; other nurses and technicians ignored her too. Though they worked in the same place they were adversaries. Their job was to keep people in; Vivian's job was to get them out.

Eventually Dr. Creslin, the monstrously tall fifty-something lead psychiatrist on the floor, buzzed Vivian onto the unit, but not without lightly scolding her for not pulling it shut behind her and pointing to the ELOPEMENT RISK sign.

Vivian apologized and proceeded to pay the price of entry: listening to his bad jokes.

"One of my patients, you know, he thinks he can predict the future. So I ask him, 'How long have you been experiencing this?' He says to me, 'Since *next Friday.*'" He punctuated this with an elbow-ribbing motion Vivian thought people only did ironically.

Vivian pointed at him while smiling. "Good one."

The unit was loud this morning. Cut to patients everywhere, walking around in threadbare slippers, talking to themselves, to nurses, to each other. You could spot the overmedicated ones—they shuffled with the slow, stiff gait of the Tin Man and looked like people coming out of general anesthesia, eyes out of focus and drooling. An older white man with gray-white, powdery debris in the corner of his mouth stared at Vivian while salivating sexlessly. Instead of street clothes, he wore full-on hospital-grade shirt and pants (without drawstrings, as a suicide precaution), which meant he was an escape risk. He could barely bend his legs. He had a sweet face, so Vivian felt comfortable touching his elbow.

"Are you feeling stiff?" she asked.

The man muttered something incomprehensible.

"Looks like you're having trouble walking," she said, moving past him while he continued to mutter. "I'm one of the lawyers here. I'll find you after you've had some rest and we can talk, okay?"

He let out an affirmative grunt.

Joey, a recently admitted actor with mania, was pacing back and forth down the hall, eager for conversation.

"You changed your hair," he said.

"I did, I did," she said, touching the ends of her still-straight hair reflexively.

Joey tapped his feet on the floor.

"It makes you look Caucasian!" he said, looking impressed.

Vivian laughed and did a full-on Jim Halpert into the camera.

Walking past an older black man with thick glasses, she got a strong whiff of urine. The man politely asked Nurse Jackson where his doctor was.

"I told you I don't know where he is and you're just gonna have to wait! Go back to your room before I call the tech!" Nurse Jackson snapped, wrinkling up her nose as she smelled him, changing the mood of the scene. A technician could be dispatched at any time to "sedate" a patient deemed to be a threat, typically with a haloperidol injection.

"What are you looking at?" Nurse Jackson asked Vivian.

"Why don't we try to speak to the patients with respect?"

"Please. They need to treat *me* with respect."

"Well, he just asked you a question and you went off for no reason," Vivian said.

Nurse Jackson gave a look like, *Who do you think you are.* "I've been doing this since before you were born, sweetheart. I don't work for you."

It was too early to be fighting with nurses, so Vivian batted her away. "Whatever, I have to see my clients," she said.

Nurse Jackson looked at Vivian as if she had made a big mistake, the consequences of which would be visited upon her later. *But what can she do to me?* Vivian wondered. *She's just a nurse.*

Doctors were hard to find; they were often holed up in their offices doing paperwork to justify their all-too-frequent use of physical and chemical restraints. It was the nurses who did the primary patient care, though it was more like surveillance. Making sure people still had a pulse and were being compliant.

Vivian knew that the nurses had been threatened, spat on, grabbed, and assaulted throughout their careers but she often found herself at odds with them and unable to empathize. At best, the nurses' behavior was of the eye-rolling variety, of the dismissing-a-patient's-valid-questions-with-hostility variety, of the gaslighting variety, of the laughing-behind-patients'-backs variety. At its worst it was the four-point-restraints-because-a-female-patient-mocked-you variety, the punishing-misbehavior-by-depriving-patients-of-food variety, the forced-seclusion-because-you-don't-like-someone variety. She would have liked to scold them through chastising speeches. The problem was that she was at work. You couldn't really stand around in the workplace publicly denouncing things while imagining yourself to be a great figure, especially at a psychiatric hospital.

The television in the dayroom was on, and patients sat watching CNN with varying levels of engagement ranging from comatose to monofocused. Vivian stood in the doorway, imagining a camera slowly tracking across the room. A heavy white woman with yellow hair slumped over, picking at her skin. A black man in his late fifties sat slack-jawed, staring at the screen, muttering to himself about the new president in looped, monotone sentences. A group of older men played cards by the wall.

Vivian heard someone playing "Onward Christian Soldiers" on the woefully out-of-tune piano in the recreation room. It was Ms. G., a former music teacher and devout Christian who had been brought to Wellhaven by the police after she'd been found proselytizing outside a bank in Manhattan about the evils of late-stage capitalism.

When not preaching, Ms. G. played piano. Hymns mostly, but she also had an impressive vaudeville repertoire. While pounding out a tune, Ms. G. would narrate on the darkest subjects. She was currently sing-talking about a recurring figure. "Ron Dent raped me tremendously in 1984," she said, over the piano, "put his filthy dick in my mouth. As a result, my phone went dead for nine months. Who gets punished? My family and me. My father is dead and I'm in this place, all thanks to Ron Dent." It was like trauma survivor cabaret.

There was an opening between songs, so Vivian slowly moved toward her and called out gently, "Ms. G.?"

Ms. G. stopped playing and turned around. She wore a long floral prairie dress with ruffles, straight out of the Dust Bowl.

"Oh hey, it's you," she said. "I haven't trusted lawyers since I was a kid. I always say I wasn't raised by parents, I was raised by lawyers!"

Ms. G. did a piano flourish and laughed loudly to herself.

"At least you were raised," Vivian said. "*I* was flattened."

Ms. G. raised an eyebrow and smirked, relaxing a little.

Vivian tried to bring up the release hearing, explaining that in order to keep her in, the hospital had to prove that she was a danger either to herself or to others. Ms. G. responded with a long, winding monologue about various rapes and encroachments. "Everyone fondled me but they called it tickling, that's how they get away with it, see? Euphemism and deceit. I've had six gynecological surgeries! I lost my vision for a year, but the day Ron Dent died it came back. God is good."

There was nothing to do but listen as Ms. G. cycled through overwhelming events. Vivian knew what this felt like, the rumination vortex. At times she was pulled into it, like when she was stoned, but often she went willingly. It was like she was an archaeologist and her violent past was the dig site: she had to pore over, process, and record every inch of land to get the job done. But as she listened to Ms. G., she started to doubt whether either of them was actually excavating anything. They were kind of just poking around.

After, Ms. G. yawned, turned back to the piano, and launched into "What a Friend We Have in Jesus."

Suddenly Vivian felt herself being looked at by Nolan, a cabbie who'd been admitted to the hospital by his union rep after several complaints of lewd comments by women passengers. He was talking to Nurse Smith, who was tight with Nurse Jackson, and when Vivian said hello, she noticed that Nurse Smith's hello wasn't as effervescent as normal. Had Nurse Jackson gotten to her already? As she passed, Nolan made elevator eyes at Vivian and said, "Look at the pretty lawyer," and Nurse Smith cackled as if they were in cahoots.

Vivian headed to the dining room to see Melissa. She knew she could find her sketching there. When she turned eighteen a few days ago, Melissa was transferred to the adult unit. She was already getting into trouble up here. Over the weekend she'd threatened a male patient twice her size for touching her shoulder.

Patients were scattered throughout the yellow room, picking at flavorless vegetables with plastic forks. Melissa sat at a table by herself, working intensely in a large sketchpad. Her long black hair was pulled back into a tight ponytail and somehow she'd given herself a perfect cat eye. Today she was in patient scrubs, but she'd still rolled up the sleeves of the top so everyone could see how strong she was.

"How you doing today, Melissa?" Vivian tried, sitting down across from her.

Melissa said nothing, continuing to draw. Now that she was up close and not fearing bodily injury, Vivian could see the adolescent acne all over Melissa's face. It didn't take away from her beauty, though.

"Let me ask you something—after that thing with the knife, how'd you get them to give you eyeliner *and* colored pencils?"

Melissa smirked in spite of herself and looked up, holding her sketchpad to her chest so Vivian couldn't peek.

"I got my social worker to tell them drawing is 'therapeutic,'" she bragged. Then, in a low whisper, "I stole the eyeliner from one of the nurses' bags. They all left the nurses' station when some lady tried to hang herself or whatever." She smiled at Vivian with her tongue between her teeth, then looked back down at her drawing.

"Good job. That's like reparations. Do you know what reparations are?"

"It's like payback, right?"

"Exactly—it's payback you don't have to feel bad about. So look, it's going to be hard to get you out because of what happened last week. These judges don't like weapons. It could be helpful, though, if maybe someone in your family could—"

"What family?" Melissa said sharply, staring Vivian down. Her eyes were weary and knowing. Fuck. She had forgotten that Melissa had been homeless for months.

"Hey, I'm sorry. Can you remind me what happened?"

Melissa looked searchingly at Vivian, trying to see if she could be trusted.

"I work for you, okay?" Vivian said. "I can't talk to anyone about what you tell me unless you give me permission—I lose my license if I do that. I just want to know your side of what happened at home and why you think you're in here."

Melissa closed the sketchpad and placed it in her lap, gripping it as she began to speak.

"My mom had This Person staying with us and he's just mean. Always nitpicking and judging me, he hates that I don't wear frilly clothes and screams at me for every little thing. It got so bad that I didn't even leave my room to eat; I'd rather stay in my room and starve than get yelled at. So we got into it one day and I called him a punk bitch and he threw a stool at my head. He missed, of course." She flashed that wicked smile again. "So then he threw my new phone. I kept waiting for my mom to step in but she took his side, and was telling *me* to calm down. So I waited a few days for things to cool off and when they thought I had forgot, I took a baseball bat and I just went off. I broke all the family photos and all his bullshit sports collectibles and bounced. My mom wouldn't let me back in unless I apologized and replaced the broken items or whatever. I didn't, and I been jumping from house to house since."

Melissa described how, after bouncing from one friend's place to another and sleeping on trains and under bridges, she ended up in Port Authority, charging her busted-up phone on the floor, trying to look like a college student at an airport instead of a homeless teen surrounded by pigeons. There were men everywhere, carrying duffel bags and plastic bags and rolling bags, eyeing her and hollering at her and sniffing around her. When one of them tried to grope her she fled, spending nights in the streets. She got her period one night and didn't know what to do, so she started buzzing intercoms. When a woman finally answered she asked her if she could come to get some pads, and the woman called the police, who brought her to the hospital, where she was diagnosed with conduct disorder.

Nolan had now entered the dining room and was sitting at a table in the corner, watching them and narrating. "Now the pretty lawyer's talking to the wild girl, now she's writing, now she's looking at me and now she's looking back at the wild girl and now she's crossing her legs."

"I'm just so tired of being scared, you know? Not being listened to and disrespected by these people. You supposed to be my protector," Melissa said, her voice wavering as she gesticulated to an invisible third person.

"But you protect *him*, not me. It's embarrassing." She looked back at Vivian. "I'm ashamed to be her daughter to be honest with you. So, fuck her. You don't defend me when I need you, you are nothing to me."

Vivian pressed her lips together as if from pain and then zoned out, looking at a half-full cafeteria tray. Dry mashed potatoes and slabs of an unidentifiable protein.

"You all right?" Melissa asked.

"I'm just really hearing what you are saying." Then, quietly: "We had a similar upbringing."

They looked at each other. For the briefest of moments, the anger in Melissa's eyes receded to reveal a teratoma of grief. Quiet discernment passed between them. It felt inappropriate, how much Vivian wanted to help Melissa then. And not just to help—to rescue.

Then when she looked at Nolan, as if to atone for some trespass, he said, with the cadence of a young boy trying to get the attention of his mother, "I saw my cousin rubbing his child's penis until it got hard!"

Melissa laughed, and Vivian tried not to.

"I put a gun to his head and pulled the trigger!" he yelled. After being heard, Nolan seemed to snap out of his ravings and walked away.

"What were you feeling, when you broke everything?"

"I felt amazing, it was like, beating someone down after they've been pressing your buttons. Only this time, they'd been pressing my buttons for seventeen years."

"Were you afraid he would hurt you when he found out?"

Melissa waved her hand away. "If he laid his hands on me, I would end that dude like anyone else who tried to come for me."

"You aren't afraid of being hit?"

Melissa shook her head.

"I'm afraid of getting hurt every day," Vivian said, shocked again at her candor.

"I'm like the girl who's still in the gang and you the girl that got out of the gang."

Vivian laughed. She was overcome for a second at how insightful Melissa was, and how self-possessed. She had a good foundation for survival. But that wasn't enough. The girl needed support, affirmation. *Come live with me,* she wanted to say.

"There's a rush to it, though," Melissa continued, shaking her head and smiling. "That guilt-free reparations, like you said."

"Is that why you took the knife the other day? Were you getting back at someone?"

"This girl kept teasing me, saying I have arms like a boy. It's like, these are just my arms. I accidentally cut that nurse when she reached out her hand. That's when I got scared and ran to my room."

"So when the judge asks you if you meant to hurt someone with the knife, what will you say?"

"I'll say of course not. The way I see it, the pictures and sports stuff I destroyed, the mattress I cut up—those are safe targets. Better I lash out at *things* than, like, a person, right?"

"That's completely right. Safe targets. I love it. So what happened after I took the knife from you?"

"Bunch of dudes barged in trying to strap me down and I don't like that shit, so I was kicking and screaming and I bit Carl in the arm."

Melissa smiled again proudly.

"Any incidents since then?"

"Nah, they just better not strap me down again, I swear."

Vivian took a risk, reaching out to touch Melissa's hand. "I'm going to make sure that doesn't happen again. But you have to try too. They can only strap you down if you give them a reason to. Stay calm, don't raise your voice, and don't threaten anyone, okay?"

"I'll do my best."

"And do your best not to take anything else from the nurses, either."

They both laughed and she left it at that. There were other clients to see and it was almost noon. She heard her stomach make noise and realized she felt faint. She dug out a baggie of roasted unsalted cashews from her blazer and popped some into her mouth while leaning up against a wall. Her phone vibrated. It was a text from Matthew.

Had so much fun the other night. hang again soon?

Vivian beamed with joy and had the urge to take this week's episode in a musical direction. To a jaunty tune played by Ms. G., she'd waltz with Joey and the newly limber Tin Men, then Nolan would lift her up onto one of the dining room tables and she'd tap-dance on it. There'd be no restraints for the day and she'd go around freeing patients from seclusion, until everyone—patients, nurses, techs, and doctors alike— was tap-dancing and strutting toward the camera in unison in an unbroken cut. For the big finale, Vivian, Ms. G., and Nurse Jackson would jump up and turn over a couch in the dayroom à la *Singin' in the Rain*, and they'd all wind up seated on the couch, giggling and nudging each other good-naturedly.

As she stood there eating and daydreaming, the camera spotted an older white balding man lifting up his shirt and yelling at a nurse, "Why do I have breasts? Men don't have breasts! WHY DO I HAVE BREASTS?" Then he squeezed his breasts provocatively, one at a time. The nurse, impassive, replied, "It's a side effect of your medication, Bill," and made a note on her chart.

Down the hall patients were lining up for pizza and music

in the dayroom. Vivian scanned the line for Linda, a native South Brooklynite in her early twenties and the most beautiful woman on the floor. She wore her black hair in a chin-length bob, the hair providing a stark contrast to her gleaming green eyes. She always had on a tight black leather jacket.

Linda had been diagnosed as bipolar and had been in and out of city hospitals since she was sixteen. Her married boyfriend had recently broken off their affair, which triggered a meltdown, and she'd been admitted by her mother after ingesting a bottle of Tylenol in a desperate attempt to win back his affections.

Linda's roommate, Angela, twenty-four, was usually near her side. Angela was heavy, with brown disheveled hair and white glasses that were being held together with tape of various colors and thicknesses. She spoke like a child.

Vivian approached them and asked when she could talk to Linda about her hearing, but then Angela interrupted to ask when *she* was going to be getting out of the hospital, and while Vivian was talking to Angela, Linda began to jump up and down in place. Vivian whispered to Angela, so that none of the other patients on the line could hear, that at the last hearing the judge had determined that she still wanted to hurt herself and so she'd have to stay at least another month. Angela's face twisted and she started crying, after which Linda stepped in front of Angela to talk to Vivian, in a kind of hammy way, which set Angela off more with the crying, and while Vivian tried to comfort Angela, Linda danced around them, grinning.

"I can talk right now," Linda said in a singsongy, bragging voice, so they walked to the room she shared with Angela, which, like all the other rooms, was minimalist and low-stimulus, featuring two twin beds on wood slats on either wall and two hospital-green armchairs. The smell of industrial disinfectant was strong. Vivian adjusted her skirt and sat on the edge of one of the armchairs and Linda plopped into the other one and began recounting, unprompted, the grand tale of her breakup with her boyfriend Brian (which she pronounced "Broy-uhn"), whom she'd met while webcamming.

"So I fell for this guy, one of my clients. He was a huge guy. Into heavy drugs, maybe some white nationalist stuff I dunno, but still a good guy anyway," she said, starting to cry. "I'm sorry," she then slurred, removing from her jacket a tear-soaked color printed photo of Brian.

"Ain't he beautiful?" she asked suddenly, looking up at Vivian, green eyes glistening with tears.

Brian was tall and muscular with angular features. Vivian made a face for the camera like, *Very attractive for a Nazi.* While fingering the photo, Linda had a look of blissed-out rapture.

"I waited my whole life for someone so beautiful," she said, and Vivian covered her mouth, trying not to smile, thinking of Matthew and the secret unanswered text she had on her phone.

"Once we started seeing each other, I said 'I love you' to him in my head a hundred times a day. I knew he was married but I didn't care. I just wanted to make him happy. So I dressed up like a little princess even though it's not my style, you ever done that?"

"Sure," Vivian admitted, recalling a year she wore pink.

"That's what girls do, right?" Linda laughed.

Vivian shifted in the cheap armchair. She didn't like to think about it that way.

"And I'd bring him other girls and watch him be with them. Then he started strangling me, sometimes with his bare hands, and once with a phone cord. He'd picked up an old landline phone and texted me a picture, saying he couldn't wait to wrap it around my pretty neck. And I let him." She shrugged.

Vivian touched her own throat as she received this information.

"Were you afraid?" she finally asked.

Linda said, "Nah. I just thought, *'Well, if I'm gonna die, at least it gets to be with him.'*"

She looked at Vivian with the world-weary honesty of the addict then, and Vivian just whispered, "Damn."

"I lived, though, ha, ha. But he wouldn't leave his wife!" Linda cried out. She folded into herself, making the loud, effortful vocalizations of a distressed child. "He threw me out like I was a used napkin. So that's when I started thinking about taking the pills." She started to collect herself, wiping her snotty nose with her hand.

"You wanted to kill yourself?" Vivian asked, like she'd been trained to do.

"Nah," Linda said, shrugging. "I just did that to get Brian back. I took the pills just so I could call him, so he'd rescue me, but he didn't answer the phone, because *she* wouldn't let him, so I had to call Ma."

"And what about now? Do you want to hurt yourself now?" Linda shook her head.

"So if the judge asks you if you want to hurt yourself, what will you say?"

"I'll say I made a stupid mistake. I want to live. And I miss my kitties. Snowball and Nugget," Linda said, and started off on a new round of crying.

Vivian told Linda to say exactly that. Linda nodded and looked into Vivian's eyes and promised she would, and they both stood. Linda thrust her arms out and embraced her. Vivian patted Linda's back briskly, like they were players on the same team, then pivoted out of the hug.

After, they walked back to the dayroom, where Linda ordered Vivian to stay with her and hang out, promising that if she did so, Linda wouldn't "lose it" at the hearing. But instead of talking to Vivian, Linda danced alone to "Careless Whisper" in the middle of the room, while the other patients ate pizza. Vivian watched her dance while leaning on a windowsill on the opposite side of the room. Linda slowly and meticulously pointed her toes, twirling and raising her hands above her head like a snow globe ballerina, while silently crying. Vivian couldn't stop looking at Linda's face, which seemed to glorify suffering as much as it reflected it, her eyes determinedly generating tears that she wiped away slowly, with both hands in synchronicity, as if choreographed. Occasionally while sniffling loudly, like a child in thrall to her tantrum, she sang snatches of the lyrics, slowly and completely out of sync with the song, before bursting out, "I miss Brian!" Angela asked, "You want me to save you a slice?" and without breaking character, Linda said she wanted sausage.

❖

Vivian ate lunch alone in her sterile, beige, fluorescent-flooded, and windowless office. She didn't hate the other lawyers she worked with so much as she dismissed them as basic and uninteresting. Most of them were older than her and had families. Their downtime conversation would often turn to a domestic sphere that Vivian had no interest in. Meredith's son was having difficulty eating and so she had to take him to a feeding therapist. Leslie struggled as a single mom raising twin girls. Nathan's son had a disability that resulted in developmental delays. They didn't share her liberation politics and often sided with the doctors. Leslie regularly mocked her clients in court, rolling her eyes as they spoke nonsense or articulated delusions. Vivian had fought with Nathan over his deference to the psychiatrists and accused him of not zealously advocating for their clients, and he'd basically stopped talking to her. Meredith was sweet, but ineffective at trials. Also, they teased her for eating the same salad every day, demanding to know how she could live without dietary variety. "I don't have time for variety," she'd said.

She shoved aside one of the many piles of medical records, legal pads, and Post-it notes to clear out a Tupperware-sized space on her desk, tore off the rubber lid, and shoveled forkfuls of Same Old Salad into her mouth (arugula, chicken, sun-dried tomatoes, and grilled artichokes). She scrolled through Matthew's Instagram and Facebook, hoping he'd mentioned meeting the love of his life the previous weekend online (he hadn't), pondering a response to his text.

She imagined being in a room filled with every kind of woman. Matthew would enter and stop at her. Since he'd casually mentioned wanting a family, she'd be holding a heretofore unwanted baby on her hip and cooking fragrant, extravagant dishes in multiple pots while wearing a miniskirt that showed off her perfectly toned gams. After having him taste the sauce, she would begin to philosophize about the concept of cognitive liberty. She'd explain that freedom of mind is the basis of all other freedoms, that every person has the right to determine whether to alter their consciousness or not, and that the state should not chemically interfere with an individual's mental state, no matter how wayward, as long as they are not a demonstrated threat to others.

Vivian locked her office door and put her hand over her warm crotch. Monologue complete, Matthew would compare her to the other women in the room and "select" her. He'd look at her the way Spencer Tracy looks at Katharine Hepburn in *Woman of the Year* and *Adam's Rib*, with ardor and reverence. The other women would disappear. They'd kiss, she would feel how big he was. No one would need to communicate any needs or preferences. He would carry her either to the bed, where he would fuck her harder than he intended to, or to the couch, where she would ride him without even taking off any clothes other than her underwear.

When she was finished, she texted back simply: yes, let's!

———◆———

Vivian was done for the day and was getting ready to head off the unit when Nurse Jackson interrupted her.

"New client for you, miss," Nurse Jackson said sweetly.

"Really?" Vivian replied.

Nurse Jackson smiled.

"Name is Lester, said he really needs to speak to a lawyer," she said, pointing to the dining room.

"He's a real sweet man," she added.

Vivian thanked Nurse Jackson and felt proud of herself. She'd admonished her earlier and, by doing so, had earned her respect. It was clear that Vivian was someone who would blow the whistle on injustice of all forms, and that she was not to be messed with.

Vivian walked back toward the dining room, which was empty but for a light-skinned man with the body of a full-back at the end of the room. His back was to her and he was eating in hospital clothes.

She called out, "Lester?"

He didn't respond.

Walking faster toward him, she said it again, friendly and nonjudgmental.

"Lester…I'm not sure what your last name is." She laughed.

The man said something she couldn't hear, so she walked closer.

"Hi, Lester, I'm—"

As she approached him from behind the man quickly stood up and whirled around, towering a foot above her.

"WHO THE FUCK IS LESTER?" he shouted, flipping up his lunch tray. Mashed potatoes hit the wall, and Vivian's face.

She turned and ran.

"His name is Andre!" she heard Nurse Jackson say. She was gripping Nurse Smith and laughing. "Thinks she's better than me," Nurse Jackson added, shaking her head. For a second Nurse Smith looked at Vivian with empathy but it was quickly replaced by mockery. While the women laughed Vivian hurried off the ward, removing her phone from her blazer and pretending to take a call, wiping the mashed potatoes off her face in a casual and unhurried manner.

FAMILY OF ORIGIN

THE FAMILY REUNION was being held at her aunt Carmen's place in Bridgeport. "It's in the ghetto," Anita had warned her over the phone. "You know your aunt loves the ghetto."

Although they weren't close now and in fact she hadn't seen her in years, Vivian had always experienced Carmen as a safe and benevolent presence. As a kid she had spent many nights at her aunt's baking cookies, listening to music, dancing. Carmen was always kind, never vindictive, and hadn't once shamed her bed-wetting.

Vivian spent a long time dressing for the cookout at her apartment, posing in various outfits in front of the mirror. At first she thought she shouldn't wear anything too revealing, but then she scolded herself—*This is a family cookout, why are you being paranoid, you can wear whatever you want*—and decided on a sleeveless fit-and-flare floral minidress. It was the last weekend of the summer!

Julio picked her up from the train station by himself. She got in and kissed him on the cheek, getting a strong whiff of Nautica. He looked like a Puerto Rican Billy Crystal. On the way to her aunt's they alternated between prepackaged anecdotes, strained silences, and talk about movies. Julio and Anita had just watched "that one where Catherine Keener's husband cheats on her with Amanda Peet," he said.

"I love that one," Vivian said.

Julio had never been abusive, it was just that he'd married her mother when Vivian was a teenager and she had already emancipated herself, at least psychologically, from the notion of a family. She'd always kept her distance.

Once they reached her aunt's neighborhood, Julio repeated Anita's "ghetto" warning. He said it as if Vivian had become so accustomed to a middle-class lifestyle that she'd be uncomfortable. That wasn't quite true, though. Mostly it was being around her family that made her uncomfortable.

Looking out the window, Vivian grimly laughed to herself, imagining how she would describe this place to Matthew. There were hood characteristics after all: discount liquor stores, woofer vibrations from myriad sources, bulletproof store windows, and a "Who's Your Daddy?" DNA-testing truck. But these were just surface details, and she wouldn't want to share them with a white person without placing them in a rich sociohistorical context (redlining, the clustering of alcohol purveyors in black neighborhoods, masculinity displays, et cetera). Julio stuck to the main roads, which, as Vivian recalled, were like a tourist area compared to the side streets, where the real hood was.

Vivian had come a long way from this place, a long way from the projects, the gangs and shootings, the empty storefronts and low-rent hotels. She was more Black Rock than east side, which they drove through now: Stratford Avenue, Seaview Avenue, Connecticut Avenue, negligently littered streets where people who looked like Vivian were already drinking themselves to death by noon, though at least they had porches to drink themselves to death on and some of the porches were grand, with columns in the Italianate style.

Vivian knew, from being told, that when she was little they'd lived in the Beardsley Terrace housing projects, a series of low-rises at the north end of the city. Her only memory of the Terrace was of being about five years old, walking around the projects on a sweltering day with her aunt Carmen listening to a portable radio, singing and dancing to Color Me Badd and Jade and SWV in the heat, feeling safe and accepted. Shortly after, the violent man had entered their lives and moved them to a house on the south side, far away from Carmen and the rest of the family.

Anita's main priority in life, always, was snagging some guy. It didn't matter how psychologically fit he was or whether he was a man of character, as long as he would be there with her at night and do all the things she didn't want to do. She needed a man to take her to work, because she couldn't drive. She needed a man to supplement the bills, because she never finished high school or any other certificate program she signed up for. She needed a man to assemble furniture, to fix the toilet, to patch up the holes where the mice got in. She even needed a man to hang up the *Head of Christ* painting that she carried with her from cheap apartment to cheap apartment. The violent man did all of these things, and many more.

After a few years Anita finally understood that if she stayed with the violent man, they would all either die or suffer permanent injury. So they made a plan to leave the next time he was out drinking, and moved to a midwestern city where the largest employer was a Catholic health care provider.

Anita's favorite cousin, Jeannette, lived there, and she intro-duced Anita to Julio, a postal worker. They quickly fell in love and were married. Vivian knew by then that you couldn't trust men at first, that you had to withhold judgment, care-fully evaluating them in a variety of contexts before you made your final determination. Because there were men who raped children and there were men who didn't, and of the men who didn't rape children, there were men who beat children and there were men who didn't. Julio turned out to be a man who didn't beat or rape children; instead, he was a man who used his status as the primary breadwinner to encourage children to behave the way he wanted. If Vivian was social and performed A-student cheeriness at a cookout, she'd get new school clothes and running-around money. But if she was moody and refused to come out and watch boxing with the family, she wouldn't get any rides to the mall. Compared to the violence before, Julio's personality felt entirely navigable, quaint even, and the solution was simple: *Fuck boxing and fuck the mall.*

After they married, Anita stopped working in the poultry plant, stopped studying to be a medical office assistant, stopped going out dancing, never learned to drive, and never left the house unless he took her somewhere. She became completely dependent and seemed to like it, relishing that she existed only for Julio, existed only to clean for him and cook for him and laugh with him and to entertain his family and friends. Vivian was grossed out by their relationship but also edged out by it—they were a twosome with no room for children, who should be seen and not heard. So she withdrew, into her room, into her music, into her journal, into boys, into school, into her head.

They had separated once, Julio and Anita. There was a year where he went back to his ex-wife. Anita was completely despondent. Didn't get out of bed, didn't eat. Vivian remembered trying to open Anita's bedroom door one morning before school, to say goodbye and ask her if she needed anything. She found Anita sitting up in bed, midsob, swaddled in her favorite color, purple—purple walls, purple sheets, purple pillows, purple nightgown. There were used tissues all over the bed and nightstand and multiple ashtrays filled with soggy cigarettes. Anita's face was stained with eyeliner and mascara from the night before. "Leave me alone!" she'd shouted, and Vivian immediately slammed the door shut and ran to school.

"It's here," Julio said now as he parked near a field. She had been expecting her aunt to live in one of the two-story row houses that were so common here, the kind with brick on the bottom and siding on top. But Carmen lived in a cream-colored duplex home with a large, welcoming porch. Since the house opened directly onto the field, it felt like her aunt owned land. People were setting up the cookout in the field, and among them was an unrecognizable teenager in a wheelchair. Another hood characteristic. It was typical there to see someone who hadn't been born paralyzed but had been made paralyzed, by the environment. There were also about a dozen neighborhood kids who were not related to her, waiting around for food. The block was lined with cheap cars with expensive rims and sound systems that made you feel like you were in a club.

Inside, Loose Ends was playing: "Hangin' on a String." The house's warmth was impressive. This was in part because of all the plants in the living room—mottled prayer plants, stringy rhipsalis hanging from the ceiling, figs and ferns in a motley crew of pots. After embracing Carmen with genuine excitement, Vivian asked her how she had grown all of them, and they walked around touching the leaves and inspecting. Her aunt said they'd all just started from clippings.

"That's how your grandmother used to do it," she said. "You know Abuela had all kinds of plants," but Vivian didn't know, because she couldn't remember. It was reflex now to compare Carmen to Anita, who did not keep any plants. She couldn't help feeling that this had some larger significance about Anita's deficiency as a caregiver.

Vivian was touched now by the kindness of her twenty-something cousins Justina and Arlene, who each gave her a long, rocking hug. She hadn't seen them in over a decade, but they seemed to know all about what she'd been up to, and they expressed unfiltered pride in her various accomplishments and in her attractiveness. "You look so different with straight hair!" Justina said. "Yeah, this is the last day," Vivian said, running her fingers through the now-greasy blowout.

Arlene's amblyopia had never been corrected—no money for surgery, no patience for patching—and had worsened over time, resulting in an extremely unflattering wandering eye that Vivian found difficult to look at. But Justina was beautiful. Her heart-shaped face bore the sweet, delicate features she'd had since she was a child. She was short and her cutoffs revealed perfect legs, straight and slender. But Vivian couldn't comment on Justina's attractiveness without implicitly insulting Arlene and she didn't know anything about their lives other than that they had both had children, something Vivian had no interest in and didn't consider to be an accomplishment in itself (you couldn't judge the success of a parent immediately, it revealed itself over time), so she just stood there smiling, receiving their kind words and saying nothing in return.

Anita hadn't yet appeared, but Vivian sensed her mother's presence in the kitchen. If pressed, Vivian would say she loved her mother in a biological way, but she didn't like her. The woman was impulsive and petulant, prone to explosive outbursts. Her irrationality and refusal to commit to therapy or any other spiritual program that might generate insight guaranteed that the bitterness and rancor she experienced toward herself would be expressed outward, curdling and distorting her opinions of others. She didn't have any friends outside of her husband and out-of-town family members, in part because of her tendency to criticize and bad-mouth everyone.

It had been two years since she'd seen her mother. Anita had visited New York and Vivian took her shopping and to the Oyster Bar. As they'd walked through Grand Central, Anita had to stop several times as she was out of breath, and she became so overstimulated that she had to sit in a bathroom stall for fifteen minutes to get her bearings. Over lunch, she refused to put her bag on the floor because it was dingy, berated Vivian for putting hers there, complained to the waitress about the quality of her water, and then, after the waitress left, replayed the fifteen-second interaction out loud, determining from the waitress's microexpressions that she'd been looking down on her. During the entire afternoon visit Vivian cycled between gently scolding Anita for her irrationality and contemptuousness, quietly resenting those qualities in Anita, trying to accept Anita for who she was but failing, and ultimately being disappointed in herself.

On the plus side, Anita could be quite funny, and Vivian had no doubt inherited her comedic orientation to life from her mother. She was a great cook and she did maternal things, like sending care packages with bunny slippers and cat-themed paraphernalia (socks, coasters, wineglasses). Vivian had fond memories of playing dress-up with Anita while dancing to Madonna. And she was very little, so Vivian wanted to protect her.

As a practical matter, of all the people at the family event, Vivian knew Anita and Michael the best. She needed to be on good terms with them today, in order to have a social lifeline. "Hey, Mom," Vivian said as she entered the kitchen and stooped a little to hug Anita, who was sitting at the table peeling plantains. Her mother looked like a short and pudgy Latina Bette Davis, only with a mustache and half a canine missing.

"Tostones, can't wait," Vivian said. "Michael here yet?"

"That hoodlum? You know he's drunk already. Outside," Anita said, gesturing in the direction of the field.

"Are you on speaking terms again?"

"Your brother's a mess. You'll see."

The event was segregated by gender at first, like a middle school dance. Men and male teenagers of various sizes and complexions were outside, drinking and grilling and listening to music. The women stayed inside at first, cooking and gossiping in the kitchen or hanging out on the porch with cocktails in plastic cups. Unidentifiable children streamed in and out of the house in pairs and trios. Some played video games inside, others played outside, still others came into the kitchen to eavesdrop on the conversation of the adults, to observe Vivian—a strange presence!—or to pick at macaroni salad or shyly ask when the other food—arroz con pollo, pernil with roasted potatoes, and all the assorted meat on the grills outside—would be ready.

At first, Vivian stuck to Anita's side in the corner of the kitchen, while Anita, Carmen, and Justina chopped vegetables. Teena Marie came on and the women all gently bopped together. It was nice. The "Square Biz" sing-along seemed predestined.

"Rest in peace," Anita said when the song was over.

"Teena Marie's dead?!" Vivian asked, immediately taking out her phone to confirm.

But then during "Portuguese Love," Anita snatched the knife from Justina and said she was cutting the vegetables wrong; scolded Carmen for putting chicken stock into the rice "like white people" instead of putting exactly half a can of beer in it, like she did; tasted Carmen's potato salad and made a face, saying, "I don't like it"; reiterated that Carmen "loved the ghetto," this time saying it to Carmen's face; made a joke to her cousin, "I can't keep track of how many kids you have!"; and said something to an older aunt about "los negros" and laughed wildly, even though her own daughter, standing dutifully by her side, was una negra.

The cycle of a serene silence and then a round of conversation followed by an insult or a mild explosion from Anita would repeat. Women would leave the kitchen and come back, desperate to please Anita. The energy went up and down like a stock market graph on the nightly news until only Carmen and Vivian were left with Anita. As an adult Vivian was often depressed while visiting her family, and for the longest time, she'd castigated herself for it. She wasn't being currently abused. So why was she complaining? But now she realized. This was why. She decided to get some air and leave the sisters alone to catch up.

Out on the porch, Vivian ran into Junior, a forty-something cousin of hers who lived in Bed-Stuy. She hadn't seen him since she was little and had no memory of him.

With a Newport dangling from his mouth, Junior grinned, saying "Wow" repeatedly while examining her. "You look good, girl," he added, and then described an incident of young Vivian "stripping" for neighborhood boys as a toddler on a coffee table, as if she had been doing this consciously, as if a toddler understood sexuality in any way, as if "stripping" were an activity that a toddler could engage in.

Vivian felt that this behavior was inappropriate for a familial interaction but knew she couldn't say a sentence like "This behavior is inappropriate for a familial interaction" around here because she'd be shamed for *taking things the wrong way,* for *having no sense of humor,* for *being antisocial and thinking you're better than us with your white words and phrases;* no, the only way to handle it was to deflect, to pivot, to change the subject, but no subjects were coming to her now, only fantasies of walking over and ripping one of the expensive rims off one of the cheap cars and walking back and beating Junior repeatedly in the head with it until his neck was a stump. But Vivian laughed, tossed off an "I don't remember that!" and hopped down the stairs, saying she was going to look for her brother.

As she neared the field, she could see Michael with his shades on, pacing and muttering with a cigarette in one hand and a cup of Hennessy on ice in the other. He was short like their mother and dark like their father, whom neither of them had spoken to in years, not *solely* because he had schizophrenia, but because he had the angry, persecutory kind of schizophrenia, the kind where you suspect your entire family of being in on the elaborate plot against you, and because he refused all treatments, treatments being viewed also, inevitably, as part of the conspiracy. Michael was in his late thirties but dressed two decades younger, a baggy silhouette, cornrows and tattoos.

It was two o'clock so she knew he must be several cups in. As she got closer, she realized he was berating one of their cousin's male children. The child must have been about five or six years old. Vivian could immediately tell that he was terrified of her brother, who was yelling at him for taking another cousin's toys. To distract him, Vivian said, "What's up, bro! Come talk to your sister," and the child escaped.

Michael hadn't fared well in adulthood. (Neither of her brothers had.) After flunking out of high school he'd gotten a girl pregnant at nineteen, then started selling drugs to support his new family. He made a lot of money but showed too much flash. He moved his son and girlfriend to a huge house in the hills that they couldn't have afforded on her telemarketer salary. Amassed an impressive sneaker collection and had a different outfit for every day of the year. Eventually, a former friend ratted on him to the police and he was sentenced to five years in a minimum-security prison. His girlfriend left him, taking their son. Michael had been released after two years for good behavior and was currently trying to get his life back on track; Vivian wanted to believe he could do it.

On the night when she'd told them all about *that*, in hushed tones at the kitchen table while looking down at her feet, Michael had grabbed a baseball bat and left the house, looking for her assaulter. His outrage created a lasting affinity and trust, even though he'd never done anything to challenge the violent man when he was being physical with her or Anita. For his part Michael had remained protective of Vivian and respected who she'd become. Because of her intelligence, how she had survived and made a success of her life, Vivian's approval meant a lot to him.

Michael was now muttering about the boy, so Vivian asked how his tattoo was going. For months, he'd been getting an elaborate back tattoo, a graveyard of everyone he'd lost. Since his hands were full Vivian lifted up his shirt herself and had him turn around. She was surprised at the scale, quality, and vividness of the tattoo, which featured bare, Halloweenish trees, menacing clouds, and several gravestones, all done in grayscale. She first noticed the gravestone for their brother, Derron. She slowly grazed it with her fingers.

Derron was a gentle soul whom everyone in the family adored. He was the one who'd played games with Vivian when she was bored as a kid, the one who gave her rides to the movies or the mall, the only one she spoke to regularly in college. He'd been Anita's favorite, too, and he spoke to her every day by phone without fail. He shoveled the ice from the walk of their house and picked up groceries for Anita whenever Julio was too sick and loaned anyone money who needed it. He was the kind of person you'd describe as good.

Derron did well enough for himself, becoming a manager at a local Tex-Mex restaurant and a favorite of the owners, who were considering him to open one of their franchises, until he was arrested for *lewd acts with a minor under age fourteen* when Vivian was in college.

When asked, Derron denied the charges, saying that one of the boys he coached was lying to the police. Trying to get back at him after being cut from the basketball team. Everyone bought the story, including Vivian, until she visited him in lockup. His posture was stooped that day, and he covered his mouth and face with his hands as they spoke through the glass. Most telling of all, he couldn't make eye contact with her. He was ashamed.

There was nothing worse than being wrong, especially when the signs were all there. Derron embraced the religious culture of the Ozarks, becoming a Southern Baptist in his twenties. He never dated, devoting all his free time to leading the church youth group and a church basketball team for teenage boys. While leading an adolescent-adjacent life that should have raised eyebrows, he would pick fights with Vivian about "homosexuality" at every family gathering. During these long, feverish arguments the two of them would speak abstractly about same-sex relationships, which Vivian defended in the pure, nondogmatic way of a liberal teen, and which her brother denounced with a little too much fervor.

More stuff came out, and he couldn't go to trial, so he pled to a lesser charge and got probation. Vivian worried for years about what he might be doing, and then he died in his sleep, ostensibly of a premature heart attack, though Anita didn't request an autopsy.

Vivian didn't attend the funeral. She went to New Orleans on a law school–funded public service trip instead, drafting legal briefs and interviewing incarcerated clients during the day and drinking to oblivion every night at her lowest weight. She started a Macy Gray sing-along in a restaurant, crashed a stranger's wedding with her friends, and danced in the street, unable to articulate her relief to anyone.

After Derron's death Vivian retreated further from the

family. She'd call every month or two, listening to their problems and cooing sympathetically but from a safe remove, like a political candidate on the campaign trail. That time Julio had lost thirty pounds due to an undiagnosed ulcer. That time Anita had a heart attack. That time Michael drove into a ravine and was trapped inside his car for forty-five minutes until a Good Samaritan fished him out. Then there was the interpersonal instability in their lives—how Michael's latest girlfriend had called the cops on him and kicked him out of their apartment under circumstances that were vague in his retelling, but that cast him as the victim, forcing him to move back in with Anita. How Anita wasn't speaking to Vivian's uncle again after he'd gone on yet another bender.

She always listened, but she rarely shared any of the details of her own life. Amid all their stress and relational dysfunction, Vivian felt there was no room for her experiences. Sometimes she thought her achievements made Michael feel bad about himself. And she could feel Anita simultaneously resenting her successes and yoking herself to them, as if they were proof that she'd been a good mother after all. The tangled knot of emotion and expectation was too much to bear, so she stopped reaching out. This seemed to make Michael and Anita, in turn, reach out to her even more, and their texts, emails, and voice mails began to take on desperate, pleading tones, as if they believed they needed to present themselves as helpless to get her to respond, which Vivian resented, as she found it manipulative, and it made her feel like she was at work.

Next to Derron in the graveyard was Scooby, a beautiful, sweet, and distinctly nonabusive cousin whom Vivian had liked a lot because he would always sit and color with her and ask her questions. He was shot in the projects when Vivian was six.

There was one for their younger cousin Alejandro, who had hanged himself in prison. They used to stay up all night playing video games until their hands were cramped and ridden with calluses. Alejandro worshipped her and was always up for her schemes. After she convinced him that eating three bay leaves would enable him to fly, they stole some from his mom, Jeannette's, kitchen and biked out to a field. Alejandro ate the bay leaves, ran as fast as he could, started jumping and flapping his arms until he exhausted himself. Vivian stopped talking to him after learning he'd punched his pregnant girlfriend in the stomach.

Jeannette's gravestone was right next to her son's. This was the hard one, the one she couldn't look at for too long. Jeannette was easily the kindest, most guileless person in Vivian's family. She never yelled, never scolded. She loved cats and was fostering several at any given time. She differed from Anita in every conceivable way. Jeannette worked, she knew how to drive, and she lived without a man for long periods, during which she developed hobbies, like contra dancing and going to yard sales. She'd died of brain cancer, and Vivian had often wished she'd been her mother.

Instead of a gravestone there was an actual tattooed image of Michael's dog, Sammy, who had been shot by the police when they had raided Michael's house on an anonymous tip and arrested him for selling drugs, but not before taking racist pre-selfie selfies with a Polaroid camera while wearing all of Michael's jewelry, some of which they pocketed, and mocking him when he was seated and in handcuffs, completely defenseless.

Next to Sammy were several spaces for empty plots, because that's the thing about a graveyard tattoo: it's never finished.

Vivian complimented Michael on his gothic achievement. The tattoo epitomized a dark sensibility they shared, despite their wildly divergent life experiences, and she wondered if it was genetic or environmental.

Kendrick Lamar came on over the stereo.

"You like Kendrick?" Vivian asked, hoping this might give them something to talk about.

"Nah, man. That kid took my rhymes."

"What? When did that happen?"

"I sent a song called 'Bitch Don't Kill My Vibe' to this producer in New York," he said, setting his drink down on a card table briefly, to light a cigarette. Michael had dabbled in rapping in his twenties. "Never heard back from him. Then, years later, I hear Kendrick doing the song."

"Damn. It was the same song?"

"It's the title and the idea, man, he stole my idea. Hey. You think I could sue?"

"I don't think you can sue just because someone stole... your idea?" she said. "Unfortunately. You made peace with Mom yet or no?"

"I wouldn't say that, but she's making me a separate pot of rice." Michael never liked gandules and always wanted his rice without, so this was a start.

Vivian headed back to the house. Junior, who had seemingly been drinking for the entire forty-five minutes they'd been apart, had grown bolder, liquor sloshing over the rim of his red plastic party cup as he gesticulated toward her, shouting, "There she is! My cousin!"

"Here I am!" she said good-naturedly.

As she walked past him and up the porch stairs, Junior lightly grabbed her arm and said, "Hang out for a sec."

"All right," she said, continuing up the remaining steps and turning to face him on the porch, making sure to be closer to the door than to him.

He was lit up, disinhibited. He asked her what kind of stuff she liked to do in Brooklyn.

"Drink with friends? I don't know," she said.

"I like to drink too," he said.

"That's clear," Vivian replied.

He asked for her number so they could hang out in Brooklyn, and when she deflected, he tried to turn her survival instinct against her, baiting her by insinuating that she thought she was too good for him and saying that he, too, was cultured, liked to do cultured shit.

"I'm sure you are, man, but I don't even have time to see my closest friends. My job is crazy," she lied.

He sternly said, "I'm your cousin," implying that his desire to hang out was purely familial and that she should be ashamed for sensing something depraved. She ignored this, asking him about his neighborhood, the changes that had occurred there, what project he lived in. Everyone, predators included, loved to talk about themselves. She managed not to disclose what neighborhood she lived in or where she worked. At a certain point when he pressed her again, she said nothing but instead cut him a look, revealing both her knowledge of his intentions and her determination not to help him realize them, and he relented.

Vivian hid out in the bathroom for a while and looked in the mirror. She'd been right to agonize over what to wear. She had intuited, had remembered, that in this social group, this "family," there were no boundaries. Men were indiscriminately carnal when they were drinking and no one admonished them.

She texted Jane: Cousin just hit on me @ family thing. Can I void the familial contract lol and then looked at Matthew's social media. He'd just posted a photo of himself with a big group of friends upstate. So that was why he didn't ask to hang out this weekend. The friends all had their arms around each other, and the woman next to him, Stacy, was a tall, thin black woman with a long Brazilian weave. She'd commented on the photo with a cat-with-heart-eyes emoji but her accounts were private, so Vivian couldn't contextualize.

When it seemed that to stay in the bathroom any longer would be socially unacceptable, Vivian hid out in her aunt's bedroom and read the internet until Anita came to look for her, mildly scolded her for being antisocial, and said she needed to come out to say hello to one of Anita's oldest friends, Miss Mary, who used to babysit Vivian when she was little. This wasn't someone Vivian recognized or remembered, so she had no idea if she'd been good to her or not. Once outside on the porch, Anita put Vivian on display, telling Miss Mary all about her degrees and accomplishments. Vivian played her role, thinking of it as the literal least she could do. Anita glowed at her while she told Miss Mary where she had gone to law school, what it had been like, how she had struggled at first but eventually emerged victorious, and finally what she did for a living. She delivered stock stories from the hospital as if she were being paid for this conversation, closing with a monologue about how our society treats people with serious mental illness. Miss Mary said Vivian didn't have to tell her.

Her brother came out worse than he went in. Then she praised Vivian for working with those people, and asked her if she had any kids.

Once Anita seemed placated by Vivian's performance, Vivian went back inside, where Michael was now yelling at the child again, this time for hogging a video game that the other children wanted to play. Standing in the doorway of one of the bedrooms, Vivian watched Michael snatch the control away from the child and give it to one of the other kids, telling the child to "stop playing around, stop doing that shit," and threatening violence if he kept it up.

"Hey," Vivian said, stepping into the room. It was a charged atmosphere. The kids were frozen in place. "Don't talk to him like that," she said. Michael looked embarrassed, not so much for his outburst, she thought, as for having been caught.

She shook her head at him and she knew he knew what this meant. The comparison she was making, the disappointment she felt.

"Go back outside," Vivian ordered. Michael threw up his hands and did as he was told. She exhaled and then sat down on the bed next to the child while a couple of the others restarted the game.

"You okay?"

He nodded. He was so small. Their arms were touching and she could feel him trembling. "I hate him," he said, on the verge of tears.

"Me too," Vivian said, staring at the wall.

The child wiped his nose and puffed his chest out, then sat back down on the floor in front of the television set, picked up one of the controls, and resumed playing. Vivian watched, briefly, as he disappeared into the desert-themed obstacle course on the screen, driving and steering and collecting coins as Mario. When he collected ten she cheered for him and walked out.

That's a material breach for sure Jane had written.

You have no idea Vivian replied, imagining herself outside this experience and describing it to Jane on her sectional, joint in hand.

The food was ready and everyone gathered together outside, plates piled high with barbecue and Puerto Rican staples, music blasting, the air loud with laughter and reminiscences. Vivian tried to settle in and enjoy her family but she was distracted, monitoring Michael. Vivian's warning to the child didn't matter, because Michael seemed fixated on him. Vivian saw Michael tease him, then later he pushed him gently, and even later he lunged at the child, contemptuously but with a veneer of playfulness to make it seem acceptable. This dynamic felt nauseatingly familiar, as did the fact that as it played out, no one did anything. The men laughed. The women handled Michael's rage by preemptively scolding the child themselves for Michael to hear, so he would feel justified and maybe back off a little. It was textbook group dysfunction.

Then Vivian caught Michael yelling at the child about scooping too much ice cream for himself. The child shielded his face instinctively with such tiny hands, near tears while Michael threatened him.

"Leave him alone, Michael! He's a little kid and you're an adult."

The child ran inside as Vivian stood squarely in Michael's personal space denouncing him.

"What the fuck is wrong with you. Bullying a kid," she said. She didn't see or hear anything else but her brother's loathsome face as she tossed out the words. It wasn't a bat, but it felt amazing. *Safe targets.*

Michael didn't know how to react. On the one hand, someone was publicly scolding him. On the other hand, that person was his baby sister, and she never went off without a good reason. But Michael couldn't face Vivian's opinion of him. It was like how Derron hadn't been able to make eye contact with her in jail.

"Aight, sis. Damn! But these kids have to learn some kind of way," he said, walking away to get another drink.

The day went on. With Vivian watching, Michael didn't go near the child again but she knew he'd probably pick it up again when she wasn't there.

The sun was lowering in the sky, people were getting rowdy, and it was time to leave. Vivian went around telling people she had to go, dutifully hugging and kissing her elders. Anita begged her to stay, Carmen said she could sleep over, but no, this wasn't possible. She had a friend staying with her from out of town, she lied, and she had to get back to her apartment to meet up with her.

As Vivian was saying her goodbyes in the field, the child broke away from the others and ran several yards to embrace her. He did not hug so much as throw his body against her, causing her to stumble backward, laughing. She squeezed him back, registered his little bones, told him she loved him. "Stay out of his way, okay?" she whispered. "And run to Carmen if anything."

THAT ALL-IMPORTANT SECOND DATE

THEY MET IN the park and walked the loop while Vivian smoked a cigarette. It was disgusting but necessary. She told Jane about Michael's disclosure from before that "things had happened" to him as a child, and everything that went down at the cookout, but withheld the decision she'd made after. It didn't feel like a decision, even, so much as knowledge of a fact: she wouldn't associate with those people anymore. Already she had started, in this retelling to Jane, to refer to Anita and Julio and Michael exclusively by their first names, rather than through relational nouns. She needed to represent the shift somehow.

"I just can't with them," she said as she finished. "The chaos. The drama. And those are just euphemisms for shit I can't even say out loud."

"Fuck," Jane replied. "Do you think that's why your brother drinks so much?"

"What do you mean?"

"What he told you before—just seems like he's carrying a lot. And it's so much harder for men to disclose."

We're all carrying a lot, Vivian thought. *Doesn't justify terrorizing children, though.*

"And shame, too, if it was sexual—how old was he when it happened?"

Vivian looked dumbly ahead and felt bad for not knowing the answer. She shrugged and shook her head. "He was vague with the details."

Jane was missing the point. The story Vivian was telling wasn't about Michael being abused. It was about what he'd done to the child. Michael was a perpetrator now.

"Maybe one day you'll be able to talk about things with him, with your mom, too. When Corinthia and I finally talked about everything—what happened to me, how our mom singled me out, how I always resented Corinthia for it—it was hard, one of the hardest things I've ever done, but it changed our relationship. More importantly, it changed me. My therapist—"

"We don't talk in my family," Vivian said sharply. "We don't go to therapy, either. Michael doesn't even have insurance and besides, you can't have a deep conversation with someone who's always drunk. And my mom? Please. She flies into hysterics at the vaguest hint of criticism."

They walked in silence awhile. Vivian loved Jane but she'd never understand how truly disorganized Vivian's family was. How could she, she grew up middle-class.

"After going through what we went through, it just makes it even *more* disappointing that he'd go off on a little kid. It was so fucked up, dude." Vivian tried to surreptitiously wipe the tears. "I honestly just hadn't realized how small children are at that age, like, physically."

Jane put an arm around Vivian as they walked, and she didn't ask any more questions.

Contemporary life is a woman working out vigorously, with a look of sad straining on her face. It was Saturday and Vivian was exercising before another date with Matthew. They'd casually texted throughout the week, eventually deciding to go out again. Meanwhile, Vivian had taken screenshots of Matthew's slender ex, Elana. She looked at them whenever she was bored or anxious or when she found herself revisiting the family stuff from the weekend before. Elana had inspired her to put a full-length mirror up against her refrigerator, to keep herself from eating garbage. Each time Vivian walked past the mirror, she stopped to look at herself.

After doing a core video Vivian stood in front of the mirror and examined how she looked in her yoga pants. The shape of her butt made her sad but because her waist was getting smaller it formed a pleasant silhouette that many men found attractive and that made a certain kind of woman jealous. Also, it seemed like the pants had gotten looser around the middle. Vivian grinned like a child, in awe of the magic of being low-carb, but then the grin faded as she wondered whether the pants were just loose now because she'd worn them for weeks without washing them. The only way to know was to measure the circumference of her stomach. In order to maintain her ideal waist-to-hip ratio, Vivian needed to measure less than thirty inches around the area below the belly button (the widest part of the stomach).

It had been a few days since her last measuring ritual. She held her breath and slowly wrapped the tape around her stomach, fingering the metal tip at one end, heart rate eventually slowing, muscles eventually relaxing, as she measured twenty-nine-point-five inches. Twenty-nine would have been even better, of course, but this was really good. After measuring her natural waist and finding that she had gotten down to twenty-five inches, she wondered what clothes she could wear now that she wouldn't have been able to wear a month ago, so she grabbed the black-and-gold tiered midi dress she used to gauge her size and saw that her stomach had flattened considerably since the last time she had tried it on and that she didn't even need to actively flex to see her arm muscles anymore. She felt excited thinking about wearing this dress outside her apartment, beyond the confines of the ritual, perhaps to some outdoor wedding with Matthew, but then her stomach growled, and suddenly none of her measurements counted, because the real measure of a body was when it was full.

She removed the dress and put her yoga pants and T-shirt back on and checked her phone. There were still several unread texts from her family. Fuck it, she thought. Better just get it over with.

I'm never talking to your aunt again. One of those hood rats stole your stepdad's ring. Call me.

Danielle called the cops on me n they r considerin revokin my probation.

Hey Vivian what are you doing this weekend? Call me, love mom.

Hey sis, u ok? Worried about u.

Vivian you only get one mother and I could be gone any
day now. Call me.

She returned to the mirror, determined to change her life.
If she could just clinch things with Matthew and get tucked
inside the couple structure, she wouldn't need a family. The
prospect of a life without their problems and their endless
need! But then, the chorus of guilt: *If I don't respond to their*
texts, am I bad? If I never speak to any of them again, is that
wrong? Under what conditions would it not be wrong? Have they
done enough for me to justify never speaking to them again?

She lifted her shirt. She could see her ribs at the top of her
abdomen, so the core videos were working, but she feared
the pouch returning. Removing the bra, Vivian flexed her
biceps, looking for symmetry, and then pulled the skin of her
right arm taut to accentuate the muscles underneath. She'd
long ago accepted that she had what were now euphemized
as "natural breasts," characterized by soft tissue, big nipples,
and some degree of ptosis. They'd never bothered her much,
and a guy could come just looking at them, so she didn't
pay much attention to them during the ritual. She removed
her yoga pants again and squatted slightly, admiring her legs,
finding them leaner than many other pairs of thirtysomething
legs and feeling proud to be a woman with a thigh gap. But
then her eyes focused on her upper left thigh, where there
was a very obvious dimple that could be seen even from the
front. When she was in her twenties, the cellulite was only
visible from the back. Now it was creeping around her thighs,
which felt *as unfair as racism,* she thought, with knowing
self-parody. Also like racism, focusing on the cellulite made
her want to cry, but she would follow this practice to the

end. She bent over in front of the mirror and touched the craterous lumps she saw there, shuddering with anticipatory embarrassment at what Matthew would see when they slept together and at her own hypocrisy, knowing that in order to conceal it (the hypocrisy), neither the ritual nor any of its attending thoughts could ever be shared.

Vivian showered and did her hair. It was curly again and she spent some time moisturizing, cupping and scrunching it, then parting it and getting the shape just right in the mirror. As she reddened her lips she saw a flash of Anita's face, then Derron's, and Michael's last. If they were always with her, could she ever be rid of them? Before heading out she rubbed her lips together to make sure they were equally stained.

—◆—

They were going to see an art exhibit at the Park Avenue Armory. According to internet articles with titles like "That All-Important Second Date," she needed to demonstrate her worthiness as a long-term companion tonight. It should be easy enough; he'd already said he was falling in love with her. She would again show him that she cared for her body and that she paid attention to dress (she'd paired a denim jacket with a long sleeveless floral dress, which, when worn with platform sandals, made her look like a moving garden). Personality-wise she'd need to strike a balance: pleasant but not obsequious; perceptive but not overly cerebral; and she had to demonstrate her originality without being overbearing.

There had been a mix-up in communication so Matthew had already gone into the Armory while she was waiting for him outside, causing him to say, when they eventually met up inside, "I missed you," and though he clearly meant that he hadn't seen her out there, she clung to the double meaning. He was wearing a dark gray blazer with a worn T-shirt of an unknown band underneath, and light gray jeans. After flashing that megawatt smile again, he hugged her in a platonic way where none of his lower body touched any of her lower body, so that she became unsure of herself as they walked around the anterior room of the Armory with plastic cups of wine.

He told her he had been out of town the weekend before, visiting some friends in Tannersville. She tried to look like she was receiving this information for the first time, and he asked her if she knew where that was.

"I've been there but I couldn't locate it on a map," she said.

Matthew seemed to pick up on her disappointment with herself.

"I'm not testing you," he said softly, taking her hand in his.

She stroked his forefinger with her thumb mournfully as they held hands, until he stopped to kiss her. Maybe she still had a shot, despite whatever thin and undisturbed woman he had undoubtedly slept with last weekend. She began to relax. They finished their wine and started to look at the art.

Vivian often felt alienated at art museums. Walking around now, pretending to be engaged, she tried to articulate why in her head. The paintings had no people in them, and they seemed to demand an emotional response that Vivian never had. Sculpture was another mystery, with artists making private connections among materials that she didn't get. How was she to understand the meaning of tar or metal, of dyed plastic, of refrigerators? Language, at the very least, had common referents.

She moved through the large gallery, perplexed and dissatisfied but, wanting to match her date's opinions, she stayed a bit behind him, monitoring his reactions. When Matthew's eyes gleamed in front of an abstract swirl, she broke the silence. "That's so cool," she said, and he agreed. This kept happening, and it became difficult to discern her actual feelings.

While they were looking at a photograph, a woman—tall and thin with long red hair and wearing white denim pants expertly tailored at the ankle and low-heeled red pumps— glided past the two of them, looking Matthew up and down while holding on to the arm of her boyfriend, who was shorter than her and less attractive. It was as if the woman was thinking they should switch boyfriends. Vivian was unable to focus on the painting in front of her as the woman's heels continued slowly and deliberately click-clacking in their vicinity.

Vivian pulled Matthew through a thick curtain and into a smaller room to watch a video that featured long tracking shots of the youth culture of Rio de Janeiro and various other modern metropolises accompanied by moody music. According to the placard outside the room there was also an accompanying thousand-page book of photos. Yet another reason for the art disdain: too much interdisciplinarity. It felt compensatory, piling different kinds of media on to cover for the fact that none of it was very interesting.

The curtain opened behind them. She heard the footsteps of the redheaded woman. Matthew looked back and Vivian imagined him seeing the woman, desiring her. Vivian grew hot, but Matthew had turned his attention back to the endless and meandering video and seemed enamored with everything; he nuzzled her and said it was a beautiful shot. The game then became to not reveal her negative feelings. Eventually they left the dark video room and toured the rest of the space. He was so beautiful. But so was the redheaded woman, who could reappear at any moment. And so, to lay her claim, she stopped in the middle of the floor and kissed him in a dramatic fashion.

They were kicked out—exhibit closed—before they knew it. Vivian was relieved. They headed back to Park Slope, where Matthew lived, and had dinner at an underground bar where they ate spicy chicken wings and dumplings and buckwheat noodles (which she allowed herself because she'd deprived herself of carbs all week) and listened to midnineties rap.

"Full Clip" started and Vivian got riled up. "He just said, 'Big L rest in peace.' Do you know Big L?"

Matthew had never heard of him, and Vivian considered this a minor tragedy, so she took the opportunity to expound. New York media people behaved as if the ethics of consuming art was a new question, she said. But where were they when Vivian was a teenager discovering her love of violent rap? Big L had probably killed people and might have even participated in a hate crime or two, but *Lifestylez ov da Poor & Dangerous* was canon. The production was relentlessly dark, and the lyrics intimidatingly good from someone so young. The album's best feature was its ambivalence. Some songs were boastful about drugs and violence, but then "Street Struck" was mournful, if not maudlin, about black boys being seduced and ultimately destroyed by the street life. At the time of his violent death in his early twenties, Big L had experienced more trauma than most people do in their whole lives.

"This is survivor music," Vivian concluded.

She told Matthew about the first time she came to New York with her parents. They stayed with a family friend in the Bronx, and at night, when everyone was asleep, she'd sneak into the living room, turn on the radio, and record all the hip-hop she couldn't get in the Midwest. She spent hours writing out all the lyrics and rapping along while looking at herself in the mirror.

Bopping in her chair to "The World Is Yours," she told him about her playlist, "Hip-Hop Piano Beats." "You could do a similar playlist of horn samples," she added, but it seemed that Matthew didn't want her to keep going on like this. Did he kiss her just now as a way of shutting her up? Then, to appear less intellectually dominant, she asked him to feed her the buckwheat noodles, smiling at him between bites.

"Who are you?" Matthew said, mesmerized. He said it was rare to find a woman both so smart and so sexy. "Usually it's one or the other."

As they ate, Matthew asked if she'd seen the How People Eat Chicken meme from years prior. She had not, and she braced herself for what was to come. He said his "Nigerian friend" had posted it online. The meme showed four different pictures of a drumstick with a caption about how a different racial or ethnic group would eat it. According to the meme, white people leave meat on the bones, black people leave no meat on the bone, Ghanaians eat some of the bone, and Nigerians eat the entire drumstick, bone, marrow, and all. Vivian glanced down at her plate, and she caught Matthew sneaking a look as well. They didn't say anything about Vivian's leftover meat or Matthew's racial essentialism.

When their dating histories came up Matthew surprised her by disclosing his first sexual experience. He said that when he was a freshman in high school he dated the twenty-year-old sister of one of his football teammates. She had seduced him and taken his virginity, and he said it was "awesome." His eyes sparkled as he told the tale, but Vivian was disturbed by the age gap.

He went on to describe what happened later in life when he tried to rekindle something with the woman, and Vivian joked that she bet this chapter took place "over winter break in college." Matthew laughed and said that was exactly right. He had returned to his hometown on a college break and the woman had reached out to him on social media. They met up for dinner at a sports grill–type spot, where he could order beer without being carded. He still felt that same attraction to her that he had when he was younger, even though he'd since been with other women, but when they'd gone back to the woman's apartment and had sex, she spoke to him as if he were still a young boy she was teaching, as if she wanted to re-create the dynamic they had had when he was fourteen.

"It weirded me out," he concluded. They never spoke again.

Vivian nodded silently, sensing that the story had some importance, that it was perhaps signaling something about Matthew's sexuality. What it was, exactly, remained obscure. Did he need to be in charge during sex? Or was he merely beginning to understand that he had been abused by that woman? If so, why was he revealing this to Vivian on their second date? She needed time to think, to process this information and devise a perfect response.

Matthew excused himself to the bathroom. Her phone vibrated from inside her bag. She glanced at her texts.

Your brother is so hateful! Said that I'm not a mother, that I'm trash. Call me.

Now mom is sayin' if I come back 2 the house I'm bout 2 b shot. Call me sis plz, if u can, I'm sleepin' in my car tonight.

Her brain was scrambled. She pressed her hands to her temples.

"You okay?" Matthew asked, startling her.

"Yeah, just some family drama."

When she glanced up at him she saw concern and an invitation to elaborate; he began to inquire. But Vivian couldn't explain the texts without using words like *abuse* and *dysfunction*, and she didn't want to use those words right now. Better to keep things light, to preserve her air of comical distance. So she said flatly, "It doesn't matter—we're not close," and he changed the subject.

Matthew, meanwhile, overflowed with personal information. A bit drunk, he said mental illness ran in his mother's side of the family and alluded to having had a breakdown in college over a "girl." He laughed nervously and blushed.

"I don't know why I'm telling you any of this," he said.

Vivian smiled and touched his hand.

"There's nothing to be embarrassed about. That kind of thing is pretty common in adolescence, especially in college, when it's the first time for many people that they are away from their primary support systems."

At some point Vivian said she was attention-seeking. It wasn't particularly true, she just thought he wanted that based on the Elana intel. But Matthew made a face. "Honestly, that's my least-favorite quality in a person," he said. "My ex was like that and it really bothered me."

Vivian felt a twinge of panic, but then Matthew said he would "have to find a way to live with" the trait she'd pretended to have, and she relaxed again. Latching onto the ex comment, she fished around for more about his last relationship, but he was evasive, saying only that they had "different priorities."

It was late and Vivian was pretty drunk when she suggested they go dancing at a nearby bar.

"Dancing is a series of poses that burns calories," she slurred on the way to the bar-turned-club, in a stand-up comedian way, laughing at her own joke.

"Dancing is, like, my favorite drug," Matthew said, also in a stand-up way, and Vivian laughed even though she didn't find it funny.

The DJ was in the middle of a New Wave and electropop set, creating an atmosphere of anthemic melancholy and gothic drama. A new mood announced itself. She didn't want to talk anymore. Vivian danced through the circular space until she reached a shallow row of stairs in the back of the bar that looked out at the rest of the room. While Matthew got them drinks, she hid her bag in a corner and began to dance alone at the top of the stairs so that she could survey the room without anyone looking at her—except for Matthew, who, when he returned, danced with somewhat awkward enthusiasm below her at the foot of the stairs. Vivian stared into his eyes, grooving along in a series of shuffles, twists, and finger snaps. Then, suddenly, she just left him, and when he started to come after her she commanded that he stay behind. It didn't matter if he liked it or not, what was important was that he obey. Spinning away from him and laughing, she sang along with the music, shuffling in circles with herself, dancing facing the wall away from the other dancers, then moving to the middle of the room to dance near but not with them, not being self-conscious, feeling, actually, at her most secure when the constant stream of verbiage and narration was drowned out by sound and rhythm. Occasionally she would return to Matthew, either facing him or allowing him to grind her from behind, and they would kiss and touch. Mostly, though, Vivian worked up a sweat by herself, determined to completely exhaust her body.

They danced for a couple of hours, then went back to Matthew's apartment and fooled around. Vivian said she wasn't ready for sex yet, but this was a lie. She was just taking advice she'd read online about not making yourself too available. Before he fell asleep, Matthew said he wanted to spend the next day with her, and she agreed.

That night she had a series of dreams about her dead brother. They each began with the same scenario: She woke up in her childhood bed, startled to find Derron sleeping next to her. Her body tensed, and she understood that she had to make it out of bed without waking him. This was the most important task in the world.

In the first dream, in a series of quiet microgestures, Vivian slowly eased out of the bed. She got the feeling that her childhood cat, Noodles, was in danger, so she tiptoed downstairs to check on him. Then she went back up to her room to wake Derron up and demand that he leave.

She turned on the light. As Derron woke up, so did she. Only, she didn't wake up in Matthew's bed but into another dream.

She woke up, startled to find Derron in bed next to her. She eased out of bed, successfully getting her feet to the floor without waking him, but as she began shifting her weight to stand up, he grabbed her arm hard and tight, and she woke up into a third dream.

Again she was startled, again he was there. This time, she made it out of the bed and turned on the light, telling Derron he needed to get out of her bed.

Laughing and with sexual playfulness, he asked, "Aren't we having a slumber party?"

Vivian sneered. "No, we are not. Go."

"But why?"

"Because I was raped as a child," she said. "And you being in my bed makes me uncomfortable."

Derron looked shocked, but he stayed in the bed.

Vivian woke up from this third dream-within-a-dream and it wasn't yet daybreak. Tears made their way to her neck. She wished she were close enough to Matthew to wake him up and ask to be soothed. That desire passed, and she went back to feeling buried alive. She lay there uneasily, clenched in the dark.

In the morning, when Matthew began to stir, Vivian did too. They kissed each other with the closed mouths of people who haven't yet smelled each other's morning breath. While they were shopping for breakfast ingredients he said he liked the way she looked, hair in a high puff, sunglasses on. It felt good to be part of a pair in public.

He made them omelets with kale and mushrooms, and

though she didn't like kale and still didn't like the mushrooms, she pretended to love it.

After dry-humping and making out, they lay in bed watching *How I Met Your Mother* and she acted interested, but every time Barney referred to "banging" a woman she scoffed. When her distaste leaked out, Matthew covered her mouth, laughing.

"No, you're being too serious," he said. "It's just a show!" For now, she wouldn't disagree.

FAMILY FEUDS

WHEN VIVIAN GOT home, Reginald was howling for food again. He trotted behind her through the apartment as she changed and peed and got water. She fed him slowly in stages while changing into yoga pants and a cotton T-shirt. After he ate, inhaling the food so quickly she thought he might choke, she petted him the way he liked, stroking his chin while he lay on his side, and apologized for not playing with him enough.

Things were going so well with Matthew that she felt emboldened, somehow, to contact her family. After sipping a tequila on ice, she called Michael. Before she could go into her speech about how his treatment of women and children was unacceptable and if he didn't work on it she wouldn't be able to continue a relationship, Michael said he'd been trying to reach her all week but she never returned his texts. "I'm your brother," he scolded.

Danielle had kicked him out again so he'd moved back in with their folks. A couple of days later they got into a fight after he accused Anita of poisoning his son against him ("She won't even let him get into a car with me") and he said that, whenever Anita was watching his son, she'd talk shit about Michael to him, calling him a vagabond, etc. Then Anita kicked him out of the house, which she'd done before, at various times in his life, without really meaning it. They'd fight, she'd kick him out, he'd sleep somewhere else for a few days and then return, and they'd both pretend like the fight didn't happen. This time, though, it had been different. He'd tried to come back a few days later but Anita and Julio had changed the locks, and when he rang the doorbell they said he needed to leave or they were going to call the police.

"I'm done with them, man. I'm never talking to them again. I'm tired of her evilness, Vivian. She has evil and hate in her heart, and I don't want it around me, I don't want it around my child, I'm just done, man."

"I feel you," Vivian said, but before she could pivot again to why she'd called he asked her if she could help him out because he didn't have anywhere to go and was sleeping in his car, and since he'd been spending so much time in the park he was being harassed by the police, and had even been filmed against his consent earlier that week, by a television crew following cops on patrol. Apparently someone had complained about him drinking in the park alone, and the cops showed up with cameras. He wasn't arrested, but he had an embarrassing and drunken interaction with the police that ended up on TV, and now people around town were recognizing him and making fun of him.

"So can you help me sue them?" he asked.

She couldn't, but she could send him some money. At this, he calmed down and half heartedly asked her how she was doing. She said she was super busy with work, and that she actually should get off now, because she had to prepare for court.

Vivian Western Unioned Michael a few hundred dollars and reflected. What had transpired between him and Anita was so severe, so dramatic, that they'd mutually cut each other off. Michael was free—free from hysterical outbursts, free from guilt-inducing phone calls and texts about Anita's inevitable death, free from her chronic negativity. She was so jealous.

She poured another tequila and thought about what she was going to say to Anita. Maybe she could use the Michael thing to her advantage. She could take his side, blame Anita for making Michael homeless. Then the estrangement would be Michael's fault! But it wasn't a position she could commit to fully.

Her mind turned to Anita's trespasses. Several years ago, the day after Thanksgiving, as Vivian was sitting in the living room watching TV, Michael's son, who was staying with Vivian's parents for the long weekend, went into the kitchen looking for something to eat for lunch. He took some leftover turkey out of the refrigerator and was about to put some of it onto a plate to heat it up in the microwave.

"That's for dinner!" Anita had yelled at him, as if he'd committed some grave offense. She snatched the plate from the child, dumped the turkey back into the roasting pan in the refrigerator, and yelled, to no one in particular, about the child's greediness, causing him to dejectedly go back downstairs to the den.

When Vivian cut in, with a gently pleading *"Mom"* regarding her tone and decibel level, the rage had turned onto her. "Oh please!" Anita yelled. "That's just the way I talk!"

"Yelling is bad for kids," Vivian snapped back.

"You've been hanging around white people too much," Anita said. Vivian spent the rest of the day in her room.

Now in her mind Vivian repeated phrases like "explosive rage," "no accountability," and "asserting my boundaries." She was justified in what she was about to do.

"I've been trying to get with you for weeks!" Anita said when she answered the phone, breathless. "Do you even care about your mother?"

Vivian fished out an ice cube and held it in her left hand as Anita spoke.

"Of course I care, Ma, I'm just super busy with work."

While Vivian squeezed the ice in her palm, Anita gave her version of what had happened with Michael. Anita admitted to telling Vivian's nephew that Michael was a good-for-nothing who refused to better himself. "Your brother doesn't believe in work!"

Vivian rubbed the ice down her right arm. "He does have a felony on his record."

"We told him the post office was hiring felons, though— he never went. He doesn't want to work; he just wants to drink, smoke, and play video games all day. Well, he's not living off me anymore. I've been taking care of him for over thirty years. Let me tell you, you aren't really a part of this family so you don't see it, but your brother has gotten really paranoid, Vivian. He's scary to be around. I hate to say it, but he's starting to sound like your dad."

Anita continued to rant, but at this mention of her father Vivian started catastrophizing, imagining the worst iterations of what could happen to Michael. Would it be homelessness and mental illness like their father? Would his justified suspicions—of white people, of strangers, of their family members—metastasize like their father's had, such that they blotted out consensual reality, taking on a menacing but seductive logic that he'd be unable to escape?

Or maybe Michael's fate would be more banal. Addiction and transience, moving from girlfriend to girlfriend and from house to house, staying fed and always in a relationship. Maybe he would get desperate and go back to selling drugs. If he did, would he get caught again, go to prison again? Would Vivian have to deal with more years of nightmares imagining him being beaten to death or otherwise murdered in prison?

Next she thought backward, seeing the entire history of black suffering, sardined bodies transported to an unwanting continent that would strip them of their traditions and customs, separate individuals from their tribes and families, and subject them to decades of oppression and cruelty that threatened to decimate the entire race, the future generations inheriting no land or wealth, only trauma, instability, violence, and poverty, and she felt angry all over again, on her own behalf, and on Michael's behalf, and on her father's behalf.

"He's jittery, I know," Vivian said eventually. "He's had two car accidents and might even have a concussion, but he doesn't have health insurance so he can't..."

"Well, if he got a job, he'd have health insurance!"

"He had that telemarketing job but then he lost it after the first car accident...It was hurting him to look at screens. I'm just saying, he's your son, he has nowhere to go. Are you really going to see him live on the street?"

"Well, Vivian, that's not my problem anymore. If you're so worried, why don't *you* take him in?"

No, she would never take Michael in. She would not have his chaos in her life.

"He texted me horrible things—he said I was a bad mother, he said I was trash, it was very hurtful. There's no manual for raising kids, and he's no saint himself. He can't even hold a girlfriend because he hits them all, and you should see the way he talks to your nephew. He explodes at the drop of a hat. Your nephew doesn't even want to be alone with him anymore, he told me, and we don't want him getting in his car because he drives drunk. You know that's why he's gotten into all these accidents, right? He's either driving drunk or fighting with Danielle."

She could see Anita's point of view. She didn't want to be around Michael either, and she wasn't willing to help. But Anita was also delusional. Sure, there wasn't a manual for raising kids but there was basic folk wisdom about not doing harm, and self-made ethics.

"But fine, take his side—none of my kids love me anyway," she heard Anita say.

Vivian didn't want to acknowledge the truth of these words, or to be moved by them. She wanted to say, *Love is earned, not freely given. I don't love or respect you. You have been a disappointment and I refuse to engage with you anymore.*

"Oh, Mom," she said instead.

"You have to call your mother." There was a catch in Anita's voice as she made this demand, but Vivian wouldn't give in to it.

"I talked to my mother on the phone every day."

Vivian remained silent.

"So when are you coming home next?"

"Well…about that…," she began.

"Oh, here we go, what now?"

"I'm not so sure I feel comfortable coming this year."

"You don't feel comfortable? What does that mean?"

"It just seems there's a lot of disorder right now, a lot of fighting, and every time I come out there, there's a lot of…yelling."

"Who yells? What yelling! Me and your stepdad are just here being peaceful, Vivian, what are you talking about?"

Vivian held the phone away from her ear.

"It's…happening right now," she said. "I just feel like—"

"Fine! You don't want to come home, don't come home, I don't care, do what you want, maybe I'll see you at my funeral then," Anita said, and hung up.

Vivian teetered to the kitchen, where she poured a tequila shot, sliced a lime, wet the burn mark between her thumb and forefinger with her tongue, doused it in salt, licked the salt off, took the shot, bit the lime, and exhaled.

———✦———

She asked Jane if she could come over. She needed to tell her what had just happened and to not be alone. But when she arrived, Collier was there too, and they were watching *Losing Ground,* Kathleen Collins's masterpiece about an ultra-rational black philosophy professor on a quest for ecstatic experience. *This is one of our movies*, Vivian thought, but then brushed this thought aside and settled into the armchair as Jane and Collier went back to snuggling on the couch.

It was right at the point where Sara (played by Seret Scott) has agreed to star in a student film. "It's a takeoff on the theme of the tragic mulatto," the student says about the film. Vivian and Jane laughed raucously, while Collier looked at them, unsure whether she could join in. Meanwhile on-screen, Sara beams back at the student, radiant in a head-to-toe yellow dress, slightly darker than Vivian and totally lean.

"I always wanted to be the only black girl at the eating disorder clinic," Vivian said wistfully. "I blame Seret Scott in this movie."

Jane smiled and Collier looked at her as if she were a member of an alien species.

While the film played Vivian felt once more the churning excitement of a creative idea. She would do in a novel what Kathleen Collins did on film. A strong black female lead with a highly developed interior. The cover would be spare, just text. No image of a thin woman. No bones, salt, or water in the title, either. She opened up her phone and wrote. Can Vivian live ecstatically, after what has been done to her?

After they talked about the movie Vivian took some puffs from a vape pen and offered it to Jane and Collier, who exchanged the quickest of glances.

"No thanks, I don't smoke," said Collier.

Jane shook her head. "I'm good."

"Wow," Vivian said, "you haven't turned down weed in ten years."

"We have an early drive out to the house tomorrow," Collier said.

"We just don't like being groggy when we go up," Jane offered.

Vivian resigned herself to smoking alone, pretending to pay attention while the two of them went on about the house and Collier's current work. Collier wore blue Dickies and a white tank top with her black bra straps showing. Her arms were quite toned (from carrying all her camera equipment, probably) and flower tattoos bloomed out over her shoulders. She kept her brown hair long, but when she put it in a ponytail, Vivian thought, she put it in a ponytail like a man. She didn't wear makeup and had a hard face, one that didn't express self-consciousness. She had beguiling blue eyes, and was capable of sustained, siren-like eye contact.

Collier was also famous—famous enough that she had been profiled on television, but not so famous as to be recognizable by the general public. She took her Siberian Husky, Wendy, with her to all her photo shoots, which centered on forgotten people: the homeless, drug addicts, and sex workers. Now as Vivian heard Collier say "Mom died" and "Nevada" she regained interest in the conversation and redirected her attention to Collier's story.

Collier was talking about being out in the desert soon after her mother died. "I hadn't spoken to my mother in twenty years," she was saying. "I left home when I was fifteen and never looked back," she explained, looking at Vivian, having noticed that she was listening. "But anyway I had to go out there, to Nevada, to take care of some stuff for the funeral. It was my job, for instance, to choose the clothes she was buried in. They gave me this task, I guess, because I'm the only daughter."

"Little did they know—" Jane began.

"—that I could give a shit about clothes," Collier finished. They all laughed.

"Sounds like a nice way to be useful while not having to interact with anyone?" Vivian said.

"For sure. So I went through her clothes and wound up donating a bunch of them, including Mom's collection of fur coats. (This was the kind of woman who wore furs in the desert.) Then I had to go call all these people Mom knew and tell them she's dead. I'm talking like four little phone books full of people I don't know. So I took Wendy, and we camped out in the desert to like, deliver death notifications."

"That sounds super intense," Vivian said, while Jane rubbed Collier's back.

"It was intense but also absurd. Many of the numbers didn't work, and even if they did, most people didn't answer at first, so I had to decide whether it was appropriate to, like, tell someone their old friend died in a voice mail? A couple of people thought I *was* my mother at first, so that was awkward. Anyway, days went by, I finished the calls, and I needed a drink. So I drove into town and ended up in this little desert bar. I look over and I see an old woman, about Mom's age, shooting pool in a fur coat. She's wearing one of my mom's coats!"

Vivian let out a gasp.

"I know! As soon as I saw her I just knew I had to photograph her. I was devastated by her face, which was so richly textured. Craggy, you know, and she was wearing this dramatic lipstick, and the fur. So I told her everything and she agreed to do a shoot with me. It was wild."

"Do you think it helped you process your grief?" Vivian asked.

"Probably. I was silently crying for much of the shoot," Collier said, laughing.

Jane and Vivian laughed too, and Jane squeezed Collier's shoulder. Vivian thought of Matthew, then of her family.

"Tell me more about not talking to your mom," Vivian

said in an Oprah-like tone, resting her chin on her hand with genuine interest.

"It was her who didn't talk to me," Collier said, looking at the floor, and before Vivian could respond she cleared her throat and said she was going to her studio. "Gonna get some work done, babe." She leaned over to Jane and kissed her forehead and Jane looked up at her adoringly.

"Have a good one," Collier said to Vivian as Jane walked her out.

She'd wanted to be alone with Jane all night, but now that they were, it felt awkward. Not natural. Vaguely strained. Vivian found herself looking around Jane's space, eyeing the plants and décor as if for the first time.

"Things are good with you two?"

"I like being with an artist, someone who actually acts on her ideas."

Vivian couldn't tell if this was a dig or if she was just high.

"We're going to work on something together."

Vivian made a face. "You're making art now?"

But Jane didn't take the bait; she just got excited. "Collier asked me to theorize her latest collection. I said okay, thinking I'd just write the wall labels, right? Provide the context and shit."

"That's what you're getting your degree in, right? Context and shit."

Jane continued, ignoring the joke. "But it kind of evolved into a curator role too? Helping to choose the photos and to position them in the cultural conversation, with my essay becoming part of the work. We want to disrupt the idea that theory is 'parasitic' or whatever," Jane said, sliding into a cheeky Black Barbie voice.

"These are the pictures of homeless people? Or Fur Coat Woman?"

"Actually...her latest work is about trauma," Jane said, pulling down a stack of photographs from a nearby bookshelf and handing them to Vivian. "She took all these pictures of women in the place where they'd been raped or beaten or whatever. They agreed to it, of course, and directed how they'd be photographed. Most of them are performers already, so they're used to expressing themselves in this way..."

Jane kept talking, but Vivian couldn't hear.

The first thing Vivian noticed was how diverse the women were: they were black and indigenous and cis and trans. A woman in a torn skirt pinned herself to the back brick wall of a grimy convenience store. Many women were in cars, either in the front with the seat kicked back or sprawled across the backseat, and one woman was kneeling by the passenger-side door with a bloodied lip. A woman in a kitchen raised her hands to her face while holding a spatula wet with pancake batter. One woman was on the floor of a nursery. Many were in bed. One was on a mattress on the floor, arm behind her head, looking at the camera with a warped smile.

Vivian was overwhelmed. It was so fucking cool, so much better than anything she'd seen at the Armory. Refusing to center white women's experiences of assault was radical in itself, but the reenactment element made the project even more dynamic. In re-creating their abuse on their own terms the women were demonstrating survival, on the one hand, but also rejecting the idea of "Survival" altogether, by aestheticizing what had happened to them, or laughing at it, or making use of it.

Why was Jane doing this with Collier, though? It was annoying.

Jane was saying, "Some of the pictures are banal, almost transactional. Does that express how the women are numbed out? Or is that just my projection? It's so complicated, right?"

"Cool," Vivian said, handing back the pictures. She was irritated at how smug Jane was being, and decided to communicate a lack of interest by not asking any follow-up questions. She didn't want to share any of her ideas with Jane and Collier. Jane and Collier didn't deserve her ideas. Jane looked a little hurt, but also like it was Vivian's loss.

"Anyway. How's your family?" Vivian asked. That ought to bring Jane back down to earth and provide an appropriate segue to Vivian's problems.

"Oh, you know, just disinvited to Corinthia's wedding," Jane said with a shrug.

"Say what now?"

"She wouldn't back down on the no-date thing. And you know, if this had been a few years ago? If I was still in my twenties? I would've actually gone for some closeted and compartmentalizing shit like that. But I'm sick of it, so I said no, I would only come if I could bring Collier. So now I'm out."

"That's some grade-A bullshit," Vivian said.

Making a pearl-clutching gesture, Jane said, "My mom is like, 'Jerome's father is a *pastor*, Jane. We can't afford to have A Scene at the wedding.'"

Vivian rolled her eyes. "Oh, here we go with A Scene. People love to allude to some Scene!"

"Yeah, like what does she think I'm going to do, start licking a white girl's pussy during the first dance?"

"LOL at 'white girl's pussy,'" Vivian said.

"MLK would've wanted it that way," Jane said.

"He truly had a dream about it," Vivian said.

The women were quiet then. For a minute and then two. Vivian knew this was her chance to process the failed estrangement attempt. But she feared Jane's judgment.

"Do you ever think about just saying 'fuck off' to them?" Vivian asked.

"What do you mean?"

"Like, middle fingers up like, just cutting them off, you know? I mean what value are they providing you? Are they providing joy?"

"This isn't a Marie Kondo book. It's my family. Can't just cut them off."

Vivian squeezed the nubby end of the vape pen. That wasn't what she meant. Why wasn't Jane getting what she meant?

"But Collier did it," Vivian said. "Gay people cut their families off all the time."

"No. We get cut out of our families."

"That's right. I'm sorry, you're right."

"The black family is under attack enough as it is," Jane added.

The air was sucked out of the room then. Allusions to racial solidarity will do that. Why was Jane being so deterministic about this?

"So there's just no consequences for bad behavior in The Black Family?"

"I'm just saying that the extreme step, of giving up on your family altogether? It seems more like something white people do. And it makes sense, they have the privilege to do so. They don't have our history of oppression. Family and, like, the church, were the only reliable structures black people had for over a hundred years," Jane said.

Vivian felt herself getting hot.

"That *sounds* right," she said. "And yet, most of the white people I know are still very much attached to their families. In fact, they seem even less likely to cut their families off—if only because of the money they stand to inherit or whatever. If you're inheriting shit, you're probably more likely to put up with narcissistic and abusive behavior."

"I don't think Corinthia is a 'narcissist,'" Jane said, using air quotes.

"I didn't say she was—"

"She just doesn't know any better. She needs time. She's made a mistake, but she's my sister."

At this, Jane went into her bedroom. Vivian heard her puttering around. Clearly this was Jane's way of signaling that the conversation was over. But Vivian didn't want it to end. She wanted to make Jane agree with her. She needed Jane's agreement. Why wasn't Jane agreeing with her? She pinched her side fat a little, waiting for Jane to come back. She felt like a menacing presence, bad and unwanted.

While keeping her eyes in the direction of the bedroom, she retrieved Jane's drug box from the coffee table's lower shelf, quickly swiped the Comfort Killer they'd smoked before, and tossed it into her bag. Then she turned on the TV and browsed the streaming options. She clicked on a documentary about meth in the Midwest. The first scene was a mom helping her adult son shoot meth inside a white van. It was a real nail-biter. Would he find the right vein? The son didn't want to listen to the mom's advice about which vein to use. As they bickered in a Mother-knows-best fashion, the son grew increasingly frustrated until he stormed out of the van. Finally the mom was able to reason with him. He poked his vein. After, he exhaled and said, "This is what it's *all* about," and told his mom that the effort deserved a hug. They hugged.

"Why were you in there for so long?" Vivian asked when Jane came out.

"I just had to return some emails," Jane said.

Vivian fingered a throw pillow. They didn't look at each other, only at the TV.

Everyone seemed relieved that a vein had been found, except for one of the daughters, who looked sad and embarrassed that all of this was being caught on video. Vivian vaped more and thought, *She has a fat face, but she's a good person.*

She refused to go home; she needed to bring the conversation back to family somehow. She swapped out issue documentaries. This time, sex work in the heroin triangle.

"Sex work makes me so *sad*," Vivian blurted out.

"Why does it make you *sad*?"

Vivian felt tension in her face. On-screen, very thin women lived in abandoned houses. The women were always cold. They waited at bus stops but never got on any buses. One of them said, of heroin, that the circuits were all dead and it felt really good that way.

"It's sad that women have to do it," Vivian said.

Jane pulled at her shirt. Her foot was shaking.

"It's something that women actually choose to do," Jane said, "so whether they should do it is irrelevant. The focus should be on supporting them in doing it, not condemning the practice."

"I'm just being honest," Vivian said. She knew it sounded stupid.

Jane looked over at her.

"Just because it's honest, doesn't mean it's true," Jane said. That stung, because it felt right.

"But shouldn't we want to imagine a world where it doesn't happen? I'm just saying it's not ideal."

"But you can't create ideal outcomes out of unideal conditions," Jane said.

"I guess it just bothers me to professionalize the objectification of women," Vivian tried.

"But any kind of labor is objectifying—what separates sex work from, like, bricklaying?"

"Well, for one thing, there's a spiritual component to sex."

"There's a spiritual component to intimacy, too, but we—well, some of us, not you, of course—outsource it to therapists," Jane said. And then, so low Vivian could barely hear: "Anyway, I did sex work after I dropped out of law school."

Vivian rubbed her face.

"What?"

"Yeah, before I went to stay with my parents. I hadn't told them yet and I needed money. I did some phone shit, some camera shit, met guys in hotels."

"You slept with men?"

"Yup."

Vivian felt a strange hurt.

"How could I not have known that?" she said. She stood up and walked to the kitchen. She felt Jane's eyes on her back and resented being watched. She poured a mug of water and stood there holding water in her cheeks.

"I mean. Did you want to know what was up with me? I would text you and you wouldn't respond," Jane said from the living room.

The mug said STRAIGHT OUTTA THE CLOSET. Vivian fingered the letters and walked back to the living room.

"I'm sorry, I literally don't remember that," she said, sitting back down on the edge of the couch.

Jane shifted in her seat and stared at a spot on the floor.

"Right," Jane said. "You don't remember that your best friend had a breakdown, that I left school and moved across the country, and that we didn't speak for months after."

Vivian took in more water and tried to recall that time period. She didn't remember any texts. Jane had left school, sure, but Derron had also died, and so Vivian flew into propulsive activity—studying, volunteering, exercising— just to get by. There wasn't any room for Jane's problems.

"Yet you can recite, with astounding precision, every single detail from every date you've ever been on with a man," Jane added.

This felt like a non sequitur, easily dismissed.

"I like going out with guys; is that weird?"

"Remember how you joked that you needed a boyfriend to get you through finals? Well, you got one, and I never saw you after. And I always just thought," Jane continued, "if you need a guy to feel stable, just say you need a guy to feel stable. But don't act like some radical feminist."

"I don't…need guys…to feel stable."

"Of course you do! Would you really be dieting and

working out so insanely if you weren't trying to, like, bag some dude?"

Vivian shook her head in disbelief. This was completely absurd.

"And why do you think you're being so paranoid lately when you go out? No boyfriend to make you feel safe— and because you smoke too much, but you're also doing *that* because you don't have a boyfriend."

"This is ridiculous. You're clearly upset at me for something that happened years ago that I don't even remember, because, if you recall, I was grieving my dead brother."

"Well, you weren't 'grieving' him. I mean let's be real, you were partying."

Vivian felt a jolt of rage. "Oh okay, you got me, *I was partying I was partying,* like why do you care? Was I doing damage to the fucking Platonic ideal of what a woman of color owes her family? Get the fuck out of here."

Vivian started to gather her bag and look for her shoes while continuing her tirade.

"And you're going to judge *me* for my commitment to feminism? I mean come on," Vivian said, laughing. "I'm sorry but I'm not going to be purity-tested by someone who—you know what, never mind."

"By someone who what?" Jane asked. "Say it."

She should have just left. But Jane had been trying to destroy her earlier with that boyfriend stuff. She put her bag back down.

"Okay, by someone too weak to stand up to their homophobic family."

"Girl," Jane said, rolling her eyes and waving Vivian away.

"It's like what we say about women being collaborators. Aren't you a collaborator in the homophobic family?"

Vivian leaned back and waited, eager for another volley. But Jane just scoffed, as if the line hadn't landed, or worse, as if it had been quickly metabolized and then dismissed as totally off base, deranged even.

"You know, you're very smart," Vivian continued, "and good at making arguments and whatnot, but when it comes down to your actions, you're as weak as others. You were too weak to handle law school and you're too weak to handle your family."

"And you're too judgmental to love yours."

"Actually, your whole family thing makes sense now. They're still paying half your rent, right? So there you go. You don't need to make it about race or, like, *ethics,* when it's about money." Vivian laughed.

"And you don't need to make your family stuff about abuse or, like, your mom's personality disorder. Really, you're just a selfish person! You can't tolerate anyone's flaws but your own. And now"—Jane stood and pointed to the door—"it's time for you to go."

Vivian needed to make a dramatic, self-righteous exit. The problem was that she was still super high. She bent over and, at a glacial pace, put on one black socklet, then the other, then picked up one of her Keds and smelled it in an exaggerated manner while looking at Jane, who just kept shaking her head.

"You're embarrassing yourself," Jane said.

Vivian tripped her way toward the door, then stopped and turned.

"They aren't just flawed. I'm not talking about a Big Five

personality trait that I don't like. Our families are fucking evil and if we stay in them we are participating in evil. I expected you to agree with me on this, but I guess your brilliant critiques are limited to movies and not, like, your own life. And I am the only one," Vivian said, "who gets to decide whether I am embarrassed."

She immediately bumped into Beyoncé the money plant, which crashed to the floor, dirt spilling out all over the floor and her Keds.

Jane refused Vivian's efforts to help gather the dirt and the ceramic planter shards, so she walked quickly to the door, pulling it hard in an exaggerated huff.

On the other side of the door, though, she felt exposed, as if Jane had seen the real her, as if Jane knew how bad she was, how incapable of sympathy. And she was still high, so high that her insides were vibrating. It was embarrassing, how scared she was to go out alone into the dark night of the city.

BAD AT PARTIES

IN THE AFTERMATH of the phone call, Anita launched a maternal guilt offensive. There were long, weepy voice mails, emoji-laden texts, and apologetic emails written in all lowercase that seemed to have been composed by a child.

Whenever Vivian received any of these correspondences, she quickly deleted them and moved on. Meanwhile, her muscles were perpetually clenched. It wasn't just her back. It was everywhere. Her jaw was tight and her abdomen, her shoulders, and her pelvic floor. She felt like a cowering child at the center of a cosmic joke, bracing for violence that never came. She ran in the park to ease the tension, but once she felt physically better she found herself in a bad mood. *Everyone in this park annoys me: the cluster of dance-walkers are slowing me down, white families with dogs don't respect my space, the swarms of male cyclists are actually just evil.* She was thick with irritation when she sat down by the lake, feeling mocked by all the happy people.

Matthew hadn't asked to see her that weekend, and Jane hadn't reached out at all to apologize. Yes, she thought, it was Jane who needed to apologize; she was the one who started with the low blows and the lazy psychoanalysis. And let's not forget the lemming-like loyalty to the family structure masquerading as politics. It's easy to maintain ideological purity from the safe remove of academia, where none of your theories are ever tested.

She decided to reconstitute herself socially. She would go to a party with Cristina, whom she'd been friends with since college, where they trauma-bonded over being two of the only brown people.

They met up at a bar near the party first.

"You balayaged your hair!" Vivian said to Cristina as they hugged and kissed each other on the cheeks. Cristina was a publicist, and she still wore heels. She was the kind of woman who read about fashion trends, believed in the power of retail therapy, and was genuinely excited to "debut" her first fall outfit: burnt-orange corduroy overalls with dark brown boots and a brown pashmina. She was heavier than Vivian but also prettier.

"You're so good at variety," Vivian said.

"I get bored, you know," Cristina said with a shrug.

At a divey bar playing mid-2000s Beach House, they ordered tequila sodas and talked breathlessly while tucked into a booth.

"I'm a woman on the verge," Vivian told Cristina after they'd settled in. "I had an amazing couple of dates with that guy Matthew I told you about, and then we texted about going out again, and now he's suddenly disappeared. Why isn't he worshipping me?" she asked, mock-shaking Cristina's shoulders.

Cristina loved to problem-solve in the romantic realm. "Why don't you text him and say 'Hey, just following up to see when you want to hang out' or something?"

"That's cute." Vivian laughed. "But no. You can't do that in contemporary dating. I don't reach out to them; they reach out to me. I have to be up here," she said, making a "higher-than" gesture with her hand.

"Wow. You are always measuring," Cristina said.

"Yeah, I'm pretty Battle of the Sexes, you know."

"And how was it seeing your parents?" Cristina asked.

Vivian broke off eye contact, said it was okay. It was easier to talk about guy stuff with Cristina than family stuff. Cristina grew up in South America. She had a deeply embedded sense of filial piety that made any criticism of the family as a unit impossible.

"I wanna order some chicken fingers," Cristina said, "but I know you won't share them with me, right?"

"No way. Got to keep it tight, especially when I might have sex soon."

"I kind of like my belly, though," Cristina said, with a sinister grin. "When David and I fuck—which is basically never, by the way—but when we do, I like to be on top and rub my fat belly while riding him. It's disgusting and hot at the same time!"

Vivian smiled in amusement. Cristina was in a years-long relationship with David, a white software developer with some kind of intimacy disorder. Their lack of a sex life was a regular topic of conversation.

"Speaking of, how are things going with you guys?"

Cristina said she'd snapped at David earlier that afternoon while folding laundry. It started when she'd told him she wanted to fuck and David demurred, saying they should do it later.

At this, Cristina had exploded. "You know what? Maybe I should just start sleeping with other guys."

David froze, holding a pair of boxers midfold.

"You would like that, wouldn't you?" Cristina continued. "You'd probably rather watch your pornos than fuck me anyway."

"You said that?" Vivian asked.

"I fucking said it all, dude," Cristina said.

"Fuck. What did he say?"

"He didn't say shit. He just looked down at the floor."

As Vivian understood it, David was so self-conscious about his penis (it was smaller than average but still serviceable, Cristina had said) that he had trouble relaxing during sex. Cristina hadn't minded at first; they had sex enough in the early days that it didn't seem pathological, and besides, she liked to help people and tended to view men as projects.

But then, about a year into dating, Cristina discovered that David had a secret Instagram dedicated exclusively to following women in the fitness industry and so-called urban models—typically black and Latina women—who posted sexy workout videos and thirst traps all day. She didn't say anything about it, not wanting to make a "thing" of it, but as time went on and David stopped initiating sex (too tired, too stressed), the secret account took on greater significance, and she began to see it as a cause of his disappeared libido. She wondered, too, what else he might be doing, so she started checking the search history on his computer and saw that he was watching porn every morning after she left for work. By the time she'd realized she was in an *Intervention* episode it was too late—they lived together and had merged their lives. He had proposed recently and they were going to get married.

When she'd told Vivian about the engagement Vivian had just said, "Wow."

Cristina had shrugged while stubbing out her cigarette. "Fuck it. I want to build equity and this is my chance. If it doesn't work out, who cares? Get a divorce and that's it." Vivian had always admired Cristina's flippancy about non-trivial matters.

"But I have to tell you what I've been doing," Cristina said now, leaning toward Vivian conspiratorially and dramatically adjusting her pashmina.

Cristina revealed that she'd created a fake Instagram account to follow David's models.

"It started because I wanted to understand why he was into these women. They are all thick Latinas like me or black girls with big breasts and huge, cartoonish butts popping out of their bikinis," Cristina said, stepping off the barstool to make breast-and-butt-shaped gestures with her hands.

"But now I don't know, dude." She looked at Vivian mischievously.

"What?" begged Vivian.

"Well," Cristina said *sotto voce*, "I'm like obsessed with looking and comparing and being jealous and angry but also kind of turned on." She waited a beat, and then, with a smile: "It's sick, right?"

Vivian laughed, rapt in the face of her friend's capacity for unfiltered self-disclosure. She didn't know what to think. "Is it sick? Or is it like a way to be close to him, maybe?"

Vivian believed she'd arrived at the key insight, but all Cristina said in response was "Yeah, I don't know, man." Then she rubbed her face and spoke to herself quickly in Spanish.

Vivian reflected on how neurochemically pleasurable it was to hear about other people's problems. *Better to be single than to be in Cristina's relationship,* Vivian thought, and then judged herself for thinking that.

Cristina now had an air of fuck-it-I've-told-you-one-thing-so-might-as-well-tell-you-the-rest, and she said that one reason she'd stayed with David this long was because she felt bad for him as a fellow survivor of abuse. Cristina had been fondled by a babysitter.

"David experienced some kind of gray-area sexual abuse, right?" Vivian responded.

"Yes, definite gray area, like his stepmother would flirt with him, you know? She treated him like a little husband. So creepy."

As they walked to the party and shared a cigarette, Cristina mentioned a recent fight she'd had with her aunt, who lived in Inwood. She'd gone up there for the aunt's birthday, and the aunt kept making mean comments about Cristina's weight. When Cristina asked her to stop, the aunt accused her of taking things too personally, and said she never used to behave this way and that maybe she should stop working so much. They ended up getting into a screaming fight.

"She's crazy," Cristina said, shaking her head.

Vivian saw an on-ramp, so she decided to tell Cristina some of what had happened at the reunion. Pulling hard on the cigarette and passing it back to Cristina, she described being borderline hit on by her cousin and shuddered.

Cristina laughed. "That's sick, but what can you do? It's your family, you know? They will be with you forever. You just gotta suck it up."

She passed the cigarette back to Vivian.

"But isn't that crossing some kind of line—"

"I mean, last time I was in my country I was groped by my ninety-something-year-old great-uncle. He was all fat and drooling and slumped in a chair. I stooped down to give him a kiss like this"—she made a stooping-and-hugging gesture— "and as I stood up, his hand slid down to my butt, dude. I was in fucking shock."

"That's disgusting," Vivian said.

"My lesbian friends were all like 'That's abuse,'" Cristina said.

They both laughed.

"Isn't it, though? Did anyone else see?"

"Yeah, my mom saw, and she was like, 'Next time, kiss him from behind.'"

"Fuck that guy," Vivian said, killing the cigarette and tossing it.

"Eh, he's harmless. Almost dead, you know, let him get his final pleasures before death, who cares?"

Vivian sorted through the vape pens in her backpack and debated arguing with Cristina about this. She started sucking on a pen with more CBD than THC—a perfect party vape— and decided against the argument. Cristina wasn't exactly a bra-burning feminist.

The party was being thrown by David's best friend, Elliott, and his wife. They lived in a huge newly constructed luxury condo in Prospect Heights. Through an immaculate lobby with huge plants they took an elevator up to the sixteenth floor and Vivian imagined her party entrance.

She would cut through the room and go straight for the drinks table, where, after making herself a gin or tequila and soda with lime, she would stand silently sipping on the periphery of a semicircle of three to five people, nodding and smiling until she felt comfortable enough to start to insert herself, little by little, into the group, contributing positive things to the conversation, making people laugh, and delivering entertaining monologues. There was an ethics to partying, after all.

Vivian followed Cristina into the apartment. It was stunning, featuring oversized windows framed by wooden flowering planters, stainless steel appliances, and a marble kitchen island. She estimated that the place cost at least two million dollars. Who were these people?

The party was fully on; the place was packed with people laughing and talking as a Sia club anthem streamed through multiroom speakers. Despite doing her best to broadcast "confident love of life," Vivian felt off. The aggregated gloom of the past month was beginning to take its toll. That, or she was high. As she walked through the apartment and took in all the mostly white faces of people in their late twenties and early thirties prattling about what they had consumed online, she felt like she was dodging enemies in an aquatic video game.

She felt desperate for a drink, and needed to do something with her hands. But before she could make it to the kitchen, she bumped into David. He had a flat face and a short nose, like a Persian cat, which caused him to look disgruntled even when he was smiling, like now. They hugged and she congratulated him on the engagement. Then she asked how work was going and tried not to think about his sexual problems.

Luckily, before things got too awkward, Cristina grabbed her arm and pointed to a fashionable-looking woman with the taut body of a dancer who had her back to them. She wore a body-hugging sleeveless navy-blue dress that hit her shins and matching navy-blue strappy sandals. Her defining feature was her hair—long, wavy, waist-length.

The woman turned around and when she saw them her eyes widened and she jogged over to hug Cristina. As Vivian watched them embrace, her breath caught. Was this Paula, Miss Competition Among Women Is Biological from the panel? The woman who said she wished she'd been poor, neglected, or abused *for the story*? She must have lost like fifteen pounds. The tightness of her dress made Vivian uncomfortable suddenly.

"Pauline, meet Vivian, my best friend from college!"

"Hey, girl," Paula/Pauline said, with the overly familiar inflection certain white women use when talking to black women. "Great to meet you." As if they hadn't already met and as if Vivian hadn't made a strong impression.

"We've met before?" Vivian said. "I work at Wellhaven, we did that panel—"

"Oh right! Of course, you do that super-important work. I remember you, duh," Pauline said, profusely apologizing.

Strike One, Vivian thought. They fake-hugged and Vivian felt Pauline's bones.

Pauline explained that she'd left her psych job several months ago ("It's the craziest thing I've ever done!"), taking a leap of faith to focus on turning her food-blogging hobby into a career. She was developing a pitch for a cookbook and had decided that it would be better to go by Pauline "to avoid any, like, Paula Deen confusion."

Pauline turned and introduced Vivian to her husband, Elliott. "This one's the sole breadwinner now," she said.

Vivian got a good look at both of them. Pauline's weight loss exposed her high cheekbones and made newly apparent the delicacy of her features. She had tiny wrists and shoulders, and a small, pinchable nose with a turned-up tip. Elliott's thick black hair, dark-framed glasses, and beard were, in theory, blatant Vivian bait, but any interest she might have in him was blocked by Matthew. She had always been like that—there was only room for one person at a time.

"What's up?" she said to Elliott, as if he were an old buddy.

Elliott had a big, open smile. He was clearly attracted to her without being showy about it.

She asked them how long they'd been together and how they'd met.

"We went to college together," Pauline said, slurring ever so slightly. Vivian realized now how drunk she was. "The girls in my dorm called him El Caballo," she said, spacing out her hands about nine inches apart. Vivian suppressed the urge to check Elliott's bulge while everyone else laughed. It was a funny comment but also annoying, because they were both white and it didn't seem like she actually spoke Spanish. They went through the preliminaries, what they did for a living. Elliott was an executive at a record company. That piano in the corner of the living room was his, he made sure to mention.

Pauline touched Vivian's shoulder and showed her off. "Bless her, she works in a psych ward," she said to Elliott.

"Doing God's work," Elliott said.

Vivian smiled and tilted her head to the side, gesturing at an imaginary halo illuminating above her head.

"Working hard to dismantle that *DSM*," she said, with an edge in her voice.

"Ha, ha. I don't know any clinician who uses the *DSM* for actual treatment," Pauline said. Her sudden sobriety was disarming. "I just saw those labels as reimbursement codes. What I actually used was HiTOP. You aren't familiar with HiTOP? It stands for Hierarchical Taxonomy of Psychopathology. With HiTOP, you don't go searching for a unifying label; you just cluster the symptoms and target them in order of severity."

Vivian was annoyed for some reason and didn't want Pauline to go on. "So why'd you leave the field?"

"I was a psychologist in acute care. You know what it's like. I was losing my hair and I'd gained *so much* weight. I went home to see my parents and they were like, *You're miserable.* They're both doctors and I guess I thought this would make them proud of me. But then they said life's too short to be stressed out all the time and I felt like I had permission to do something else. Part of me misses helping people (and being self-righteous about helping people). But overall, I'm much happier now."

As Pauline spoke, Vivian had a peculiar feeling. It was as if Pauline was speaking to her subliminally. She'd touched Vivian's arm when she said the self-righteous thing. Why would she do that, unless she thought Vivian was self-righteous? Had something leaked out at the panel that night, or later at the bar? Now Pauline seemed to pick up on the fact that Vivian was thinking negatively about what she'd just said, so she added, "But you *love* what you do, right?"

This felt like mockery, like condescension, like Pauline was boxing her in to a response. "It's a thankless job in some ways," Vivian said. "But I'd rather do something about injustice than, like, tweet about it."

Fuck. Well, now she really did sound self-righteous, and Pauline knew Vivian was creating a straw man and was probably about to say as much, so Vivian pivoted.

"Anyway, I'm a writer too. Working on a novel based on my experiences at the hospital."

At this, Elliott perked up. "A lawyer *and* a writer. So impressive," he said, looking at her hair.

Pauline shifted in place. "A fiction novel?" she asked, with vague skepticism.

"All novels are fiction," Elliott said in a mildly dismissive way while making eye contact with Vivian as if to signal that they were in cahoots against Pauline.

Having successfully renegotiated her identity, Vivian went to make a tequila soda and looked around the living room. Cristina was telling her engagement story to a semicircle of rapt women in their thirties. David was talking to his and Cristina's mutual friend Denise—a Haitian American DJ and sculptor with a high-top fade and a nose ring—about contemporary film.

While making her drink, she tuned out the party and plugged into the up-tempo love-your-body anthem that was playing, hand-dancing briefly with various cocktail-making accouterments.

Someone tapped her on the shoulder while she was rhythmically cutting a lime and she turned to see her and Cristina's mutual friend Max, a corporate lawyer who'd done some pro bono work at the hospital. They hugged and Vivian exhaled. "An ally has arrived!" she said.

Max practically lived at his Midtown office these days, keeping late hours doing document review and finding typos in legal briefs defending every corporation from BP to Apple.

He had just bought an apartment in Harlem and was planning an epic, *Call Me by Your Name*–inspired trip to Italy. She told him about Matthew and how she was currently about to have a nervous breakdown because he hadn't texted her in days.

"He'll reach out," Max said.

Then, after a beat, "Unless he doesn't."

Vivian laughed.

"In which case," he said, cupping his hands around his mouth like an announcer, " 'Next!' "

Vivian vocalized carefree assent to Max while feeling abject; then they both watched a woman mindlessly shovel handfuls of tortilla chips into her mouth at the end of the snacks and drinks table.

"Ugh," she said to Max in a low voice. "I'm so jealous of people who can eat massive amounts of carbs without a care in the world."

Max laughed, running his fingers through his dirty-blond hair. She knew it was safe to say such a retrogressive, weight-conscious thing around Max, a former fat kid who struggled to maintain a body that met the high standards of other gay men.

"I'm sorry, but all of these snacks are homophobic," he said, pointing at the spread of chips and cookies. "It's still beach season somewhere."

"I gotta get my body back, man. For three weeks last year," Vivian said, with a comically embittered tone, "I didn't have to wear a bra," and Max laughed.

Vivian looked around mock-suspiciously and said she knew they'd rightly be accused of fat-shaming if anyone overheard but, now tipsy, she said, "What's at the core of us wanting to be thin, though? Shame. So when you think about it, anyone who accuses us of fat-shaming is really engaged in shame-shaming."

"That's a good take. Wouldn't share it, though."

Before Vivian could respond, Pauline appeared at her side in the kitchen.

"You're black and Puerto Rican?" she said, looking at Vivian with an awed expression while putting ice cubes into a wineglass.

"Yeah...Why, Paula?" Vivian asked, using what she considered the woman's "real" name out of spite.

Vivian watched with morbid intrigue as Pauline poured rosé into the glass.

"Cristina just told me. That's so cool," Pauline said cheerfully, and then walked back out into the living room.

Vivian stood there stunned.

She turned to Max.

"I think I just got drive-by ethnicized."

"By someone who puts ice in her rosé," Max said.

"What kind of *She's All That* bullshit is this? I met that woman last year and she looked like a completely different person. Also, *et tu, Cristina?*"

Max's phone vibrated. "I have to take this, I'm so sorry, but let me know if you need me to make a witness statement?"

"Hysterical," Vivian said as Max walked down the hall, taking the call in some bedroom or bonus room or other. She looked out into the living room at Cristina, who flashed her such an endearing and welcoming smile-and-wave, eagerly beckoning her over to join what looked like a rollicking conversation, that she couldn't be mad at her.

But this was certainly Pauline's second strike, and Vivian needed space. She sought refuge in the bathroom, pulling out her phone so quickly that it dropped on the floor, cracking again. She shimmied her pants down and sat on the toilet even though she didn't have to go. If Matthew wasn't texting her, what was he doing? *Who are you with right now and is she thinner than me?* She stood back up and looked into the mirror, closed her eyes, and mock-screamed.

Max was still on the phone so she was forced to rejoin Cristina, Elliott, and Pauline's group. Pauline was going into the minutiae of a recent multicourse tasting they'd had.

"It was incredible. Yellowfin tuna with foie gras; delicate, barely cooked scallops; charred octopus; lobster lasagna; everything on white plates, all arranged with different textures and colors—we felt like we were looking at great art or something."

Kurt, an independently wealthy gay fashion photographer whom Pauline had introduced as her "bestie," said, "It probably has a similar effect on the brain—looking at gorgeous food."

White people whom Vivian hadn't been introduced to nodded in agreement. Vivian nodded too, while thinking contemptuously about how much money they all probably spent on food, and about what she would do with all that money: voice lessons, a personal trainer, time to write that novel.

"Speaking of which," said Pauline in a conspiratorial tone. She held up a finger to the group and then jogged to the kitchen, returning with a plate of vanilla and chocolate cupcakes.

"Homemade!" she squealed.

The circle of whites began murmuring in unison over the cupcakes. Pauline proudly held out the plate for each person to grab one. While they dove in, Vivian looked around the apartment uncomfortably. There was a fluffy white rug in the living room with a glass coffee table on top of it. Vivian hated glass coffee tables. They reminded her of her childhood. She thought of someone's face being shoved against it without warning, and recoiled at her own thought.

"That look on your face!" Pauline said to Vivian.

"Huh? Oh, it wasn't about anything you said, what were you saying?"

Pauline offered Vivian the last cupcake.

"No thanks," Vivian said. While holding her drink with her right hand, she pinched at a roll of belly fat with her left. Well, it wasn't quite a roll. But it was certainly more flesh than Pauline would be able to grab.

"Really?" Pauline said. She gave a disappointed look, her tone mildly pleading.

"I try to keep a low-carb diet," Vivian said.

There was a microexpression of discomfort on Pauline's face.

"Oh come on, it's my birthday!"

"I also actually don't want one," Vivian said.

"Okay..."

Pauline turned to Kurt, raised her eyebrows, and said, "Fine, I'll eat it myself." She oohed and aahed about her own cupcake with every bite.

"I just love food too much," she said again to Kurt with a mouthful of sweet carbohydrates, "to deprive myself of anything."

Kurt laughed conspiratorially. "Yeah, who cares?" he said. "It's the weekend anyway. I'll go back to my diet on Monday."

Vivian called the third strike.

"So, you don't eat rice or bread?" Pauline continued, wiping frosting off the wrong side of her mouth.

"Not really," Vivian said, resolving not to tell Pauline about the frosting residue.

"I could never give up bread—it is literally life to me, especially in the winter! It's so comforting!"

"I don't miss bread," Vivian said wearily.

Pauline noticed the leftover frosting on her face and Vivian felt that she was licking it off in a distinctly taunting manner. The partygoers, meanwhile, were orgasming over the cupcakes and complimenting her.

"These are so fucking good, dude."

"This is like the best cupcake I've ever had."

"What's the recipe?"

"Are there any more left?"

Pauline explained the provenance of the recipes, how she'd gotten them from another food blogger on Instagram but had, over the course of an entire week of baking test batches, tweaked the recipes to her own liking. Her boring tale afforded Vivian another opportunity for appraisal. Thin face, long neck, straight torso. The A-cups would allow her to wear plunging necklines without being ogled, and her arms were sleek. *Pilates arms,* Vivian thought. It was as if Pauline's body had risen to the occasion of her hair.

When Pauline started off on how to make a piecrust from scratch in laborious detail, Vivian left the group to go to the bathroom again. You can't bake away the stresses of modern life.

Safe by herself with the door closed, Vivian checked her email. New email from Anita, no subject. call your mother I miss you. Delete.

After turning on the vent fan, she stood on the toilet and vaped, blowing smoke into the vent like a fifteen-year-old. *Much fucking better.* After, she riffled through a basket on the floor. Unread *New Yorker*s and a book of interviews with Woody Allen. Definitely Elliott's. How many times at a party throughout the aughts had she titillated a certain breed of North American white intellectual man with her opinion of a Woody Allen film. Men always got hard over *Crimes and Misdemeanors,* but she preferred *Another Woman.* Most people, even die-hard Woody Allen fans, had never seen it.

She Googled Pauline's Hierarchical Taxonomy and frantically tried to memorize its basic concepts, then looked at Pauline's Instagram and saw that it combined two of her hates: foodie-ism and fine photography, and there were no pictures over a few months old. She scrolled through photos of brightly colored vegan tarts, carefully arranged acai bowls, and endless variations on avocado toast ("seriously yum!") that Pauline had expertly photographed on the terrace of this apartment, which, Vivian thought now, she had no doubt bought with family money. Vivian used her thumb and forefinger to zoom in on Pauline's pale white regularly manicured hand holding a spoon that slowly drizzled semen-like yogurt dressing onto homemade sex-organ-like falafel balls.

Pauline had tens of thousands of followers and she promised to deliver to them, through pornographied photos, recipes, predigested summaries of popular wellness books, and endless lists of "bests" and "essentials," the keys to health and happiness. Many of her posts were accompanied by the hashtag #foodisart.

"Oh my fucking God," Vivian said aloud to no one.

Vivian was the real artist here. She was the one who was going to write a book so good that everyone would know her name. All of Pauline's meals would be shat or vomited out, but Vivian's brilliant book would last forever. Pauline promised her fans that if they just learned how to make the perfect soufflé, they would be loved and validated as creative visionaries. But this sort of thinking was a mistake. Elaborately designed food was not a fucking art form; it was a way to broadcast one's social status.

Vivian clicked on a filtered photo of lasagna. In the accompanying post, Pauline wrote about her privileged childhood, characterized by weekends baking with her grandmother, an Italian immigrant with whom she seemed to have a close and nontraumatizing relationship. Now that Nonna was gone, Pauline alleged, she kept her spirit alive every Sunday by baking an elaborate, carbohydrate-rich meal.

But Pauline had transformed her body into one that looked great in light denim, in a white dress that fit like a glove, in an actual bikini. No way she ate lasagna. Not regularly at least.

Next Vivian looked at Elliott's profile. His music industry job took him all around the world. Here he was in Italy, in Mexico City, in Barcelona. His was a life of leisure, of happiness, of fun. During his travels he would visit and photograph every site, posting dozens of photos from whatever place he visited. This false belief that Elliott seemed to have, that if he did not take pictures of a place it was like he had never been there, or if he did not record an experience it was like it had not occurred, filled Vivian with hot resentment as she sat on the toilet scrolling fervidly. These people had so much fucking time. On the plus side, Elliott's profile offered rare glimpses into his wife's pre-Pauline persona and body, which Vivian pored over as if they were evidence she could use to charge Pauline with a nebulous crime against womanhood.

Just as she was zooming in on an image of a heavier Pauline wearing a one-piece in Tulum there was a frustrated rap on the door. Startled, Vivian wiped herself and flushed out of habit. She'd been discovered being crazy, it seemed.

Vivian returned to the party with a refreshed drink and a re-newed sense of control now that she had identified everyone's social media accounts. As she inserted herself awkwardly into Elliott and Pauline's circle she felt Elliott looking at her again with interest. She pretended not to notice, but the attention had an alleviating effect.

Pauline was saying that she was close to her mother and they talked on the phone every day. "She is the rock of my family," Pauline said.

Vivian felt like she was being trolled, so while Pauline's maternal encomium went on, she imagined the woman's upbringing. As a child, Pauline must have been well-cared for by her parents. If she scraped her knee after a tumble on the playground, say, she had a mother who would run over, kiss it better, and apply a decorative princess Band-Aid that Pauline could run her finger over whenever the cut throbbed. Over time, the consistent reassurance of her parents combined with the crutch of wealth encouraged Pauline to believe that there was a larger, kind force out there monitoring her, a force whose benevolence Pauline later internalized, leading to a feeling of groundedness and optimism about both other people and her own future.

Still, Pauline insisted, she had problems. She was "super worried" about what would happen when her parents died. It would be up to her to dispose of their assets. "It's all going to be on me. I don't want the responsibility of deciding where all the cars go."

Vivian tried to make eye contact with either Max or Cristina but they both seemed to take Pauline's complaint as legitimate. Max looked amused, and Cristina seemed amazed, finding this one percent conversation pleasurable precisely because it was so rare. It was as if Pauline's wealth in itself made her a person worth knowing.

Vivian wanted to look up at the ceiling in a "Please God" gesture of exasperation but she held back, resolving, though, that as soon as this conversation about family ended, she would demonstrate her superiority and get revenge upon Pauline, by embarrassing her in front of her husband. She wasn't even interested in Elliott particularly, but she was fucking bored.

"Bold move to keep that Woody Allen book in your bathroom," she said to Elliott eventually, trying to lure him into a private conversation.

With a bashful smile he turned his body toward her.

"What can I say? He's a genius. Can I ask how you feel as a woman," he said, leaning closer, "about the allegations?"

Vivian laughed and pivoted toward Elliott, pretending to hold a microphone. "Well, as a human who cares about women and girls and knows what a predator is, I can say that they aren't *allegations,* they are *facts,* and to society I would say, where were y'all in the eighties because this news literally dropped way back then, but no one cared about women and girls then, and y'all only care now because being anti-misogyny is cool, and none of this changes the fact that *Another Woman* is brilliant and—"

Denise interrupted with, "I'm sorry but I just can't. If I ever get tempted to watch *anything* he makes now, I just remind myself that he molested his daughter. That usually gets rid of my desire to watch *Annie Hall* or whatever movie you're talking about."

Vivian felt her neck getting red. She hadn't wanted this to be a big-group sort of conversation.

Max said, "I've never been invested in Woody Allen but this comes up for me with, like, David Bowie raping people."

"Who did David Bowie rape?" Vivian asked.

"A young girl, I think. No one talks about it. It's weird which sexual abusers people latch onto and which ones people don't. But I do the same thing as Denise—get tempted to listen to *Station to Station* and then think about him raping someone."

Cristina said, "I'm so scared of being caught listening to or watching something by someone who has been canceled, now I just Google everyone first before I consume anything."

"We need an FDA but, like, for rapists," Vivian said, to Cristina only, and only Cristina laughed.

Kurt sighed. "I just don't care what the artist does or doesn't do in his personal life. Once the thing is out there in the world, it's mine. The artist I can take or leave."

Denise turned to face Kurt. "But there's money involved— your consumption is allowing a pedophile to get richer. Don't you see a problem with that? The art and the artist can't be financially separated."

"I don't care about my money supporting them," Kurt replied. "Because the issue isn't that abusers are artists. I mean abusers are everywhere. They do everything for a living. So you find yourself inevitably supporting them."

Elliott cleared his throat and said, "For me it depends what the art is about. If the art is actually about whatever the artist is being accused of, then I can't make the distinction between the art and the artist. So, like, I can watch *Crimes and Misdemeanors,* but I can't watch *Manhattan*. It's too close."

Vivian tongued the inside of her cheek as they spoke, different parts of her clamoring for attention. One part was happy this conversation was happening, but another part was enraged. She was the one who had been talking about sexual violence for years when no one else was; she had better opinions on sexual violence than any of these people. She should be a sexual violence pundit on TV, really, or the sexual violence consultant to the President. At the very least she should be writing sexual violence explainers that would be widely read and shared online. But what was she doing instead? Standing at a party completely unheard, unappreciated, and unrepresented!

There was a moment of expectant silence that comes when everyone in a group has given their opinion about a topic and they all want to be the one to say the next brilliant thing about it, to offer the one take that everyone can rally around, to have the one interpretation that sticks.

Vivian jerked up into this void, dramatically sloshing her drink around in her cup and taking a gulp before speaking. "Look," she said, "pedophiles can make important movies about women."

She took a beat.

"*Another Woman* is brilliant, Gena Rowlands's performance is legendary and there just aren't many movies that portray an intellectual woman grappling with the limitations of her own personality.

"I'm the most feminist person here," she continued with self-aware vanity, holding her right hand to her chest and making eye contact with each person as if they were the members of some jury. "And my love of that movie doesn't negate my loyalty to the cause. Maligning a pedophile's work product? That's the morally easy thing to do. For me, when we're talking about moral duties, the real test is what you do when you know or suspect that abuse of women or children is going on *in your life,* in your actual life. I'd like to see the people who refuse to watch *Manhattan* or *The Cosby Show* or *Two and a Half Men* reruns actually have their moral construct tested when someone close to them turns out to be an abuser, because we all know someone who is abusive, whether we're aware of it or not. On the far end, *your father could be out there molesting people,*" she said, pointing at Pauline, "but at the very least, we all know toxic people who must be stopped. Do we stop them, though? I think we fixate on the ethics of aesthetic consumption because it's easier than dealing with the moral trespasses of real life. It's easier to denounce an artwork than a family member, right? Or a friend? So ultimately, for me, all this talk about whether we should watch *Annie Hall* or dance to 'Ignition Remix' or whatever is a distraction from the larger problem: How do we prevent the mass rape and abuse of women and children? And what do we do with the offenders?"

It was a solid speech. Very *high school oratory.* Very *opening statement.* Very *militaristically vanquishing the enemy.* She took a triumphal sip of her drink, surveyed her lands, waited for applause. But she didn't get any. No one knew what to say and she didn't understand what she'd done. She had to read their faces.

Pauline was looking at Vivian like she was crazy. Denise's face indicated that she was puzzling over Vivian's remarks and couldn't speak until she had a rebuttal. Elliott seemed sympathetic but perhaps felt it was too soon to express his sympathy; they had only just met and Vivian had suggested that his father-in-law could be a pedophile. Max looked like he was watching a reality show where women compete against each other, and one of the women has just come for another of the women in a crossing-the-line manner that was also true, and so, while he was slightly disturbed he was also thinking, *She's not wrong.*

She probably shouldn't have mentioned abusers in their lives. Maybe some of the men in the circle *were* abusers and maybe some of the women in the circle *had been abused* and maybe even one or two of the men in the circle *had been abused* or maybe it was just the social taboo *against mentioning abuse* but now it appeared that no one wanted to say anything, because she had made things "too real" by going down this road, like years ago when she would make things "about race" around a group of white people, before it had become socially acceptable or even cool to make things about race, and now here she was, out there all alone looking, she felt, like someone who had been abused as a child. She had outed herself, she felt out of control, her face was getting red, the sludgy feeling was returning. Could they all see?

Pauline spoke first, as if she had to, being a psychologist in the presence of an unstable person. "Well, anyway. I'm not sure how we got from *Annie Hall* to people having abusers in their family and 'mass rape,'" she said, looking at Elliott, determinedly not looking at Vivian, but clearly directing the comment toward her. Her quotation marks felt like rubber gloves being used to protect her delicate social ecosystem from Vivian's hazardous concepts. What she was really saying was *This is my birthday party and I don't want to talk about this stuff. I've Hi-TOPped you, and you're mostly a fearful and distressed internalizer with a thought disorder, but you also tend to antagonistically externalize in social situations. In other words you're creepy, afraid, depressed, and bad at parties. Stop bringing down the mood.*

"These days, I just watch TV to be entertained," Pauline continued. "It's nice to have at least an hour away from all the horrors of the world. I left all that *righteousness* in the past—doesn't it get exhausting?"

"But you write about food. What horrors do you engage with now?" Vivian asked. But before Pauline could respond, Max said, diplomatically and with an ironic air, "This is a safe space for *all* opinions."

As a feint, Vivian walked away once the subject had been changed and the group was laughing. In the bathroom again, vaping again, she felt oppressed by basic whiteness.

After, to make herself feel better, she took Max aside and brought up the topic of Cristina and David's relationship and the two of them talked about it while looking at Cristina, who was talking and laughing with Pauline across the room.

"I shouldn't say this, but fuck it. I am so sick of women being in sexless relationships. Our friend deserves to come, you know. I'm tipsy and high but you know what I mean. Pretend it was more eloquent than that, and rooted in psychology or feminism."

"I feel like the theme of my thirties is watching each of my straight friends make a huge mistake that will likely ruin their lives without saying anything," Max said.

Vivian paused to think this over, then nodded slowly.

"That's pretty deep," she said. "And sad. What about your gay friends?"

"Oh. We make the same mistake over and over, in rapid succession."

Vivian nursed her drink and did a thousand-yard stare, quickly devising a path for herself and Cristina. If she could rescue Cristina from her relationship, her whole life could change. Cristina could enter therapy to understand why she was attracted to men who were incapable of sexual intimacy, getting to the root of her own fears of intimacy and sex, which no doubt had their origins in her Catholic upbringing. It would be hard for Cristina at first, but Vivian would be there for her. Cristina could stay with Vivian while she picked up the pieces of her life. They would be single best friends like women on TV in another era, going out and looking for men and having adventures. They'd become each other's greatest confidantes and would replace men in each other's lives. Vivian would write her novel, Cristina would start that screenplay she'd always wanted to write, and they'd launch successful creative careers that had nothing to do with men.

"On the other hand," Max said, "Cristina's a pragmatist. Maybe sex isn't the top priority right now."

"It's true; David does provide stability. And he always takes Cristina's side when she fights with his mother."

"Also, he's a founding developer at his company. Once they go public, he'll get a windfall from the stock options alone."

Vivian felt that, by positively reevaluating Cristina's relationship, she had successfully counteracted her earlier hostility, thus proving that she was a sane and normal person, so she went to get another drink.

In the kitchen, as Vivian poured her tequila and soda and cut up a lime to drop in, Cristina and Max talked about a Twitter controversy that Vivian couldn't find a way into. She didn't recognize the author of the tweet in question, didn't understand the brand of humor contained within it, and, though tempted to belittle the app and its addicts, being openly anti-Twitter was a stance that had already been metabolized by Twitter. She laughed in their direction out of politeness before turning her attention to a neglected bowl of baby carrots while they chatted on, riffing about a TV show that wasn't funny, a woman singer who overemphasized her sexuality, and a violent movie Vivian found unredeemable. She slowly and methodically placed the baby carrots on a paper plate, then busied herself finding a spoon to dole out hummus, all while feeling that particular loneliness that arises when everyone around you is engrossed in a topic of conversation that you have no interest in. When you don't care for the people, you are able to buffer that loneliness with judgment and disdain. But when you love them, the loneliness is tinged with grief. She crunched on a single carrot before putting down the plate, turning to Max and Cristina, and then announcing, "The vibe inside me, formerly known as The Mood, has gotten dark again, so I will leave now but I love you." They all hugged.

＊＊＊

Standing outside the rich couple's building waiting for her car to arrive, Vivian took in the night's activity while shivering. It was almost jacket weather. A drunk guy huffed on a Citi Bike and couples lovingly lapped up their last outdoor ice cream of the season. She heard a woman say, "I wore this outfit as a joke," and thought of Jane, who, at a party once, had joked that her oversized sweater paired with the oversized bohemian dress she was wearing "as drag" made her look like an actress in a nineties sitcom who gets pregnant while playing her role at a time when pregnancy wouldn't make sense in the character's story arc and so the actress is forced to hide her baby bump in ways that get progressively more absurd as the pregnancy evolves. Jane had really committed to the bit, too, grabbing items from the party host's apartment to use as props-to-hide-the-bump: laundry basket; paper bag filled with groceries; stack of towels.

She laughed a little and decided to smoke some of the Comfort Killer. It would make her feel closer to Jane. "Let's go," she said, taking a few puffs.

By the time her car got there she was very high, and her slow, awkward wobble into the car made her intoxication apparent, such that she felt immediately at risk. Shortly after she'd settled in for twenty minutes of unity with the world, her Eastern European driver asked her, "How long have you lived here?"

His icy blue eyes were trained on her with a hungry expression. He was a tall man in a short person's car, with long, spindly fingers like a fairy-tale witch. He had a nice face, but she wasn't in the mood.

"Ten years," she said. She put in her earbuds.

As they got onto the FDR she remembered Anita's email and how she had deleted it. She leaned her head against the window and thought about her family. It hadn't all been bad. On holidays they'd watch TV together in the living room. A *Twilight Zone* marathon, a *Soap* marathon, a *Dark Shadows* marathon. They had good taste. Eventually they'd fall asleep. Vivian would drift in and out of consciousness, curled up in her favorite armchair. No one would touch or disturb her, and even though she was intermittently awakened by a family member's snores she wouldn't go to her room to nap because actually there was no place she'd rather be than with them. Julio played Scrabble with her for hours even though she beat him every time, and no matter how tired or sick Anita was, she always left a plate of food out for Vivian when she came home late and the food was always delicious. She actually felt safe sometimes with them and it hurt her heart, actually, it was too much, so she put on *Kid A* and she turned it up so loud that it drowned out her primeval longings, allowing her to focus on the city's soaring buildings and their relentless rectangles of light.

When they reached her neighborhood the driver interrupted her again.

"You live by yourself?"

She pretended not to hear, but then he asked her again. *Forcefully,* she thought.

He wanted to hurt her, that was clear.

She took out one of her earbuds and lied.

"No, I have roommates. Three roommates. One's a guy," she said quickly.

He told her she was his last fare for the night. After dropping her off, he was going home to Staten Island, where he lived with his brother.

"Nice," Vivian said, putting her earbud back in.

But she'd opened the door to conversation and he wouldn't stop. He asked her where she was from.

"All over," she said.

"Ah. So you moved around a lot."

"No. I was moved around a lot. Like a chair."

He laughed, but Vivian didn't.

The street they were on now intersected with Vivian's street, though they were a mile away from her apartment. He'd turn left onto her street and it would soothe her nerves. Soon enough she'd be home and could put this night behind her.

But suddenly the driver sped up and passed her street. He didn't make the left. Vivian intuited that she had to get out of the car and so, even though it was still moving, she started to pull at the door handle.

"What are you doing?" the driver asked. "We are not at your destination yet!"

Vivian said she had to get out of the car and he needed to let her out.

He slowed the car but the door wouldn't open. "Why the fuck isn't it opening!"

"I don't understand what is happening," he said innocently, exaggerating his accent so she would not suspect his intent.

Noticing that the car had power windows, Vivian acted quickly. She lowered the window, unbuckled her seat belt, hoisted herself through the window, and jumped out of the car.

Now the driver was yelling incomprehensibly. The voice sounded worried at first, but then it curdled into anger. Vivian littered the back of the car with bills of unknown denomination and ran away from the car as it peeled off into the night.

The street was quiet and Vivian realized how late it was.

She was a ten-minute walk from her apartment and still

quite high, so she ran to the only place that was open, an auto body shop. An older white mechanic with the body of a 1980s newsman in dirty overalls was sitting on a crate in the brightly lit shop working alone. "More Than a Feeling" was playing.

Vivian ran in and said, between breaths, "I think someone's after me!"

She told the mechanic everything that had just happened to her, that the driver hadn't made a left onto her street but instead took a detour down a darker, narrower road, that she had tried to get out of the car but the door wouldn't open, that finally she had to crawl out, that she littered the backseat with bills, that he knew where she lived. As she spoke the mechanic looked at her the way Vivian looked at her clients in the hospital, with pity.

Then he said, "There's no left turns on that street, sweetheart. They can lose their livery license if they disobey the traffic laws."

Vivian didn't believe him, so he got up and motioned for her to walk with him to the entrance of the garage. He pointed.

"See there? There's a sign that says No Left Turn."

Vivian looked and it was true, there was a sign that indicated that a car could not turn left onto her street. She was so high and disoriented that she'd forgotten. In horrified relief and confusion, Vivian followed the mechanic back into the shop as "(Don't Fear) the Reaper" started and he offered her a crate to sit on. She needed to recalibrate and to give the driver time to get far away so she sat down, trembling, cracking her knuckles and inhaling the grease and motor oil smells while the mechanic told her it was going to be okay.

When the song went "la la la" and he offered her something to drink, though, she stood, choked on a waft of petroleum, and said, "I have to go!" while running out of the shop.

As Vivian walked home a light rain started to fall. It was one of those nights that she loved so much, where it felt like she was walking in mist, but she was too afraid to enjoy it. There were too many cars parked along the sidewalk, and she feared being dragged inside one of them. So she started walking in the middle of the street instead. Then, flashing again to the fact that the driver knew where she lived, she returned to the sidewalk, thinking that less visibility made more sense.

At first she was able to pay attention to the environment around her. There were sirens in the distance. A paper bag rustled in the wind and she heard bottles clanging against one another, and it was unclear whether they were being collected or discarded. But then Vivian noticed a male figure leaning with his back against a lamppost up ahead, in front of one of the two-toned Craftsmans. He didn't belong there. This was a deeply residential area. She was sure she saw his hand moving back and forth vigorously out of the corner of her eye. It made no sense—he was standing in front of a private home directly under a streetlamp. It seemed *highly,* some part of her thought, *unlikely* that the man was masturbating there. But that didn't mean it wasn't happening. Vivian's face got hot as she stepped closer to the lamppost. She walked quickly past the figure, keeping him in her periphery, unable to look directly at him. As she passed he drifted from view without touching her.

Vivian listened to the wind rustling the leaves and tried to focus on the shadows of the trees. Then as she walked by a car she thought she saw a hunched figure in the back, waiting for her to walk by. Too scared to confirm or deny her suspicion, she acted upon it instead, quickly crossing the street to avoid the maybe-figure. She looked into the illuminated homes, with their promise of safety and comfort, and felt singularly apart.

The street was so deserted that she was shocked nothing had happened to her yet. It would be so easy for a man to jump out and cover her mouth, forcing her into a secluded area. What did it mean that no one was attacking her? Did the fact that she had never been attacked on a dark street mean she should be less afraid? Or should she be more afraid, since through the laws of probability she was not safe from the event happening until it happened to her?

Somehow, Vivian reached her building and lunged into the entranceway. If she could make it into the lobby she'd be safe. When she couldn't find her keys immediately she panicked. She would either be attacked in the antechamber before she found them or she'd find them, drop them, and be hit from behind when doubled over.

Finally Vivian found her keys and opened the door to her building. She ran to the elevator, went up, and shut herself inside her apartment. While leaning against the door she briefly considered sliding down it in filmic grief, but decided against that, laughed weakly at the idea, then imagined an intruder waiting in the dark. Reginald ran to her, howling like he hadn't eaten in five years, but she pushed him aside, gently, with her foot, remembering a story from the eighties about a man who'd spied on a woman for weeks from the roof across from her building and how one night he'd hoisted himself up the fire escape and crawled into her bedroom through the window. There was nothing out of the ordinary about Vivian now instinctually and automatically walking from room to room opening all the doors looking for an intruder while Reginald padded along behind, begging.

Once she'd completed the sweep, Vivian fed Reginald, rolled out her yoga mat on the living room, and lay down looking at her phone while her back spasmed.

She had an idea for a story.

> *A woman under the influence of drugs becomes convinced that her cabdriver is going to rape-murder her and so she bails on the ride early, shortchanging him, after which he waits outside her apartment and violently assaults her, not due to misogyny but due to his anger at having been ripped off.*

She had a second idea for a story.

> *A woman under the influence of drugs becomes convinced that her cabdriver is going to rape-murder her and so she bails on the ride early, shortchanging him and running to an auto body shop, where she begins talking to a nice-seeming mechanic, who, once he realizes she is under the influence, closes the garage door to the shop, trapping the woman inside, and sexually assaults her.*

And a third.

> *A woman under the influence of drugs becomes convinced that her cabdriver is going to rape-murder her and so she*

bails on the ride early, shortchanging him and running to an auto body shop, where she talks to a nice-seeming mechanic who loves classic rock, whom she also comes to suspect of plotting against her, so she runs home, only to be attacked by a stranger waiting for her inside.

SO ORDERED

"MORNING, OFFICER MCCREADY," Vivian said as she moved through the windowless courtroom to sit at one end of a long conference table facing the elevated judge's bench. McCready grunted without meeting her eyes. He was completely uncharmable, but he was also huge and heavily armed with a gun, a nightstick, pepper spray, and a handheld two-way radio that could be used to call a med tech if anyone acted out, so Vivian smiled through the affront. When Judge Mitchell arrived, McCready would spend the morning stationed next to his bench, which was adorned with various judicial tchotchkes: scales of justice in various sizes, assorted decorative gavels, and a framed sign that read: BECAUSE I'M THE JUDGE AND I SAID SO.

John, the hospital lawyer, sat at the opposite end of the attorney table. Her adversary was a man of late middle age, a heavy smoker of disheveled appearance who'd thirty years ago found a job where he could really coast. The mental health laws never changed, defense counsel were too underfunded to mount any real challenge, and, she imagined him saying, the patients were certifiable. He was home by four thirty.

"How are you doing this morning… *Veronica?*" John asked.

"It's Vivian? I've told you that like five times," she said, still erring on the side of good-naturedness, though she would have liked to reach over and pull John's sagging neck waddle back like taffy, then quickly let it go, so that it would snap back and knock him facedown onto the table.

"I'll get it eventually," John said, riffling through a Bankers Box of case files with liver-spotted hands. "Besides, you keep changing your hair. Last week it was straight, now it's curly. I can't keep up." Vivian said "Ha" to avoid seeming demeaned. Blood pooled around his crushed nose in the fantasy.

The vibe in the courtroom was bleakness tinged with absurdity. Members of the public were scattered throughout the pews: family, friends, another group of law students researching a paper. Patients were clustered on benches, some as restless as children before an exam, others nodding off, a couple just averagely suffering and embarrassed. Linda was braiding her hair. Melissa seemed weakened without her sketchpad, and the cat eye was gone too. Vivian smiled at her affectionately. Andre hadn't been brought in yet and she avoided thinking of him for now.

There were over forty cases on the docket—the hospital churned through Medicaid patients and the federal payments that flowed through them—and although just a few were Vivian's, she liked to watch the other hearings. *I am part of the civic fabric and do not reside on the internet,* she thought.

"Medication is the new lobotomy!" Ms. G. blurted out as Dr. Creslin took a seat, ready to testify in his white laboratory coat. Linda stopped playing with her hair and looked at Vivian, giggling in that way she did, like they were in on a secret.

Vivian laughed too. "Thanks, Ms. G. It was too boring in here anyway."

Ms. G. was so unused to benevolence at the hospital that she didn't know quite how to take this, but John shot over a disapproving look.

Judge Mitchell was a light-skinned older black man, tall and lean and always well barbered with a low-top fade. Today he sauntered into the courtroom from chambers twenty minutes late, wearing sunglasses and carrying a Starbucks cup, looking like an athlete at a postgame signing. Everyone stood respectfully as he took the bench, expecting the proceedings to begin immediately, like they did on television. Instead, Judge Mitchell flipped through a legal news rag like he was the one waiting on them, then began chatting up McCready and his law clerk. Kaleisha was in her early thirties, wore a finger-wave wig, had impeccable eyebrows, and shared her boss's disdain for patients' lawyers.

"Hurry up and wait, right?" Vivian whispered to John. He pretended not to hear.

A cell phone rang in the gallery. McCready broadened his chest, looking out with contempt as the phone's bright, tinny synthesizers blared on. Seeing the judge shift in his seat (subtly revealing his irritation at a perceived slight), McCready demanded the phone's owner turn it off *NOW*, and though it wasn't her phone, Vivian felt like she was going to be hit.

She turned around to try and help. People squirmed and twitched with embarrassment, but no one responded.

Then Vivian watched as an older Latina woman in the back of the courtroom struggled to dig a small burner phone out of her oversized bag; once she found it, she dropped it, and once she finally picked it up, she couldn't find the button to turn it off, despite holding it up an inch away from her face.

"Turn the phone off, ma'am!" McCready said again, walking toward the back of the room.

"She doesn't speak English," Vivian said, rising.

"She *knows* English," McCready insisted, motioning for her to sit down and escorting the woman out of the courtroom as the offending phone looped on.

Vivian felt an impulse, inchoate and obscure. She tucked into her phone, first pretending to send a text by typing nonsense into Notes and then, once her heart slowed, scrolling through Matthew's texts. He was sick and they'd been texting all week while he was home from work. Watching Friday Night Lights and thinking of our first date he'd written earlier. Waves of quiet tenderness momentarily took her away from her life.

Rather than call the court to order, Judge Mitchell resumed chatting with his staff and Vivian tried to listen without looking like she was listening. She heard him explain that there were two separately incorporated municipalities known as Kansas City—"Didn't you learn that in school?"—then Kaleisha laughed and play-slapped Judge Mitchell's shoulder as he smiled with his tongue between his teeth and Vivian bet that though he was probably sexually harassing her it didn't matter, because Kaleisha didn't perceive it that way. If a tree falls, et cetera. Vivian looked over at them and then at the clock and thought of how much of everyone's time the judge was wasting and how she couldn't say anything about it because he was the judge and then Kaleisha caught her looking at them and so she smiled but Kaleisha didn't smile back and Vivian hated herself for being so ingratiating.

She went over her notes on Melissa's case. The bright spot of the day was her confidence that Melissa would be getting out. Not only had the two of them perfected the girl's testimony, but Vivian had a secret weapon: she'd convinced Melissa's mom, Ruby, to testify today. Ruby had kicked the violent boyfriend out after another altercation, and she said she wanted Melissa to come back home. Ruby was prepared to say all of this on the record, and to affirm that Melissa had no history of mental illness and didn't need medication. No way the hospital could keep a minor in under these circumstances; *The presumption that a child should reside with their parents,* Vivian prepared to say, *is a cornerstone of juvenile law.*

The only wrinkle was that Vivian hadn't been able to tell Melissa about Ruby, since Melissa had been in seclusion the past couple of days after getting into it with another patient. Now, looking around the courtroom and not seeing anyone who resembled the girl's mother, she didn't think it was a good idea to tell her just yet. What if Ruby didn't show?

Finally Judge Mitchell swore in Dr. Creslin and Vivian felt a familiar blend of conviction and futility.

Creslin had practiced for thirty years, and by this point whatever idealism he might have brought with him into the profession had been replaced by cold pragmatism.

Take, for instance, this first case. Homeless black guy brought in by the police after some tourists called. He was swinging a metal pipe at people in Times Square, claiming to be a sultan and a king. As Creslin ticked off the criteria of the patient's schizophrenia diagnosis and justified keeping the man in, Vivian followed the subtext. What Creslin was really saying was that this was your garden-variety paranoid schizophrenic black male. These guys come in floridly psychotic, claiming to be the president or otherwise adjacent to power, or that they are being followed or their minds are being controlled, too disorganized to give any meaningful personal history that might provide a diagnostic or therapeutic road map. They won't take meds outside the hospital and they don't have the insurance to fund anything more psychodynamic and, even if they did, they have no social support to reinforce any progress. No family, or no family that wants anything to do with them. This one has been homeless for years and he prefers it that way. Try to connect him to supportive housing and it won't take, he'll be back on the streets in a month. He's "wholly unassimilable," in the parlance of Creslin and his kind.

"So, Your Honor," Creslin concluded. "The goal here isn't recovery, it can't be. All we can do is try to resolve the acute crisis. Treat him with haloperidol to reduce the hallucinations, mute out some of the aggression. When he's stabilized, we discharge him back to the street, and he'll be back in a couple of months."

"Lather, rinse, repeat huh?" Judge Mitchell said. "He'll be recommitted, and given haloperidol as the doctor suggests. It is so ordered. What do we have next?"

The next patient was a homeless black woman who believed she was a fashion designer. She said she needed to be released immediately because she had a very important meeting—with Donna Karan.

"Her delusion is very intriguing," Creslin testified. "It's not how grandiosity typically presents."

Creslin had a weakness for those patients that could form the basis of a case study. He loved to encounter a rare condition or unique delusion. Studies turned into papers, and papers improved Creslin's professional standing while also securing additional funding for the hospital in the form of research grants.

"We've had our presidents and our gods and the earlier gentleman who thinks he's a king," Creslin continued. "But we're starting to assemble a cluster of patients with quite fascinating mechanisms of ego protection that you don't see in the literature. You remember, Your Honor? We had the woman last week who wears certain colors to protect herself on the street?"

"That was a very interesting one," Judge Mitchell agreed. "What are you using to establish that she's a danger here?" he asked John. The hospital had to meet the danger-to-self-or-others standard for every patient they intended to keep in.

"We can say she's homeless," John ventured.

Now it was Vivian's time to shoot a disproving look.

"Don't say that in front of defense counsel," Judge Mitchell joked. "You know the standard."

"She's unable to provide for her own welfare," John said, like a student who'd found the right answer. "Isn't she, Dr. Creslin?" The men all began to nod.

"Yes, that's right. Her homelessness…in itself…is a form of self-neglect, and as a woman out there, spouting delusional beliefs, she runs into the wrong person, she could be assaulted."

It was decided then. "This respondent will be recommitted and sedated as Dr. Creslin desires. She should meet regularly with the doctor and his team for interviews and analysis as needed, and we'll keep her in at least until the study is complete. It is so ordered."

Next, Judge Mitchell called Linda's case. John stood and

buttoned his suit jacket, picking through an uneasy tower of files and stray pages before feeding Creslin questions from a crumpled script. Linda resumed braiding her hair, seeming not to hear while Creslin redescribed her reality. She and Brian weren't in love, she *had an erotomaniacal obsession with him.* He hadn't invited her into his house, she'd *broken in and drawn hearts on the bathroom mirror in pink lipstick.*

"Does she have any insight into her illness?" John asked.

"Not currently. This type really resists having their delusions challenged," Creslin marveled. "You can point out any logical inconsistency and they'll inevitably incorporate it into their little world view."

"I got one," the judge said, rubbing his hands together. "Where's your engagement ring?"

Linda received the question and quickly conceived a response. "Brian said I can only wear it when we're together. His wife has spies, you know, and if she finds out about us, she'll have me killed."

Creslin and Judge Mitchell exchanged amused glances and Linda returned to her hair.

"Then, she ingested a bottle of Tylenol."

"Suicide attempt?"

Creslin shrugged. "It's common for erotomaniacs to seek attention in dramatic ways in order to lure back the object of their fixation. They'll feign injury or that they're in danger— in one case, a woman faked *cancer.* She was a nurse, and she went so far as to self-administer chemo."

Judge Mitchell chuckled. "You don't have to tell me about seeking attention—I have three daughters."

"And I've got a couple of ex-wives."

Judge Mitchell laughed; then, glancing at Vivian, caught himself.

"Just a little good-natured humor, Counselor."

"Erotomaniacal delusions are very rare," Creslin continued. "If we keep her in and study her, we'll have a unique opportunity to update the literature. It will be great for the larger psychiatric community."

"Not to mention for Linda herself, of course," Judge Mitchell said.

"Of course, Your Honor. We can keep her in as a danger based on the break-in alone."

Vivian leaned over to Linda and apologized. "Unfortunately, there isn't much I can do for you right now, but with a couple of weeks of good behavior—"

"They want to study me?" Linda interrupted, perking up.

"More than they want to help you," Vivian whispered.

But Linda looked enraptured. "You'll write about me, Doc? Put me in a book or something?"

"That's a definite possibility," Creslin said.

Linda said she'd love to participate.

Vivian threw up her hands. "Why would you want to stay in here?"

Linda smiled. "For the attention."

It was settled. Linda would remain in the hospital and take the risperidone; she also agreed to make herself regularly available to Creslin and his research team. In exchange, she was guaranteed a spot in the hospital's group beauty class every week. While walking out she smiled and winked at one of the male law students, who blushed in return; then Ms. G. blurted out, "We're all guinea pigs!" to the delight of the spectators, and Vivian felt that sudden indefinable impulse again.

As Melissa's hearing started Vivian was relieved to see that a woman who looked like a fortysomething version of the girl had arrived in the courtroom. Same chiseled features and willowy frame, same big brown eyes. She mouthed, *Ruby?* And the woman nodded. Melissa, noticing her mom, said, "What is she doing here," with fear and suspicion in her eyes but Vivian assured her that it was okay, he's gone, you can go back home, and relief came over her face at the prospect of safety.

After some time John found the papers with Melissa's name on them and Creslin described Melissa's propensity for aggression, how in addition to snatching the knife she'd threatened a patient for touching one of her colored pencils, that she had an unhealthy attachment to said colored pencils, that she'd been observed engaging in "repetitive drawing be- havior," in fact. "She's certainly a danger to others," Creslin concluded. "If she doesn't hurt someone soon, she'll provoke someone into hurting her. My thinking is, let's get the behavior under control with a sedative."

Judge Mitchell nodded in a that-seems-perfectly-reasonable manner and began writing notes that he'd likely plan to use in his final order.

Vivian wobbled a little as she stood. She thought McCready looked at her lustily as she pulled her blazer down and adjusted her pencil skirt, which was riding up. He had a wet mouth. Judge Mitchell assessed her too. She imagined their sexual thoughts while trying to look over the notes on her legal pad, which was shaking almost imperceptibly.

She began her cross-examination with the diagnosis itself. "You've diagnosed Melissa with conduct disorder. Are you aware that black children are three times as likely to be given such a diagnosis? Whereas their white peers are more likely to be diagnosed with oppositional defiant disorder or ADHD, conditions with a more favorable prognosis?"

"Objection," John said. "This is irrelevant and an attempt to prejudice the fact-finder against Dr. Creslin."

"I'd argue that the diagnosis itself is prejudicial. Labeling Melissa as antisocial beyond redemption based on one incident? Not every black kid who acts up has conduct disorder."

Melissa laughed as Creslin shrank back and John stood, faux-outraged, objecting to Vivian's objection and to her characterization of Creslin. A back-and-forth ensued, during which Vivian elaborated on diagnostic racism, "the invisible third party whenever a white doctor examines a black or brown patient in distress," and Judge Mitchell threatened to find her in contempt.

"If your unit finds itself on the receiving end of additional funding to hire its own medical expert who can testify as to such matters, I'd be happy to entertain it. Until then, let's stick to the normal line of questions, Counselor."

"Understood, Judge." This was all grandstanding anyway, meant to show Melissa that she was there to protect her, that she didn't believe what Creslin said about her. The truth was that Ruby would win this hearing for them, not critical theory.

"You stated that Melissa threatened to hit another patient. But she never followed through on that threat, correct?"

"No, but—"

Vivian put out a hand. "Stop there, you answered the question."

She watched Judge Mitchell touch his fingertips together,

McCready shifting from left to right as if uncomfortable, and Creslin just looking at her, waiting for her next move.

"And in fact, aside from the accident with the knife she hasn't hurt anyone, in all her ten days on the ward?"

"No, but I—"

"Please stop there." Vivian stepped forward.

"No you don't," Judge Mitchell said. "Let him finish." Vivian looked back again at Judge Mitchell, McCready, then Creslin.

"But Your Honor, I asked a yes-or-no question. He doesn't get to elaborate."

"He does if I want him to," Judge Mitchell said, with a quick glance at McCready and then Kaleisha, who smirked and rolled her eyes at Vivian.

"Go ahead, Doctor. Don't shake your head at me, either, Counselor."

Vivian apologized.

"I believe she's dangerous, based on her past behavior. The greatest predictor of future violence is past violence."

"You 'believe' she's dangerous?"

Judge Mitchell let out an exasperated sigh and removed his glasses as if for effect. "Now, why are you repeating what the man just said?"

"It's a cross-examination style, Your Honor. I'm trying to remind the fact-finder of what was said earlier. It's hard for me to get into a flow with all of these—"

Judge Mitchell chuckled. "Style? Flow?"

Kaleisha and McCready laughed too, as the judge looked at his watch.

"This isn't a rap video. Not the Supreme Court, either." More laughter. "We don't have time for style and flow. I've got to get through thirty-five more cases before lunch." He put his glasses back on. "Make your points. Fast."

So Vivian gave up trying to humiliate Creslin and called Melissa to testify, getting Melissa to describe how her mom's conservative boyfriend mocked her for not wearing dresses, how he wouldn't let her go out with him and her mom because of it, how he said that if she was going to "dress like a boy" then he would treat her like one, how the next time she'd stepped to him he threw a stool at her head and how if it weren't for her quick reflexes he could have broken her jaw, how she'd been thrown out by her mom and become homeless at seventeen, how the first night outside was the scariest night of her life, how she got her period when walking the streets and she couldn't find pads, how she'd gotten tired of folding a paper towel between her legs to catch the blood so finally she buzzed some white lady's apartment and the white lady had called 911 and she'd ended up here, and that she'd grabbed the knife quickly because someone said she had muscles like a boy and it brought her back to the day with the stool, that the knife thing was an accident, that she hadn't meant to hurt anyone, that she wanted to go home but she didn't have a home, that she was sorry for crying, that she was sorry for everything, Mom. It was a beautiful testimony, perfectly calibrated to encourage the judge's empathy. Now she just needed Ruby's; the hospital couldn't retain a child against her mother's wishes.

Ruby was nervous on the stand. She needed water and had difficulty making eye contact with Vivian, and it looked like it hurt her to look at Melissa, which made sense, given Melissa's wrenching testimony and how they'd left things. Once Melissa got out, Vivian would recommend that the two of them enter family therapy together. One of the social workers had mentioned a feminist therapist who specialized in helping women overcome the aftereffects of violence.

"Why are you here today?" Vivian asked Ruby.

Ruby took a sip of water and cleared her throat.

"I'm here to help my daughter," Ruby said, just like they'd discussed over the phone. She finally looked at Melissa, with genuine concern and affection. "I'm here to tell the judge...more about what's been going on at home, and what we might do to make things better."

Melissa exhaled. Vivian put her hand on her shoulder and felt her relax a little more.

"And what's been going on at home?"

This was when Ruby would corroborate Melissa's version of events, introducing mitigating factors to contextualize her daughter's recent behavior.

"Honestly, I don't even recognize her anymore," Ruby said quietly.

Vivian was confused. This wasn't what they'd discussed on the phone. She had no choice but to ask Ruby to clarify what she meant by that.

Ruby's tone changed, then, and she said that Melissa was jealous of her fiancé and that Melissa had destroyed his property unprovoked, because, Ruby said, "Melissa can't handle that it's not just the two of us anymore." She said she was afraid of Melissa and that she didn't want her in her house, especially now that they had a baby coming, her and her fiancé, and so, given all that, she thought Melissa should stay in the hospital for a time, do what the doctors say. And that, in the meantime, Ruby could see if maybe Melissa's grandmother would take her, when she got out.

Vivian was stunned into silence. She felt her face get flushed. She didn't know what to do.

"No...further...questions," she said.

"Sucks to have your own witness turn on you," John whispered. She pretended not to hear.

As Ruby got down from the witness stand Vivian looked into Melissa's eyes and saw briefly the girl's renewed disappointment at her all-too-limited mother as well as a secondary and almost worse disappointment in herself, for having believed that her mother could change. But just as it appeared it was gone, a wall went up, and Vivian was shut out. Melissa screamed out, "This is some bullshit," and she knocked all of John's files off the table as her mother walked by, and Ruby looked at Vivian and said, "See? I have to protect this baby," and Melissa stood up looking like she was ready to do more to her mother, who hurried out.

"Excuse me, young lady. Sit down!" Judge Mitchell bellowed.

Melissa refused to sit, shoving the conference table and knocking down her chair in the process.

As McCready moved stealthily toward Melissa, Judge Mitchell said, "She'll be held by the hospital for a minimum of four weeks and medicated as Dr. Creslin advises. It is so ordered."

"That's not right!" Melissa cried out.

"I decide what's right in here, young lady. These people are trying to help you, and your own mama said you need all the help you can get." He looked at McCready. "Now get this out of my courtroom." McCready moved fast, and suddenly a second officer and Carl the tech had pounced on Melissa and were carrying her out while she kicked, screamed, and cried, begging not to be restrained.

Vivian followed them into the hall and told Melissa to take a deep breath.

"You promised me they wouldn't strap me down!" she yelled at Vivian, tears streaming down her face.

Vivian pleaded with Carl. "Be gentle with her, she's scared!"

But once Melissa spotted the gurney loaded with restraints, she panicked and bucked like a horse resisting its rider, kicking McCready in the chest. The looks on their faces said it all. Melissa was done for.

"You promised me they wouldn't do it! You promised me!" Melissa screamed while McCready tightened his grip, clasping her arms behind her and instructing Carl to grab her legs. Melissa stared holes into Vivian as the men handled her, placing her on the gurney. Once supine, she thrashed against the gurney with such force that Carl had to pin her down. She was screaming, cursing, and crying all at once, struggling to get free as Dr. Creslin insisted that the restraints were necessary to protect her. Vivian watched in shock as they applied the leather straps to Melissa's wrists and ankles; then Dr. Creslin prepared her arm for a haloperidol injection.

Melissa screamed at Vivian as she was wheeled away. "You ain't shit. You're useless. Useless!"

"I know," Vivian said quietly, watching Melissa bang the back of her head repeatedly against the bed.

"Get back in here, Counselor," she heard Kaleisha say. She was holding open the door. "The judge doesn't have all day."

Melissa's screams followed Vivian back into the courtroom and she remembered a dream from last night. She was walking on a long bridge for what felt like hours. She never reached the other side.

More cases were called. A black man got into a fight with his mother while high on PCP and began repetitively drawing the Star of David on the walls of their apartment; despite his attorney arguing that he was suffering from temporary drug-induced psychosis he was ordered to be recommitted. But the white lawyer who had a manic episode after not getting a job offer from the law firm of his dreams, said manic episode leading him to punch the security guard at said law firm in the face? His family came to the hearing and vouched for him, and he was released to their care.

At Ms. G.'s hearing, she testified that she was a prophet sent to the hospital by God to warn people about the dangers of the mental health system.

"And why don't you want to take the medications the doctor is suggesting?" Vivian asked robotically.

"They gave me some drug with an 'H' as an excuse to take off my clothes. It's the equivalent of a date rape drug!"

Judge Mitchell looked down into his lap as if to keep from laughing, then ruled that Ms. G. would stay in the hospital.

At this point Andre was brought into the courtroom. She watched him shuffle past. He had shackles around his ankles but his hands were free and in fists. His facial features seemed built by testosterone: a prominent forehead and thick jaw. His eyes were hostile. They sat him slightly behind her, just a couple of arm lengths away. Vivian's stomach knotted and she felt a flash of heat at the back of her neck as she thought of his uncuffed hands. The best predictor of future violence is past violence. Unassimilable. It suddenly seemed completely absurd that she was in this room, so close to a violent man again. Not a supposedly violent man, but an actually violent one. After the mashed potatoes incident, he'd been placed in seclusion for attacking another patient while waiting in the medication line. He was less than six inches away from her. She had never heard a human being breathe like that. Andre actually *was* a danger to others, and going through the humiliating rigmarole of the hearing felt like a waste of everyone's time.

Dr. Creslin spoke quickly, explaining that Andre had been in restraints most of his time in the hospital. Andre was impulsively violent. He was hyperreactive to stimuli. He'd punched another patient in the back of the head while they were waiting in line for meds and had made multiple threats to the staff. While Creslin testified, Vivian thought about how easily Andre could overtake her, how quickly he could choke her out with his large, bearlike handcuffed hands.

Judge Mitchell, immediately grasping the urgency, ran quickly through the standard questions about his hospitalization and whether he knew why he was here, what the psychiatrists were saying about his aggressive and threatening behavior on the unit and how they were proposing to treat him.

But the word "treat" set Andre off and he responded to the judge in threats and swore that if this wasn't over soon he was going to "lose it" and hurt someone, most likely Vivian, she thought, because as he spoke his right elbow touched Vivian's arm, and he probably thought she was working with the State to detain him, and so she tried not to move, to pretend she was not afraid of him, to make him understand that she thought he was a human being worthy of being treated like a human being and not a rabid animal. As Andre unleashed his tirade of threats all the muscles in Vivian's body contracted. She needed to sit down but the situation called for her to remain standing in her suit like a lawyer, and to argue as best she could the reasons that Andre should not be medicated over his objection. It became difficult to think or speak in sentences. It became difficult to stay present. She felt herself simultaneously there and not there, she had an urge to leave the room crying, she had an urge to ask for help. The game then became to freeze all the muscles in her face into a position that did not suggest extreme fear as the judge issued his ruling, the game became don't burst into tears, the game became don't lose it in the insane asylum. Andre was ordered to continue to be detained and to be medicated and Vivian couldn't understand the names of the medications. She closed her eyes and almost fell into a trance, staring at the deep red at the back of her eyelids. Andre was being taken out of the courtroom by four court officers, who were moving their mouths in her direction, but she couldn't make out the words. Back into her body she heard Andre call her an Uncle Tom on his way out of the room.

Vivian gripped the table as a lightning bolt of pain passed through her lower back. She couldn't tend to it, couldn't be alone yet, had to stand there and look the part of the professional while Judge Mitchell apologized to her, saying he still had to have a hearing even though it was clear that Andre was seriously ill, due process being what it is, he said, and then he told her she had handled herself so well throughout the hearing, that she didn't seem scared at all.

After, she jogged to her office, where she grabbed her desk drawer key from under the keyboard where it was always hidden, unlocked the bottom drawer containing her bag, grabbed it, logged into her computer, cleared out the cache on each of the three different internet browsers she used at work, deleted the worst of the gossipy emails, shut down the computer, stood up and snatched off the decorative postcards, greeting cards, and pictures she'd tacked up on the bulletin board next to her desk in order to project an image of a creative, well-read woman who is beloved by her friends, tossed them all into her open bag, tossing also, carelessly, multiple pushpins into the bag, ripped her hospital ID off her neck and threw it onto the thousand-dollar black ergonomic chair she had been sitting in for three years, shut off the lights in the office, put on her sunglasses, and walked out of the hospital for the last time.

GOOD AT SEX

AT DINNER WITH Matthew she orchestrated a champagne toast. "Here's to freedom from all responsibilities!" Vivian couldn't wait to start seriously working on her novel, and she spoke about it with the excessive exuberance of someone who hasn't started writing yet. "And novels matter, you know? They aren't like cookbooks or whatever." The oblique non sequitur required a Pauline-related rant, after which Matthew gave her the kind of look that men give women whom they perceive to be adorably unhinged.

Back at his place they kissed for a while on the couch and then Vivian straddled him. Feeling how big he was under her, she was turned on, fearful of injury to her cervix, and committed to overcoming the fear and successfully accommodating him all in equal measure. He moaned as he undid the buttons on her dress, taking her breasts in his mouth one at a time, looking eminently present.

Out of nowhere, as if gripped by an inexplicable urge, he picked her up and positioned her on the couch and got onto his knees, his face disappearing into her, though she hadn't asked for it. Vivian awkwardly ran her fingers through his long hair, trying to relax by staring at a lampshade, unable to say that externally imposed wetness made her uncomfortable and that she preferred digital stimulation. She let him do it for a while before tapping his shoulder. Sensing his disappointment, she kissed him and explained that although she would not be able to come from that, it felt really good.

Vivian wasn't ready for the main event and she was unsure what to do next but Matthew didn't let her think for very long. He pulled her back on top of him and asked her what she wanted. What Vivian wanted was for no man to ever ask that question, and instead to just do what he wanted within certain parameters so that she could then find a way to come, wait for it to be over, or object. She couldn't generate ideas of what to do in sex, only opinions on what was being done to her.

(It had to be admitted—but never out loud—that when Vivian was attracted to a man, she didn't mind being objectified by him. She was not alone in this. And, to be clear, it wasn't that when she was into a guy, she no longer felt herself being objectified: she absolutely did, and she liked it. She could go into bimbo mode when she was in the bedroom with a man who knew how to touch and kiss her and who made her feel safe. In bimbo mode all bets were off and she was only an object of pleasure, which was itself pleasurable. Being just a body was nice, if that was what you wanted to be.)

Unable to answer Matthew's question, she stalled with more kissing and moaning and Matthew continued this thread, saying into her ear that he wanted to focus on her. This felt gross, as if it were a line he had read in an online forum, a line meant to encourage a woman to get really "wild" in bed, which she resented. (The concept of being "wild" in bed was fraught all around. If she sensed a man strategizing to get her to be "wild" or assuming "wildness" because of her ethnicity, it made her just want to lie there like a corpse instead, like she imagined white women doing, just to fuck with him.)

A note on the lighting in the living room: it was horrible. Overhead lighting that accentuated every flaw, a dysmorphic's nightmare. So that when Vivian got a tickly feeling indicating that she had to pee, panic set in, and she agonized over how she would orchestrate getting up. To get to the bathroom, she'd have to turn her back to Matthew, and the light was so garish that when she turned he would see all of her subcutaneous fat and the illusion of her perfection would be shattered prematurely. Okay for it to be eventually shattered, but it had to be on her terms.

Things were stagnating, so finally she blurted out that she had to pee, but as soon as she said it she was immobilized, so she kept on kissing him mechanically. She figured Matthew was getting impatient with her, and, beneath that: anger and the possibility of violence. His impatience was confirmed when he stopped kissing her and said, "You should go." At the prospect of her humiliation she was tempted to start crying but instead she slowly got up, sort of ducked and sort of ran to the bathroom in three quick jumps.

As she peed she imagined what Matthew had seen. Each time one of her feet made contact with the floor her cellulite would have radiated up her leg, vibrating like a string that had been plucked. Matthew must have recoiled watching the puckering appear, then disappear while she was in the air, then reappear when her foot touched the floor. Her stomach tingled with shame. After, she looked through his medicine cabinet: aftershave, earwax remover, cold medicine, floss. No medications, nothing weird.

Vivian sucked her stomach in as she returned to the living room. She put Matthew inside her mouth to distract him from the back-of-the-leg rippling. He was too big to fit all the way and she gagged but she liked it. He told her to go slower and to use her hands less and she felt that she had failed some kind of test. She was used to being good at sex, with no criticism. She asked him if he had protection (again, as a distraction) and he happily went to get condoms.

Vivian tried to lower herself onto him but her body wouldn't cooperate. She was nervous and clenched, intimidated by his size. Matthew kept saying "Look at me." No one had ever asked this of her before. They had to go really slow to get him inside and Vivian trembled slightly, which she tried to deflect by kissing his neck and licking, then nibbling, his earlobes. But then he whispered that it was okay, baby, if she needed to go slow, because he liked to go slow. This allowed her to relax and to start fucking him on top, "perfectly," she thought, like she was used to. He must be a really good teacher.

When Matthew decided that he wanted to, no, "needed to," be on top of her, he picked her up and said, "Let's see if we can do this without" him falling out of her. They did it successfully and he fucked her, hard, as hard as she wanted to be fucked, and she told him it hurt, but it felt good, and she thought of the women's faces in porn, clenched in pain, and how she used to have an overtly crude feminist analysis of that, but that now she saw that it was possible to be hurt and to like it, in this limited way.

When they were finished they went to his bedroom, a tiny rectangle containing a double bed pushed under the sole window, a nightstand, a bookshelf filled with sheet music, and, at the foot of the bed, a keyboard and chair. Although Vivian had enjoyed herself she was relieved that it was over. He was the biggest guy she'd ever slept with and she wasn't sure this was sustainable. The concepts of casual dick and boyfriend dick existed for a reason. But he was so hot. He sat on his chair and she got on his lap.

"So. Did you miss me?" she asked.

"It's always good to see you," he responded, kissing her and telling her she looked beautiful. "You look like a ballerina with your hair like that. Have you ever danced?"

"No, but flattery will get you everywhere with me."

Vivian said that all she wanted was to be treated like a special person. It would be easy for him to game her, she said, if he just made her feel unique.

"I would never 'game' anyone," he responded. "How about we just interact and you just say what you're going to say and I respond to it?"

They lay down in bed and started kissing again. He went to the closet to get something to cover and dim his lamp. She watched him hesitate slightly while trying to figure out what to use to cover the lamp. He used a towel and she felt mildly embarrassed for him. She wondered if he felt her feeling that, and what other women might have done or said.

He got back into bed. She started sucking him off again and he told her how to touch him. She wanted to make him come harder than he had ever come in his life but she didn't know if following his instructions would be enough. She felt almost afraid of her desire. He was so big, and she liked it so much. He wanted her in his mouth while she was sucking him so she sat on his face until he just needed to get inside her. He got behind her this time. Each time she reached over for the lube with hesitation he would whisper something like, "It's okay, baby" or "We need that, we've had a lot of sex tonight." Shame didn't seem to be something he experienced during sex.

A détente was reached. It was over. They kissed and touched each other in a restless way. Vivian felt rapturous in Matthew's bed, high on a drug that couldn't be bought, only earned: oxytocin! His attention gave her permission to exist. She was desperate not to lose it.

Matthew had a framed poster of Sonny Rollins in his room and, due to her prior backstalking, she was able to reference his masterwork *The Bridge*. Matthew jumped out of bed and opened his laptop to play her a part of it that he loved. Vivian dissociated during this; though she loved jazz, Rollins wasn't for her. She wanted to mention the jazz artists that she did love and say something brilliant about bebop, but she couldn't think of any of their names. When it was over Matthew said she was the only girl he'd ever dated who knew Sonny Rollins or *The Bridge*.

"And here I thought I was a woman."

"What other kind of stuff do you want to do to me?" he asked suddenly.

Trap you into loving me forever, she thought.

"I've loved all of our sex tonight, of course, but my favorite position is probably being on top. I love the exertion of it all, the calorie burn. It's like exercise with an orgasm at the end."

While she laughed at her own jokes, Matthew traced over her oblique muscles with his index finger.

"You have a very fit body compared to me," he said, grabbing his stomach. It was true. He had a long torso that ended in a domed belly, and no biceps to speak of.

"I love your body," Vivian said, trying to bring the word "love" into their conversation.

But Matthew just nuzzled her neck and asked, with a playful tone, "Do you have an eating disorder or something?"

It was as absurd as the little ballerina remark. If she had an eating disorder, wouldn't she be smaller? Wouldn't she not have puckering on her legs?

"No. Why do you ask?"

"You make a lot of jokes about calories," he said. Vivian monitored Matthew's expression. She wasn't sure, but he seemed annoyed.

"Don't all women?" she asked, laughing it off.

"The past couple of women I've dated had eating disorders. They both dumped me." He said this as if he were delivering a punch line.

"How could anyone dump you?"

In response to this overture, Matthew rolled away and stared up at the ceiling.

After a while of both of them lying there, unsure, and not saying anything, Matthew got out of bed and sat at his keyboard. He played a hesitant version of "Summertime" as if he were practicing by himself. It was clear that piano wasn't his first instrument, and he couldn't play without looking at his hands, but the slow tempo had the effect of enhancing the song's already mournful qualities. She considered the tension between the hopeful lyrics and the melancholic composition, and fell into a languorous trance. As he got into it, Matthew added improvisational flourishes, which made Vivian laugh through the tears that were now flowing unchecked. She thought then that if he let her, she would spend every day of the rest of her life loving him.

"That was so nice," she said into his chest. He held her close. They were quiet for a while, and then Matthew said he wanted to get to know her better. Vivian got excited. They could really go in on music now, maybe process the profound experience she'd just had listening to him play. That, or she could articulate her theory that grunge was not a real music genre. (Nirvana was a noise band, Alice in Chains played metal, and Pearl Jam? That was just rock music.)

"Ask me anything," Vivian said. And she meant it.

"Okay. What I really wanna know about you is... What's your favorite color?"

Now it was Vivian's turn to roll away and stare up at the ceiling.

"I don't know, black?"

"Wow, okay. What about your favorite fruit?"

"Avocado, I guess." High in protein, low in carbs.

"That doesn't count!"

"Fine," she said. "Oranges, I like oranges the best."

"Me too!" Matthew said, excited as a puppy, nuzzling and kissing her. Granted, she hadn't eaten an orange in months. But before she'd started this low-carb thing, she really did love oranges. She liked to slowly peel them, to be lightly sprayed with citrus oils.

Vivian yawned.

"I guess it's getting to be that time," Matthew said.

"Yeah," Vivian said, slowly sitting up and looking out over the bed to find her clothes. "I should start heading out."

"I'd love it if you stayed, though," Matthew said softly.

"Okay!" she squealed, falling back into the pillows, feeling like a grand prize winner.

They talked sleepily about bedtime rituals and temperature. "I'm always cold," Vivian said. "And I have nightmares sometimes."

"What kind of nightmares?"

"Oh, you know, the kind where I'm about to be attacked."

Matthew laughed and turned off the bedside lamp. "I thought you were going to say something crazier."

She resented this. Here she was offering up a psychological jewel, a key that could unlock the mystery, and he demonstrated no curiosity. In fact he'd seemed more interested in her answers to his rudimentary, first-day-of-learning-a-new-language questions. But then he stroked her hair and she lost her critical faculties, falling into such a softened, relaxed state she thought she might sink through the bed. The last thing she heard him say was "I have a feeling you're going to sleep really well tonight." And she did.

They woke up at sunrise to Matthew's work alarm. He left the room and came back a few minutes later with a plate of sliced oranges.

"Surprise!" he announced.

"So sweet," Vivian said, humming with anxiety at the prospect of dietary rule-breaking while also smiling, feeling genuinely touched. "These are like nature's solution to morning breath." They ate in bed and Matthew bopped his head back and forth like a kid. Vivian ate slowly, methodically biting into little sections with prolonged chewing, relieved each time Matthew reached for another slice. After getting through her second piece, Vivian said she was done and needed to wipe her fingers off. Matthew took the plate from her hand, put it on his nightstand, and began to kiss, then to lick, her fingers. It was on. He wanted her on top, and she wanted it too but she didn't want to be looked at so early and ungroomed, so she shook her head no. It was comically difficult for him to get inside her at this hour with no lead-up, so when she begged him to come it was as much for her safety as it was for his pleasure. It ended and he kissed her all the way to the door, where they embraced. "Every time you come over," he said into her hair, "I don't want you to leave." Though the air was cool, the sun was insistent.

How would Vivian describe her mental state, if asked? *Exhilarated*, maybe, though that reminded her of skydiving. *Euphoric* and *ecstatic* felt too ravey, and though it was true that she'd "never felt so alive," it wasn't original enough. All Vivian knew was that as she walked home, she felt neither fear nor judgment. She was inside a protective golden orb, convinced of her own goodness. She was loved. Matthew loved her.

Gradually this confidence led to a sudden determination: She would end her relationship with her family once and for all. It was taking them too long to die.

She paced around her apartment for a while, then sat on the edge of her bed, changed her phone number, and blocked all three of them. The relief was immediate, but it didn't last.

For a while, she felt guilty. She writhed around her bed at night in a sweat. *What have I done What have I done What have I done.*

She searched her mind for precedent, trying to remember if she knew anyone who had cut off their family. She'd heard about someone from college, a friend of a friend who'd stopped talking to his mother recently, but apparently it was because she was moving to the far right and being unabashedly racist online. It wasn't a helpful analogue. Vivian's family may have been caught in a cycle of intergenerational abuse that, among other things, made them a danger to women and children, but they were staunch Democrats.

She imagined what Cristina might say. *It will be very hard on your mother, you know, as she's already lost a child. Your brother looks up to you, so this will crush him. And your stepfather has always been good to you, no? Estrangement in our culture might be worse than death.*

Jane would be unsparing in her criticism. *You are selfish beyond belief,* Jane would say. *Of course you didn't go to your brother's funeral. You were relieved he was dead. Is this really about a little boy being scolded and your mom's histrionics? I think you were looking for a way out. You always seemed embarrassed by your family. I begged you years ago, to meet your brother. "He sounds like a trip," I said, but you wouldn't allow it. It feels very much like a class thing to me. You're a professional now, honey, and it's time to leave those losers behind—is that it? But then, I can't rule out racial shame, either. Remember my joke, that bit I do about never being able to trust light-skinned girls due to various betrayals from childhood, and how you were the exception to that rule? Well, now I'm not so sure. Could you be on the run from your own blackness? I wonder, too, about the work you've been doing. Altruism doesn't square with your personality. It's as if you're atoning for your own selfishness, a reaction formation. Why not perform the same psychological sleight of hand here? You're the only upwardly mobile person in your family. Look at all the problems they have. So your mother has moods and your brother has a drinking problem—*

you're privileged enough to deal. Everyone's family drives them crazy—that's why therapy is a multibillion-dollar industry. If all the upwardly mobile people of color abandon their families then we will never get anywhere.

No, Jane could think what she wanted, but Vivian knew she was right. Her feelings on the matter had clarified. She didn't have to stay in painful situations. What does an adult child in a toxic family system owe that system? For Vivian, the answer was "nothing."

If anything, she decided, it was the ghosting that was wrong. They'd worry about her and wouldn't have closure. She had to give them closure. But she'd already changed her number, so now she'd have to send them a text from the current number and then immediately block them, while changing the number again. She composed a text while sitting on the toilet.

> *Hi everyone. It's Vivian. I have decided that I no longer wish to communicate with any of you. The chaos and dysfunction are just too much. Please do not contact me for any reason about any issue. I wish you all the best and ask that you respect my wishes at this time.*

Vivian clicked Send with a pounding heart and immediately blocked Anita's, Julio's, and Michael's numbers and emails again. She went to her cell phone carrier's website to change her phone number but because she'd just changed it a few days ago, the site wouldn't let her change it again, no matter how hard she banged on the Enter key.

She called the customer service number only to be greeted by an automated voice that doled out an endless series of numerical options, none of which applied to her particular cutting-off-contact-with-the-family situation, and when tapping "0" didn't work she yelled, "Speak to a representative!" into the phone with the histrionic delivery of Julianne Moore. Next the automaton informed her that before she could speak to a representative, she needed to enter her PIN, a numerical combination she hadn't thought about in nine years. She tried various possible combos such as her birthday and high school locker combination but none worked, so she shouted at the phone that she'd forgotten it.

The operator identified herself as Michelle. Her voice was calm, sympathetic, and nonjudgmental. Vivian made her request in a stream-of-consciousness torrent, ashamed of the whiny voice she heard, accompanied by tears.

Michelle asked Vivian for the last four digits of her social security number and for her address, but even then she wasn't able to access Vivian's account; it had been locked after the PIN debacle. She gently let Vivian know that she would have to step away to speak to a supervisor.

Vivian poured a glass of water and slowly pushed down the condensation with her fingers with the phone on speaker. The hold music was Celine Dion. "That's the Way It Is." After she'd found the harmony, Michelle came back and said she would be able to help but that she would have to send a security verification to a reliable email address. Michelle asked if she had access to an email address at the moment, Vivian said yes, and Michelle put her on hold again. After a couple more minutes of Celine she returned to tell Vivian that she had sent the verification email.

Vivian wiped away tears on the way to her desk, feeling as if her family could see her, as if they stood around taunting her with that line, *Blood is thicker than water,* as if they were going to reach out and grab her through the phone. She shook while obediently opening her email on her laptop and clicking on the verification link within the email.

Michelle said that this didn't work, unfortunately, and she had to resend the link. Vivian rubbed her forehead and smoothed her eyebrows while watching her inbox. Finally, the new email arrived and she clicked on the second link.

"It worked!" Michelle said; she'd gained access to Vivian's account. She asked Vivian to select a new PIN, and Vivian told Michelle a set of numbers she didn't think she'd be capable of forgetting. Michelle then said she was ready to generate the new phone number. Vivian requested a 917 area code, explaining to Michelle that 917 conveyed how long she'd lived in New York, and that she couldn't imagine a non-917 situation. Michelle laughed and said they did have a couple of 917 numbers left, actually, and Vivian picked one that was relatively easy to remember.

Michelle then put her on hold again and Vivian bit her nails as tears fell, feeling as if her family were there with her watching her cry, and then feeling ashamed of her childlike, primal state, all to the tune of "Prayer for the Dying" by Seal.

Michelle came back on the line and told her that her phone number had been successfully changed. She instructed Vivian to turn her phone off and then on again, and said that she'd call Vivian back at the new number in five to ten minutes to confirm that it was receiving calls. Vivian did as instructed. Ten minutes later Michelle called her at the new number, and Vivian pushed out a sigh. "Oh thank god," she repeated, stroking her forehead.

"Is there anything else I can do for you today?" Michelle asked.

"No, you've been great, thank you, you've been so great."

She wept with relief. She had done it; she had gotten out. It almost didn't feel real.

She scrolled through her recent calls and her finger hovered over Jane's name. But she couldn't do it. She knew what Jane would say, knew how she'd judge her, and she couldn't subject herself to that, not now. Besides, Jane didn't want to speak to her and probably wouldn't even answer her call. She considered trying Cristina, but she was firmly in the *family is everything* camp too.

Finally she thought of Matthew. It was time to take the next step in their relationship. To be more open, more vulnerable, more real. She'd start by being honest with him about her family situation on their next date.

She texted him, Hey it's Vivian, got a new number!! Also I kind of miss you, which is weird. Hang soon?

He didn't respond.

THE GLORY OF SONG

CRISTINA AND DAVID held their engagement party at a karaoke bar in Koreatown. Neither of them had a particularly good singing voice, but they were both hams and loved to sing together.

They'd rented the biggest of the fifteen disco-ball-and-laser-light-filled rooms. Black couches lined the walls. At one end of the room was a screen where the videos accompanying the songs were projected. On the other end was a stereo and control station that allowed the singer to change the key of the song by half-step increments. The room was practically empty and no one was singing when Vivian got there. They hadn't had enough alcohol yet.

Vivian was happy to see Cristina, though not yet ready to explain what had transpired with her family. They embraced and tucked themselves into a corner of the couch. Vivian said she was so excited about the night and that she'd missed her. Cristina complimented her on her outfit. Vivian had chosen black trousers and a black soft-knit cropped cardigan with gold buttons. When she held the microphone, everyone would be able to see her midriff. When asked how she was doing, Vivian proclaimed her emancipation from the capitalist workweek to everyone in earshot.

"And how are things going with the musician?" Cristina asked.

Vivian made a face.

"It's shit. He fucked me four times and then he dumped me by text."

A few days prior, Matthew had texted Vivian to say he had reconnected with someone from his past and was "going to pursue that," a fact that he knew must be "surprising" to her after their "great time."

"Great time," she'd muttered to herself, while her identity shattered, her face seemed to slide off, and she plummeted into apocalyptic darkness. Her body, with its clenched stomach, sensed, primordially, that what he'd said was just an excuse. In reality, she hadn't lived up to his expectations.

She'd spent hours composing a face-saving response of perfect length—three sentences—neither too short nor too long.

> That *is* surprising. We had so much fun together! But I wish you the best.

The text was meant to convey that blitheness she had worked so hard to achieve on their dates. Nothing bothered her, she was like water, she accepted the chaos of the world.

After reviewing the texts, Cristina handed Vivian back her phone.

"We gotta get you a drink," she said, causing an ice-cold bottle of soju to materialize. Vivian poured them each a shot and they cheersed.

"So how have you been since then?" Cristina asked, riveted by Vivian's dejection. "What have you been doing?"

As they nursed their drinks Vivian explained that she walked the Prospect Park loop every day, blankly observing her surroundings. (It was late September, and the trees were mostly still green, with some yellowing outliers. By the lake, clumps of honking geese were a constant presence, and children quarreled over whose turn it was to feed them. Various members of the stroller mafia edged Vivian off the trails without apology, and men were cruising in the woods.)

She wore all black, she told Cristina, sunglasses on, listening to the most depressing mixes ever, bearing titles like "Sad (Mostly White) People" and "Breakup," featuring all the great breakup albums: *Another One, Back to Black, Bachelor No. 2, The Boatman's Call,* lots of the Smiths, every Fiona Apple and Elliott Smith album, and various pathetic songs like "Heartbreaker" by Dionne Warwick and midcentury standards that captured a jilted woman's desperation, like "Glad Rag Doll" by Johnnie Ray. In particular, she played "Red Red Red" and "Everybody Cares, Everybody Understands" hundreds of times, indulging in her misery, trying to figure out, paraphrasing Fiona Apple, whether it was okay or if she was lacking something.

"Fiona is great for a breakup," Cristina said.

"It's like all she writes about," Vivian replied.

Figuring out what was wrong with her seemed like the most important question of Vivian's life and it wasn't even a question she had posed. The question, despite her atheism, felt as if posed by God. And it wouldn't matter what any therapist or friend or even Matthew himself said, she knew it was something about her that had ruined her life. She went about her days with a constant hypervigilant awareness of her phone as the metonymic connection to Matthew. She'd open the message window and stare at it, waiting for an ellipsis that never appeared.

The nights were similar, only spent in an intoxicated haze. While smoking two to three bowls a night and drinking homemade martinis straight out of *Mad Men,* she cycled between checking Matthew's social media accounts on a loop, searching for women in his life to compete with, and scouring breakup threads online. For hours she read the stories of people of all ages, genders, nationalities, ethnicities, and dispositions, explaining to the internet why they had dumped someone. She was frantic to understand the mechanism of rejection, and whether it could be undone.

She Googled *the one that got away*

She Googled *the one that got away came back*

She Googled *men ever regret dumping someone*

She Googled *why did he disappear?*

"The internet," Vivian declared in summation, "is the greatest breakup resource of all time. Never before in human history have we had such far-reaching access to so many people's opinions and experiences."

"Why do you think it was you?" Cristina asked. "Maybe it's true, the story about reconnecting with the ex. That kind of thing happens all the time, right?"

It was Vivian's intelligence. When she'd thought she was demonstrating her brilliance to attract a mate, Matthew had thought she was showing off. Her volumes on the entire history of hip-hop music, for instance. Vivian didn't allow him to relax at all. Matthew couldn't have an idea without Vivian adding to it or subtracting from it, editing it in some way, letting him know she was superior, her thoughts more interesting, more dynamic. What person wants to be with someone who makes them feel like that?

It was her narcissism. Why did she have to emphasize her accomplishments all the time? She had even called herself a narcissist. She'd meant it as a joke but she should've known that Matthew wasn't the type to think that was funny. She should have known what kind of jokes Matthew would like and would not like.

No, you know what, if anything, it was her obsequiousness! That was it, it was that she was too available, she showed that she liked him too much.

And she hadn't done anything to create an aesthetic atmosphere for him. Maybe if she'd learned *Gymnopédie No. 1* on piano like she had meant to, she would have been able to spontaneously play it for him that night in his apartment, causing him to fall in love with this odd woman who had taught herself to play a single song on piano. It would highlight her genius and her tragedy at the same time! But she hadn't learned it. One summer she had meant to, and even started practicing, but she got distracted by a beautiful ex-Hasidic man with whom she had great sex but wasn't really compatible.

Finally, she flashed to the moment at his place when she'd been forced to turn her back to Matthew to go to the bathroom. The possibility of his thoughts about her, his silent acknowledgment of her hideous backside, the hideousness of who she was, terrible being, dark creature, was too much to bear.

That was it! It was her ugliness! He'd seen her ugliness

and hated it. And it wasn't merely her body! Her face was definitely involved! When they were together he'd probably caught a glimpse of her making an ugly face. He'd seen the strabismus, or the grotesque way she looked when she laughed, or her horrible profile.

No, it wasn't only her ugliness, but her blackness! Because she was black and had cellulite he had been deterred, and she had been dumped. That was it. A sense of omniscience about her blackness and her ugliness being the reason, her black ugliness being the reason, surrounded her like an impenetrable fog.

"And I'm light-skinned, you know. Better odds, dating-wise. Still, I got fucked," she told Cristina, who didn't know what to say and poured her another soju.

On cue, Pauline approached them, flaunting facial symmetry and the benediction of whiteness. Her formfitting dress was burgundy this time, a corduroy zip-up number paired with matching pointed toe boots with a stiletto heel.

"You look cute, girl," Pauline said, again with that put-on inflection. Vivian didn't have any time to recoil from her embrace; she was just in Pauline's arms suddenly.

"You look great too."

Vivian hugged Elliott and he leaned in to kiss her cheek.

"Hi, *bella*," he whispered, and something happened between her legs.

She remembered his nickname, El Caballo, and blushed. Here was a delicious opportunity to forget the past month. She wanted to turn to Cristina and say "I could just kiss you!" like they did in the movies.

Cristina begged her to get the singing started. Best to start off with group numbers, so she asked Cristina what she wanted them to sing together. "Nineties female singer-songwriters!" Cristina shouted.

"The bride-to-be wants Lilith Fair vibes," Vivian said, grabbing a microphone and rapidly queuing up songs.

She started it off easy, wiggling her hips to four-note Joan Osborne, holding the microphone in her right hand, soju and soda in her left hand, lips perfectly reddened. She snuck a peek in Elliott and Pauline's direction every now and then. Elliott's eyes held admiration, Pauline's held fear. Vivian dipped into her head voice with Sarah McLachlan to let them know her vocal range, feeling powerful for a moment before Matthew's text flashed in her head. Then she went Lisa Loeb on them and they loved it, and, since she'd laid the foundation and they'd had a couple of drinks, they began to shout along with her, until finally someone requested the second microphone. Next she busted out "Zombie" and "What's Up?" and everyone screamed together into all available microphones and up into the ceiling and away out of the room, Vivian screaming about her fucking life, the others screaming about God knows what, hands raised to the sky, drinks sloshing wildly, occasional eye contact. By the end of the run, a mob of women who hadn't really known each other at first were baring their souls in unison to "You Oughta Know" and Pauline was doing a weird interpretive dance while they all laugh-sang to Meredith Brooks's "Bitch."

Vivian was the center of it all, she had created this experience for the group and she could feel everyone in the room loving her, except for the people who were jealous of her, but they also loved her, they just blocked that love from consciousness. When her final song played she beamed and looked proudly around the room until it was too much stimulation, her eyes lost focus, and she walked to her seat, downing the rest of the second drink quickly and then pouring a third, also quickly. Vivian sensed that Elliott wanted to say something to her from across the room but she couldn't make the necessary eye contact. All the people in her vicinity, sitting to her right and left on the couch in pairs and in threes, intermittently complimented her and she smiled and thanked them while looking at the floor, behaving as if it were no big deal, like it was just another Saturday at karaoke, like she did this all the time, which was true.

The group sing-along had given her a powerful feeling and the soju was doing its thing, so in between the whites singing off-key versions of "Say My Name" and "Waterfalls," Vivian started putting on songs to sing alone. She easily crushed "Let's Dance" by David Bowie, in a stronger tone than before, channeling Bowie's androgyny to be erotic in a different way. No more wiggling. She felt Elliott staring at her and was simultaneously flattered and annoyed—now she had to control her face, freezing it to look attractive, and this was exhausting—so she used feints to throw him off, like laughing at the video that accompanied the music or at Cristina, who was cheering her on, to get him to look elsewhere. When she finished, Elliott grabbed the remote and entered in a bunch of songs in succession, like she had done earlier.

Elliott first sang "Ashes to Ashes," which he asked David and the rest of the group if they wanted to sing with him. Vivian declined, saying she didn't recognize it, and got up to go to the bathroom, partly because she had to go and partly to make him desire her because of her apparent lack of interest. On her way out, she saw that it was a David Bowie song and knew that this was a response to "Let's Dance." It was a sign, an enticement.

When she got back, a bunch of food had been delivered to their room, and Pauline was handing out homemade heart-shaped engagement cookies. "Don't worry, I'm not offering you any," she said with a wink. Elliott was midway through a song with beautiful arpeggios. She looked up the lyrics and saw that it was "The Killing Moon" by Echo and the Bunnymen and made a note in her phone. He was singing with more emotion now and it didn't matter that he wasn't hitting all the notes.

"Wait. Is this song about rape?" Vivian yelled at Cristina, who laughed and shrugged.

After, Elliott and David sang "Piano Man" together with their arms around each other. Vivian wasn't a Billy Joel person so mostly she kept her head buried in the songbook. Every now and then she'd sway on the couch, smile at Elliott, and sing along with them. His smile in return was everything.

Elliott came and sat next to her when he was done, while a group of his and David's friends sang from the *Hamilton* soundtrack.

"You've been holding out on me—I didn't know you were a singer," he said, nudging her with his shoulder. She told him she'd grown up singing but hadn't sung in a choir since college; nowadays, karaoke was her only outlet.

"You should totally join a choir now."

She said it seemed like he had good taste in music and asked him what he was listening to. They had areas of connection—Future Islands, Kate Bush, Nas, and Solange—and areas of fierce disagreement. For instance, Elliott loved early Joanna Newsom and he wistfully recalled the first time he heard her eerie voice singing "Sprout and the Bean."

"No way," Vivian said. "She was straining her voice on that whole album! It hurts my vocal cords just to listen to her. She didn't get good until she learned how to sing on *Have One on Me.*"

"What?" Elliott said with mock outrage. "You're completely insane."

"Dude, she *could not sing* before *Have One on Me,* in fact, she had to have vocal nodules removed from her throat from straining, after which I'm sure she got some vocal coaching for the next album."

"Have you seen her play?" Elliott asked.

"Yeah, she's incredible, I saw her at Pitchfork years ago and I love how she—"

"Grimaces!" they both said at the same time.

"Yes! I love how she makes all those faces when she plays, like she doesn't care about looking unattractive at all. It seems so freeing to not give a shit what anyone is thinking about what your face is doing."

"Who are you guys talking about?" Pauline asked, sitting next to Elliott with a plate piled high with bulgogi, fried chicken, and her own cookies.

"Joanna Newsom—do you know her?" Vivian asked, not without condescension.

"Is that the medieval one?" Pauline asked Elliott between bites. "Ugh, no. She's lame!" She looked like a dumb child-princess who thinks she wields more power than she does.

"What kind of music do you like, then?" Vivian asked.

"I like music that sounds good, like Fleet Foxes and Bon Iver," Pauline said. Vivian cringed a little and said nothing, then Pauline whispered something into Elliott's ear before turning to talk to a friend.

"See, this is why I miss college," Vivian said, when Pauline was out of earshot. "I miss making mixes for people and sitting around talking about music. Now all anyone wants to talk about is Netflix."

"Yeah, I fantasize about leaving the corporate life and living in a commune where TV is banned."

"Can I come live in your commune?"

"Oh, you're on the top of my list of people to invite."

Vivian laughed and then turned toward the front of the room, where Cristina was singing Kelly Clarkson off-key. Occasionally Elliott would turn toward Pauline, who was sitting to the right of him, and they would talk in the private, inaccessible manner of couples. Whenever he shut Vivian out, she would idly flip through the karaoke book or close her eyes and listen for the quality of the vocal tone of the singer, and sometimes she would join in from her seat. In particular she found herself singing along with "Take a Chance on Me" by Abba in Elliott's direction, while he was patiently explaining to Pauline the difference between Nickelback and Hoobastank. Vivian's vague goal, which felt as if it had been set by an external, undeniable force, was to distract him from the conversation with his wife by golden-throatedly singing in his left ear. Vivian liked the propulsive quality of the song, and how honest the speaker was about what they were trying to do, which was to make someone fall in love with them, which is all anyone is ever trying to do.

His lecture complete, Elliott turned to Vivian and gently touched her arm, slightly drunk.

"Sing some songs with me," he said.

Her smile was big and natural. She was entering a new space, an aesthetic realm without consequences, like that moment in the superhero film when the villain turns to the dark side.

So Matthew had dumped her, so what? It didn't have to be the end of her, it could lead to something exciting, an affair with a married man, a bit on the nose for a thirtysomething woman but she'd never done it before. Why not rack up an experience?

You want me to sing "Jolene"? she thought. *I'll sing "Jolene."*

They sang "Jolene," and in between verses she whispered into Elliott's ear, "It's hard for me to sing this!" It was a boring song.

"But you're killing it," he said. "You're killing everything!"

"Yeah, but I identify with Jolene, not the narrator," she said.

Elliott laughed and laughed.

Next he put in "Sweet Dreams Are Made of This" and "Don't You Want Me," which they sang in decent harmony. Elliott looked at Vivian like she was his new best friend and she had a superpower that only he knew about. She knew these songs so well that she didn't need to look at the screen. She commanded the entire square-shaped performance area, spinning around Elliott while he sang, constantly moving, singing on autopilot. Vivian's dancing was severe, determined to match the music, but every once in a while she'd say fuck it and twist down low, or move her arms around, or shake her head like a dog shedding water. She snapped and shuffled toward Elliott, implicating him, and when he caught himself dancing with her, as opposed to dancing in the same area as her, he automatically looked at Pauline, who looked away, holding what appeared to be a second plate of food.

What was marriage anyway? Just another social structure that Vivian didn't believe in.

She was getting drunker, though, and on one of those twist-downs, she started to wobble and struggled to get back up. "Time for a *little* break," she said into the microphone, as Elliott pulled David onto the floor to sing "Sweet Caroline." Vivian needed to be as far away from Neil Diamond as possible so she went out to the main bar, where free public karaoke was happening, and ordered another soju. A group of queer friends were singing "Head Over Heels" by Tears for Fears, with a muscular woman with shaggy blond hair straight out of the seventies and winged eyeliner on the lead. The woman was sexy without being sexual, she was the type of woman who could work on your car, she looked like heaven, she reminded Vivian of Jane, *a white Jane,* she thought, remembering one of Jane's texts, sent from the Jersey outlet mall her mother had dragged her to: Am I disinterested in the makeup and bags at Nordstrom Rack because the gender binary is compulsory or because I'm depressed?

Vivian joined in with the white Jane surrounded by queens, yelling "I fucking love Roland Orzabal" into the woman's ear while clapping and singing the la-la-las, experiencing a rare sense of positive group feeling.

"I found you," she heard Elliott say from behind.

"Had to change up the vibe," she said, grabbing his hands, dancing at him and then dropping them, dancing away.

White Jane's friend put in Depeche Mode and handed Vivian a microphone. As they sang "Personal Jesus," Vivian struck powerful poses. She told Elliott, "My gender is Depeche Mode!" and he laughed.

"I have no idea what that means," he said, looking like he was in love with her.

As they sang, the newly formed group danced in a circle, thrilled at their own spontaneity. The vibe was zero fucks. No one was judging anyone. Vivian held eye contact with Elliott as she sang until he broke away and when he looked back, she stuck out her tongue at him. She danced with him platonically, grabbing him by the shoulders and twisting him with her, and then, for an instant, nonplatonically. They finished the song with their arms around each other, and he gently squeezed her side.

After the song was over she complimented the ragtag band of singers and engaged in small talk with them, Elliott glued to her side.

A straight white dude wearing a sports cap put on "Lose Yourself" and just as Vivian was about to start in with an "Oh boy" and an accompanying disdainful monologue, Cristina came up to her and said, "Hey, do you wanna go to the bathroom? I need to talk to you about something."

"What's up?" Vivian asked. "Are you suffering from an allergic reaction to that horrible Eminem performance? When will white men learn?"

Cristina laughed halfheartedly.

The bathroom was empty when they got there and Vivian went into a stall to pee. Cristina stayed outside, checking her makeup, and asked Vivian if she was okay.

"Of course I'm okay, it's karaoke. I'm in my natural habitat!"

She could sense Cristina making a face.

"I'm just being performative."

"Let's get you some water, I'll be right back."

Vivian stayed on the toilet for a long time, slipping in and out of consciousness.

Awhile later she heard a woman's footsteps enter the bathroom. They were different from the Cristina footsteps. She didn't want to interact with anyone else so she lifted up her feet so they couldn't be seen. This was going to be a lot to commit to, considering that she hadn't emptied her bladder all the way.

The woman entered the stall next to her. She recognized Pauline's burgundy boots. The boots didn't turn around, instead they remained pointed in the direction of the toilet. Vivian heard gagging, then spurts of liquid going into the toilet. This lasted for a couple of minutes, during which Vivian beamed with the satisfaction of someone who had been Right All Along while also making every effort not to let any pee dribble out. It reminded her of law school. She'd hear vomiting in the bathroom in between classes and have to come out pretending not to have noticed.

Thankfully the gaps in the stall door were minimal, so when Pauline got out to stand in front of the mirror she couldn't see Vivian sitting there.

Vivian heard Pauline unzip her bag, pull something out, and twist a cap. She gargled and spat into the sink, then Vivian heard the familiar clinking of cosmetics. Pauline sniffled a little, preparing herself to be seen, and walked out of the bathroom.

Vivian grinned, tapping her feet excitedly. She couldn't wait to tell Max about this.

Cristina returned and handed Vivian a plastic cup of water under the stall.

"That took forever?" Vivian said.

"Sorry, I got roped into a musical medley."

Cristina paused, then said, "So, what's going on with you and Elliott?"

"We are bonding through the glory of song," Vivian said, taking a sip of the water and flattening out a wrinkle in her pants.

"Seems kind of flirty, though, no?"

"No way," Vivian said, flushing for emphasis.

She exited the stall casually, and the two of them reapplied their lipstick in silence.

"Love that color," Vivian said, and Cristina relaxed.

"It's called Daringly Nude," Cristina responded.

"I'm more of a Reluctantly Naked kind of gal," Vivian said, then blanched at her own bad joke. "Should have kept that one in here." She pointed to her head.

"Anyway, I just don't want my friend to think you're after her husband, you know," Cristina said.

"Nobody is after anyone," Vivian said. Besides, she thought, according to Pauline, if Vivian had been inciting a competition, her lizard brain was to blame.

Back in the karaoke room, the descent into madness had begun. Pauline dropped her drink while dancing to "Girls Just Wanna Have Fun" and so, in response, Vivian sang "Walking on Broken Glass" and dedicated it to "everyone sitting in the corner" where Pauline had been standing. This got a big laugh, so Pauline was forced to take the dig in stride, but later she got Vivian back by taking pictures of her while she sang. The more Vivian protested the more pictures Pauline took, with a degree of impunity, given how fucked up everyone was. "Make a face like Joanna Newsom, grimace like Joanna Newsom!" Pauline kept saying, until Vivian's irritation was replaced by something else: a feeling of superiority, because while Pauline seemed unhinged, Vivian was still in control of her faculties.

After, Vivian handed Elliott her cup, silently ordering him to refill it with soju. "That will be my last drink of the night," she declared. "So, I noticed you guys have a piano at your house, can you play?"

He said yes, and that he was currently working his way through some Bach.

Vivian squealed at the coincidence. *So the universe is just out here handing me Bach-playing studs,* she thought.

"Do you know how to play *The Well-Tempered Clavier?*"

He said that actually, that was what he was teaching himself.

Vivian jumped up and touched Elliott's shoulder. They both knew what was happening as they took turns gushing about their favorite versions of the different pieces. She said Gulda couldn't be matched, pulling out her phone and holding it up to Elliott's ear intimately. He countered with the Tureck recording. She hadn't heard it? "I'm slightly disappointed," he said teasingly. "I expected you to lecture me on how The Woman's Version is the best."

She suddenly lied and said she was actually writing about Bach in her novel. Could he play for her sometime?

Elliott said that yes, they should hang out, he'd love to play for her.

As he put her number into his phone, Vivian forgot the crowded room and all her worries. She felt vindicated and secure, if only briefly.

VIVIAN AT THE WEDDING

CRISTINA AND DAVID'S wedding was held in late October at a beachside resort on Florida's Gulf Coast. They rented out the entire place for the wedding party and guests: twelve beach houses for family and the wedding party, and an eighty-room bungalow-style hotel across the street for everyone else. Vivian was staying at one of the beach houses with Max, and Pauline and Elliott were just a couple of houses away at the main house, since Elliott was the best man.

She'd flown down a day early by herself to spend some time at the beach. Now she set up her umbrella slowly, paranoid that others were looking at her body. Her muscle spasms had returned with such regularity and intensity that she hadn't been able to run in weeks. She could feel the weight collecting. Specifically, as she bent over now there were three distinct fat rolls bulging and coiling out of her midsection toward the ground.

Now that Matthew had broken it off, he had taken on an outsized role in Vivian's interior life, and she'd spent the last few weeks having highly specific fantasies about their future encounters.

In the I'm Still Single While He's a Father fantasy, Vivian

would encounter Matthew with one of his children—a girl—at a farmers' market in late summer. Vivian would be wearing espadrilles, her hair long and wavy. Matthew would be all smiles in his Sunday dad clothes, and he'd touch her shoulder, telling her how good she looked. Their bodies would betray a lingering and unspoken mutual attraction, like Holly Hunter and William Hurt in the final scene of *Broadcast News*. Just as in that film, their affection would be all the sweeter for not being expressed. Matthew would say they should get lunch some time and then, as father and daughter were about to leave, his daughter would say to her, "You're pretty."

In the Book Signing fantasy, Matthew would approach her after a dazzling reading. Later, over drinks, he would apologize for running away from the relationship. Vivian would tell him there was no need to apologize. His rejection, she would explain, had allowed her to face her fears of abandonment and write her book, a book which had propelled her somewhere beyond him and, in fact, any man.

"The feelings in the book…those are *old* feelings," she would say.

They would drink more and he would start touching her here and there. She would permit these silent advances and then, when he said something funny, self-deprecating, and beautifully phrased, she would smile and rub her hand up and down his back. When he kissed her, it would have a cache clearing effect. Any inadequacies—real or imagined—would disappear.

One day Vivian was in her apartment hunched over her phone spying on Matthew's various social media accounts when she noticed that he was endlessly reimbursing a new woman on a digital wallet app: Diane. She clicked on Diane's profile and before she knew it she was Googling "Diane Jones," scrolling to the bottom of her Instagram and creeping on the profiles of the woman's closest friends and family.

Diane was a black woman, at least twenty pounds heavier than Vivian, and according to the internet, she and Matthew were in love. She looked at them dancing together in New Orleans, while a brass band played. She watched a video he made of himself playing romantic jazz to her and started to cry, imagining their happy, vigorous life, with music and creativity at the center of it. A life she'd failed to make for herself.

A musician and a poet, Diane had recently put out a self-recorded Alt-R&B album that Vivian listened to, on a loop, until she fell in love with it. Astounding harmonies. Her poetry left much to be desired, but Vivian couldn't be mad at the idea of free verse about racial oppression. What interested her most about Diane was that she admitted to struggling—with depression and with her weight and with perfectionism. These issues were laid out for everyone to see in her blog, her social media, and her creative output itself. Vivian had been so guarded, and for what? What was the point of all the effort? To appear perfect, to perform at all times, to get lean? None of it mattered. None of it "worked." It was as if she were playing *Mario Bros.* and had just been told that the princess was in another castle. She cried at her own pathetic state, recalling Anita trapped in the purple room, and thought, *I hate being like this, so much.*

Days later, though, Vivian thought of Elliott. Their great conversations about music, their adoring eye contact while singing, his offer to play Bach for her. She'd initially dismissed him as someone who was fun to flirt with, with the added bonus of messing with his wife, but she should really pursue something with him at Cristina's wedding. They were way more compatible anyway.

Once her umbrella was finally in the sand she sat in her chair drinking rosé out of a plastic cup and tried not to look at women's butts. It seemed that everyone had been placed there specifically to annoy her. Men were doing intolerable things with balls and discs on either side of her. Kicking. Throwing. Grunting. Children were children-ing, wild and unpredictable. A grandmother, who was small like Anita, called after one of them. Vivian sank her feet deep into the sugar-white quartz sand, always cool to the touch, no matter how hot it was. She looked up into the abundant sun. Seabirds were gliding in circles. She wrote fragments of her irritable internal monologue and then judged herself for her inability to write about the observable world, until she banged her toe repeatedly against something and looked down and saw that it was a blue tampon applicator. She wrote then, *This blue tampon applicator being alternately covered and uncovered by sand is me.* It wouldn't amount to anything, a part thought. But some other part continued writing.

Vivian wasn't exactly happy for Cristina and David, or for anyone else. She kind of couldn't believe it was actually going forward, and a wedding was the literal last place she wanted to be. But the prospect of Elliott's returning attention gave her a sense of renewed hope. A successful seduction would operate the way a swallow of NyQuil did in commercials, warmly easing any aches it found along the way. Sensing a superego droning on about Elliott's marriage, she turned toward it and laughed. The sanctity of Elliott's marriage was a nonissue. Ethics were a nonissue. Vivian now firmly existed in a reality beyond ethics, in the dark side. She didn't care what happened to anyone, herself included.

"Apparently it's one of the warmest Octobers on record," Vivian read to Max from her phone as they walked onto the beach the day of the wedding.

"It hurts to look up," he whined.

Max was wearing a pale blue suit with a dark blue polka-dotted bow tie and a jaunty agave brooch. Vivian wore a sleeveless navy-blue minidress with four fluttery tiers of chiffon that she didn't identify with in any way and only wore because its layers covered her growing belly fat. She'd paired the dress with pointy yellow flats that were quickly filling up with sand, causing her to shift uncomfortably from side to side as they walked to the bar tent.

Max ordered a negroni while Vivian went with a skinny watermelon margarita and they reminisced about their favorite reality show moments.

"When Aviva threw her leg!"

"'Scary Island.'"

"*Intervention* Allison huffing duster while crying about wanting a father."

"Kandi ugly-crying and screaming *I will drag you in this, bitch.*"

"Now that was a good one."

"Iconic."

The best thing about a beach wedding is that it's socially acceptable to wear sunglasses, and so when she saw Pauline, she was able to hide her jealousy behind colored plastic.

Pauline wore a yellow midi dress with spaghetti straps and an exposed gold back zipper with matching yellow wedge sandals. Her hair was styled in beachy waves and was even longer than it had been last time. She looked like a model; her long tan legs and braless nipples were an indictment against Vivian's entire existence.

Elliott looked super hot in his dark blue blazer and khakis; they hugged and she got a whiff of the scotch he was holding and his signature scent, Sexy Pine Forest. Drinks in hand, they beamed at each other, and while Pauline chatted with Max, Elliott told her she looked amazing.

"And you look great, as always. How's Bach and the commune going?" she asked.

"Haven't thought of the commune in a while," he said, clearing his throat. "But Bach is going fine, doing a little every weekend." They continued to catch up amiably, but Vivian sensed that he was being distant. It must be because Pauline was around.

"Have you heard the news?" Elliott asked.

She shook her head and he turned to Pauline, who grinned uncontrollably.

"Pauline got a book deal!" Elliott said, glowing.

"That is quite the accomplishment," Vivian said, while wanting to break off a piece of her wineglass and stick it in Pauline's carotid artery. And then she couldn't even enjoy the petty thrill of revenge fantasy because Pauline performatively undermined her own success, saying, "It's just for a vegan cookbook. Not literary or anything."

The only way out of this was utter magnanimity. "You should be so proud of yourself. Are you, like, the happiest woman in the world now?" Vivian laughed. "I would be."

"Actually, I'm super stressed. I sold the book on the basis of six recipes and thousands of followers. But now I have to test all those recipes, perfect them, and come up with dozens more, to test and perfect."

"That sounds intense," Vivian said.

"But it's nothing compared to what you do," Pauline said.

"*Did*," Vivian said. "I just quit! I have some money saved, and I'm finally going to buckle down and get serious about my writing. Maybe one day I'll have a book deal!"

They clinked glasses and Vivian wondered about the truth of what she'd said. As a lawyer, she could always use her lack of time as an excuse not to write. Now that all she had was time (well, six months, until her savings ran out) she realized that writing was utter misery. She'd sit in front of her laptop in clenched, hesitating postures, one leg wrapped around the other, right hand over mouth, just staring at the page. Eventually she would begin to type but it was always so halting, so much apprehension behind each sentence. She felt like a baby mammal trying to walk and collapsing in a mute, weak pile.

Even if she did write, when she read back what she'd written her stomach would seize and she'd get so jittery she'd have to stand up, make herself a drink, get high, and watch something on the internet. Hours of angry watching would go by until the day was over.

"I feel like I need to start smoking weed or something, to, like, deal with the publication pressure," Pauline said. Vivian smiled supportively, like a sidekick whose sole purpose is to glorify the main character. She touched Pauline's elbow and whispered, "Well, you know I have some, *girl,* so if you want to smoke just let me know."

She then made a swift exit to the bar tent, where she

started sucking down tequila sodas like a 1950s housewife and plotting. That *girl* was a genius touch, she thought, making Pauline feel like she was proximate to blackness. During the bonfire tonight, Vivian decided, she would smoke Pauline out with the Comfort Killer. Pauline would lose it! She'd either embarrass herself like she did at karaoke, or she'd go to bed, leaving Elliott all to Vivian.

"Is Elliott secretly gay?" Max said, sidling next to her.

Vivian laughed and looked around to make sure no one could hear. "I'd hope not, considering that we're about to start an affair."

"Well, he just made a joke about Grindr, so I *think* he's going to be my new boyfriend," Max said.

"Did he invite you to his commune, though?" Vivian asked.

"May the best woman win," Max said.

They raised their glasses.

At the ceremony, Cristina's face was tensed and slightly grimacing. She didn't look like a person in love; more like a dog that had been crammed into an outfit by its owner. She kept nervously touching her hair and trying to cover her body with her veil. Vivian cracked her knuckles, trying to figure out whether Cristina was uncomfortable with the attention, anticipating the judgment of the spectators, or skeptical of romance in general. Instead of looking at each other, Cristina and David kept their eyes on David's father's best friend, John, who was marrying them. John spoke of marriage as a covenant and a promise and a sanctuary and advised the couple to never go to bed angry.

As they exchanged vows, David promised that he wouldn't watch their shows without her, Cristina promised that one day David would get his three-car garage, they referred to each other as their best friend, they referred to each other as their favorite person. There was nervous laughter and some of the women in the audience dabbed at their faces. Vivian thought of all the couples out there who weren't having sex but stayed together to lower their rent burden, all the couples who were more like siblings but were couple-presenting, all the couples who got married so they wouldn't be alone as they slowly marched toward death. Beyond the ceremony tent, Vivian could see swimmers scattered about in singles, duos, and trios. She focused on the sizes of their bodies until her eyes glazed over and her mind lost time; then her attention returned to the waves lapping the shore, constantly washing. When David kissed her, Cristina seemed to shrink back a little before freezing into a pose that would photograph well. The ceremony had ended.

Vivian adjusted her purse in an *on-to-the-next-scene* manner, put on a party face, and waded through the crowd, looking for Elliott. Not finding him, she chatted, seemingly earnestly, with the endless parade of Cristina's family members, including her parents, whom Vivian didn't have any interest in, though when she met them, she acted enthused.

"You must be so proud," she said, kissing Cristina's mother on each cheek and introducing herself.

"Felicidades," she said to Cristina's father.

"You look healthier in person!" Cristina's mother said. "You were too skinny in the Facebook photos."

At the cocktail hour, Vivian kept up the sidekick routine, complimenting Pauline on her dress, brainstorming book publicity ideas, asking for details about her recipes—just waiting for Pauline to mention wanting to get high. It had to be her idea.

Throughout the dinner, Vivian wanted to talk to Max, Elliott, and Adam, one of David's friends, but it seemed there was some gender divide at their table and she got stuck talking to Pauline and Adrianna, Adam's girlfriend. Adrianna kept making self-deprecating comments about her weight, remarking for instance on how the unflattering head-to-toe blue jumpsuit she was wearing made her look five to ten pounds heavier than she actually was, and how she didn't want to look like a pig for eating a second portion of bread, but she was going to do it anyway. Each time Adrianna did this, Vivian looked over at Pauline, wanting to catch her having some twisted reaction. But Pauline just did the thing women are supposed to do, telling Adrianna she was beautiful, that she looked great, that she should eat whatever she wanted to, especially bread.

"Vivian doesn't eat bread," Pauline said playfully, buttering a slice. "But that's her loss."

Pauline eats it, but then she throws it up after, Vivian didn't say.

Because of all the body talk, Vivian felt compelled to look down at Adrianna's thighs as they ate. They were aggressively untoned and took up the whole chair. This poor woman was looking for reassurance and didn't deserve Vivian's insane fat-phobic gaze, but Vivian couldn't help herself, could only see the polyester-encased flesh spreading out on the chair, hiding her knees, hiding her vagina, Vivian thought, thighs seeming to increase, to take up more space as she went on. And she had a habit of removing her round-toed flat with her right foot, and repeatedly putting the shoe back on and taking it off, on and off, drawing Vivian's eyes to the foot, and to the swollen ankle and calf it was attached to, and she became distracted by the mass, inexplicably distressed by it.

Vivian looked around for Cristina, needing something else to focus on. She noticed Cristina going around to every table, asking people if they were okay or if they needed anything. Vivian called her over and after she'd had a moment with everyone else they embraced.

"Why are you carrying forks?" Vivian asked, laughing.

Cristina whispered to her, "My mom is freaking out, dude."

"About what?"

"She found spots on some of the silverware on the place settings and she went off, demanding to the head of the catering company that she wants the whole reception to be free!"

"Oh boy," Vivian said.

"So now I'm going around looking at all the settings just to make sure, and gathering up the dirty ones to tell the staff to clean so she won't notice more."

Vivian laughed. "Cristina, your mom just needs to chill."

"Well, it's easier to just clean the silverware, you know, I'll spit on it myself to avoid that woman going off."

"Bussing tables at your own wedding—what a day to remember," Vivian said. "How are you feeling otherwise?"

Cristina inspected a dinner knife for smudges, then added it to her collection. "I'm ready for the after-party."

"Well, I love you, friend. Congratulations."

Vivian craned her neck and tried to hear Elliott, Max, and Adam's conversation, but all she could hear were phrases in the vein of "I'll send you the link."

Out of nowhere, Adrianna grabbed Vivian by the shoulders and said, "Your shoulders are so little!"

"And you have great tits," Pauline said.

"Want some?" Vivian said, looking down at them. "They make me look bigger than I am."

"Do your nipples face the floor?" Adrianna asked, with a hint of provocation.

Vivian blushed. She felt looked into but also relieved to find that poor Adrianna wasn't so innocent. She was participating in an exchange of judgment.

"We know hers don't," Adrianna said, pointing at Pauline. "Hers are like Drew Barrymore on David Letterman's couch. You have a perfect bikini body."

"It's my genes," Pauline said.

Vivian snuck looks at Pauline's plate here and there, but it wasn't like at karaoke when she'd kept going back for more. This time Pauline spent a lot of energy cutting up her food into little pieces but didn't eat much. Toasts happened; glasses were raised. Vivian snuck looks at Elliott, too. His hair, his smile, his beard. NyQuil. Her phone buzzed. An eggplant emoji from Max, who'd caught her staring. Their eyes met across the table.

"What are y'all laughing at?" Pauline asked.

"Not what, but who," Vivian responded, shaking her head.

The sun sank lower and everyone watched the sky put on a show. First it exploded into deep oranges, with scores of sea gulls gliding in circles and crying in unison, pelicans dive-bombing from above. Then, a glorious crescendo of pink and purple bands splashed with smoke. Finally, it was time to dance. Vivian might not be as thin as Pauline, but she could incinerate the dance floor. She danced throughout the tented dance area with ease, impressing elderly and toddler guests alike. But she began to notice a pattern: whenever she danced near Elliott, he would dance away to another section, or leave the dance floor altogether. *It's his passion for me,* she told herself. *It's too strong.*

She danced and sang along with Max and Cristina to "Call Your Girlfriend," joined all the thirtysomethings storming the dance floor at the first bars of "This Is How We Do It," and felt a sense of intergenerational community during "Cupid Shuffle." When "Like a Prayer" came on, Vivian thought of her mother, feeling waves of tenderness and grief and shedding tears that were undoubtedly exacerbated by all the alcohol, and which she tried her best to pass off as related to the wedding.

After the exodus of the family members, there was a bonfire by the beach with close friends only. Max got an email from a law firm partner that sent him back to their room to work, so Vivian was left alone with the three couples. She lit sparklers, made a s'more and took one bite before burying it in the sand, and continued drinking. Pauline, shivering in Elliott's suit jacket—which she'd draped over her shoulders perfectly, emanating chic power—walked over to where Vivian was sitting and whispered in Vivian's ear, "Can we smoke now?"

"Let's do it!"

Vivian announced that she'd brought weed as a party favor and the friends all cheered, then launched into a conversation about short-form online videos she'd never seen. They discussed the video of people walking in structurally unsound footwear, the video where a sweet cat is danced around in a nine-frame filter to the tune of "Mr. Sandman," and the video where a squirrel seems to dance in time to Missy Elliott. Grateful for the distraction, she looked down into the darkness of her bag. Inside, there were two baggies of weed. She fingered the one with the skull and crossbones on it.

Under normal circumstances, theft of the weed

notwithstanding, Vivian was a strict adherent to stoner ethics. She believed in warning people about the severity of a strain, for instance. But Pauline had had an unfair advantage in every way. White and desirable, wealthy, so able to collect and discard degrees, supported by her parents, making endless professional reinvention possible. And she kept coming for Vivian, in ways that were illegible to everyone else. So what Vivian was about to do—encourage Pauline, a clear lightweight, to take several hits of some weed containing the highest level of THC that Vivian had ever encountered—wasn't this justified? Couldn't it be recuperated as one of Jane's feminist pranks, or as a kind of social reparations?

Vivian handed Pauline a bowl filled with Comfort Killer and said, "Here you go," gently.

Pauline said, "Me first?"

"New smokers always get the green," she said, gesturing to the bowl. Pauline innocently asked for instructions, which Vivian was happy to provide. She watched Pauline inhale and then exhale a thick smoke once, then twice, then three times.

After, Vivian dumped out the death weed and replaced it with some regular old kush for the others to smoke. All she had to do was wait for Pauline to start to experience low- to midlevel psychosis. White nontraumatized womanhood would be destroyed, vengeance would be hers, *et cetera*.

The party moved to the main house, where Cristina and David were staying with the bridal party. It was a six-room suite with double decks facing the water. Inside, a huge open-concept living area was predictably decorated in turquoise and white and an all-white kitchen boasted stainless steel appliances. There were starfish and anchors everywhere. Vivian hovered near David's friend group on the deck, pretending to be interested in their conversation about the history of their friendship. They were all okay embarrassing each other, which irritated Vivian because she had organized her life in such a way as to avoid embarrassment. No roommates. No long-term companionship. No family. Elective relationships only. Yet, they had all done it. Traveled together and annoyed one another. Seen each other through sickness and broken hearts, witnessed each other's worst mistakes and failures, met each other's dysfunctional families. And none of them had stopped loving the other or at the very least hanging out.

Vivian tried to focus on Pauline, who should have started freaking out by now. But in defiance of all chemical and psychological laws, Pauline seemed fine. In fact, she seemed to be having a wonderful time. Whenever Vivian would go back inside to refresh her drink, she caught glimpses of Pauline *holding her ground*, she thought, on one of the hideously beachified teal chairs in the living room as a larger conversation went on around her, at one point laughing with her entire body, long "hec-hce-hee-hee" laughs, as those in her circle laughed with her, then later explaining not only how silly she felt but why, with an endearing recital of the various neurochemical pathways the marijuana was taking inside her brain, then finally rocking back and forth, squeal-ing, her pupils dilated, still alert to Vivian's and Elliott's every move on the deck outside.

That weed destroyed me twice, Vivian thought. *But this one has the giggles and is going on about cannabinoid receptors.*

Vivian needed another plan. She excused herself to "reapply her lipstick" and snuck into Elliott and Pauline's bedroom. Their clothes were heaped in warm piles around the room, which smelled like damp towels. She walked in with a frown, tempted to sniff their things like a dog, but instead she went into the bathroom and shut the door, casually inspecting the medicine cabinet.

Pauline's makeup bag was sitting on the toilet and Vivian looked through it, enjoying the click-clack of bottles, compacts, and lipsticks making contact. She unscrewed the cap on Pauline's liquid foundation and rubbed a glob between her fingers while having petty thoughts. Growing up, it was so easy for Pauline to find the right foundation for her skin. There had been rows and rows of options, catering to the nuances of whiteness. Vivian, meanwhile, could never find a shade that worked. The medium-cool was too cool, the medium-warm was too medium. Her adolescent face and neck were always different colors. She wondered whether "cosmetic privilege" was a concept she could use to justify her behavior.

There were pill bottles in there too, nestled in between several blister packs of laxatives: Klonopin, Zoloft, and Adderall. So Pauline was addicted to laxatives, huh. And she had anxiety, depression, and problems paying attention. Who didn't? After reapplying her lipstick, she stole one of Pauline's pink lipsticks, three 20mg tablets of Adderall, and three 10mg tablets of Klonopin, blue and yellow as a baby's nursery, and put them into her bra. Further reparations.

As Vivian walked out of the room every muscle in her face tugged downward, and her eyes suggested permanent suffering. If another person had seen her they would have been seriously concerned about her mental state, but seconds later she was demonstrating cheeriness and ease as she descended the stairs to rejoin the party.

She spent the next two hours waiting Pauline out, sipping tequila sodas and at one point taking an Adderall, but the woman just wouldn't go to sleep.

She couldn't take it anymore. She walked up to Elliott and asked him if he wanted to smoke with her on the beach. He instinctively looked over at Pauline but then said, "Sure!"

As they walked on the sand, Vivian said her hands were cold. Elliott didn't pick up on the signal, but Vivian had to commit to the performance so she started to blow on them. They passed her bowl back and forth and talked about work.

The wind blew and Elliott said he could smell the ocean, and Vivian's hair. "It smells so nice," he said, looking into her eyes.

She waited for him to kiss her. But he was too nervous.

He asked her if she was seeing anyone and she explained, briefly, that she'd been seeing a guy but it didn't work out.

"I bet he was intimidated by you," Elliott said playfully.

"What? Me? No way," she said, fishing.

"Of course he was, you're gorgeous and brilliant. I'd be intimidated. I am intimidated," he said.

She stopped in the sand and he stopped too. She touched his face gently and leaned in to kiss him, giving it all she had.

But his lips were a tensed barrier. He pulled away and sort of pushed her.

"No!" he burst out, wiping his mouth and face as if he'd been spat upon.

"Why not?" Vivian asked.

He held up his ring finger.

"But you said I was gorgeous."

Elliott looked at her with a quizzical expression.

"And brilliant."

"I was just being nice. You seemed bummed out about that guy dumping you or whatever."

"No, that's not it," she said, shaking her head. "You've been flirty with me ever since I met you."

"Flirting doesn't mean anything," he said, as if he were lecturing a small child.

It occurred to her that things were not going to turn out the way she had hoped. She again felt that she was losing her identity. She could no longer maintain her cool demeanor; she had no jokes at hand. *Flirting means literally everything,* she thought. She couldn't be looked at. She turned from him, crossing her arms and digging her nails into them.

"Let's just forget this. I'm going back," he said.

"That's fine," Vivian said, barely audibly.

When he was a safe distance away she turned and watched him walk back to the house. She let him get a ways ahead before following, reflexively circling her fingers around her wrists. She decided to just say her goodbyes to everyone and head out. She'd be leaving tomorrow, and no one would ever have to know about her humiliation.

But when she got back to the house, Elliott was talking amiably to David as if nothing had happened at all. When he looked at her, he did so dismissively, as if she were nothing but a failed seductress. Pathetic. Delusional. *So that's how he's going to play it,* Vivian thought.

Instead of leaving, she poured herself another drink and stood at the threshold of the living room, where Cristina and the other bridesmaids were asking Pauline, who'd now sobered a bit, about her cookbook.

"You're, like, the most famous person I know," one of the bridesmaids said.

"What if you get a cooking show?" another one of them squealed.

"OMG, it could be called *Baking with Pauline,*" said another. The women erupted in laughter at their own stupidity.

"What would you even bake, though?" Vivian asked.

The women shifted in discomfort but were too weak to condemn Vivian's tone.

"Because you don't actually eat baked goods. I mean, not without throwing up after, right? That's the only way you can stay at that size."

Pauline looked slightly stunned. She seemed incapable of listening to what Vivian was saying.

"Vivian—"

"Stay out of it, Cristina, I swear. I'm trying to tell the TRUTH here, God," she said, losing her footing slightly.

"So really, when you think about it, your show should be called *Not Eating with Pauline.* No, no—*Baking, Eating, Then Regurgitating with Pauline!*"

Vivian laughed with contempt at her own jokes. The women looked at her, then at each other, then back at her. They didn't know what to do.

"It's evil, you know, the hypocrisy of it all. Pretending to love food, writing a cookbook, force-feeding people cupcakes and then trying to make them feel bad when they don't want a cupcake and being like 'Oh I just LOVE CARBS,' but really, it's ALL A LIE. You are a scammer. A carb scammer! You restrict and work out and make yourself vomit and shit just like the rest of us. To deny that—it's abusive."

Vivian watched Pauline's face for a reaction, a display of shock or self-recognition, anger even. Some physical indication that Vivian was right about her, that this exposure was justified. But Pauline just looked at Vivian like she was a wounded animal in need of care.

She pushed on. "Why aren't you saying anything? Why isn't anyone saying anything? Isn't anyone going to stand up for Pauline or, like, for human decency? What the hell is wrong with you people? Completely useless!" she said to the ceiling as if calling out to a god.

"Girl," Pauline said, "Come on—"

"I'm not your girl, bitch," Vivian said, and though she only meant to throw her drink at Pauline, she overestimated how much force this would require, and this overestimation, combined with the condensation on the outside of the glass, caused her to lose control of it and the glass flew out of her hand toward Pauline's head, and though Pauline quickly ducked and the glass shattered just behind her on the linoleum floor, the mood in the room shifted and people screamed and covered themselves and moved away from Vivian and toward Pauline, as if Pauline had in fact been hit.

Men entered the room to protect their mates. Elliott ran to a shaking Pauline, rubbing her back and whispering something into her ear. David put his arm around Cristina and she snuggled into him, not taking her eyes off Vivian; in fact, they were all looking at her this way, as if she were a danger to them, while murmuring that she should calm down, that things had gone too far, that she'd had too much to drink.

"There's your adversity story," Vivian said to Pauline. "I know how much you wanted one." Then she turned and walked out onto the deck. The couples standing there moved aside to let her go and she felt them watching her. She didn't want to seem embarrassed so she stood on the deck for a second and finished someone's unattended drink without looking at anyone, setting it down on one of the deck's wooden beams, which her fingers now grazed sadly, but exaggeratedly. Vivian walked down the stairs slowly, feeling the sciatica flash down her right leg again.

On her way to the water, Max, returning for a nightcap, asked her if she was all right.

"I know that walk," he said, and Vivian smiled, simulating "not-suicidal," and insisted that she was okay.

"They're gonna tell you some stuff," she said, pointing back in the direction of the house and teetering in the sand. "Let them know, though, that I'm already making jokes about it," she added, refusing tears.

While looking out onto what was now a roaring ocean all by herself, Vivian was reminded of a wood engraving by Winslow Homer called *On the Beach—Two Are Company, Three Are None*. In the engraving, a woman stands in the foreground of a beach looking back on a couple about to go out into the ocean on a boat. Nothing in the woman's face suggests unhappiness, and if it weren't for the title, you'd either think she was blessing them or just watching them dispassionately as part of the ocean scene. But the title frames the woman's plight as one of being deprived relative to a pairing, and so it had been with Vivian tonight.

Drunk and high, yet alert because of the Adderall, she stood out there looking at the water in the cold, shaking her head, confused and resentful. No one understood her and everyone was garbage.

Vivian took out her phone and wrote, THINGS I'VE BEEN WRONG ABOUT. 1. Matthew wanting a thin, vapid person. 2. Elliott wanting me at all. 3. The Uber rapist. 4. The mechanic rapist. 5. The subway rapists. 6. Ruby testifying (bad idea). 7.

Pauline's weed tolerance. 8. The force required to throw water in someone's face. 9. The circumstances surrounding Jane leaving school. 10. Pretty much all of my priorities.

———•⊷•———

Vivian bolted up at dawn. Her mouth felt full of crumbling chalk, and she was being attacked by bedding, which she now kicked off. In the other bed, Max was out cold. She reached into her bra and threw the rest of the Adderall she had taken from Pauline's bag into her mouth. Flooded by shame, she crawled around the room, silently packing her things, and called a car to drop her at the airport, where she'd pay $350 to switch to a 10 a.m. flight back. Though she remembered her failed seduction attempt and monologue from the night before, she didn't remember the beach portion and had to look through all the pictures of the ocean she'd taken on her phone in order to understand how long she'd stayed on the beach by herself.

While waiting for the car, Vivian sat on the porch of the bungalow with her eyes closed, praying that Max wouldn't wake up before she got out of there. She'd really fucked up now, and it would be clear to everyone that she was insane, unfit for friendship. She had tried to induce psychosis in another woman in order to sleep with her husband—someone she wasn't even that interested in (this part was a little funny, she had to admit). Then she'd exposed the woman's eating disorder. Then she'd *attacked* her, thrown a glass at her. It didn't matter that it was an accident. There was no way to salvage this.

She imagined everyone staying late up into the night

discussing "Vivian's outburst and attack." Using information gleaned from the internet and podcasts but no direct experience, she figured, they would ultimately decide that calling the police was unjustified. It would serve only to reify the overcriminalization of the black body. Besides, now they all had a great dinner party story with which to explain to their friends how contemporary race relations intersect with gender in the United States.

At the airport bar she ordered a tequila soda, despite the early hour. Great thing about the airport: there is no judgment. She had always felt the most herself there. Anonymous, lonely, and trapped in the hellscape of her own mind. She watched people, alternately jealous and disdainful of their relationships. Mothers and fathers looking benevolently at their children, old couples bickering, and the women. Oh, the women. Women in pajamas, women in wedges, women wearing sunglasses indoors, women clomping around like camels. She claimed to love them. But let one of them stand between her and a guy and she would be hated, and it would be imperative that she be destroyed. Jane was right about her. She covered her face with her hands.

WHERE THE BOYS ARE

DAYS AFTER THE wedding, Vivian sat slumped on the couch watching true crime, stoned out of her mind, absent-mindedly eating stale kettle corn for breakfast. On the show, an old man had found a steel barrel deep in the crawl space of his home. Inside it were human remains. Cut to a human hand, a woman's skull. The autopsy revealed that she'd been seven months pregnant at the time of her murder. At the bottom of the barrel, a purse covered in mysterious sludge and then, inside the purse, an address book that might hold the key to—

THUMP. THUMP. THUMP.

Vivian startled. Someone was at her door.

THUMP. THUMP. THUMP.

This wasn't the low, hesitant tap of the exterminator or the curious knock of her super. This was forceful, insistent pounding.

THUMP. THUMP. THUMP.

She walked to the foyer and stood there, listening, too frightened to look out the peephole. She gripped the bag of kettle corn as if for protection.

Then, hesitantly, "Who is it?"

A voice, deep and male.

"It's the police. We need you to open the door."

Her scalp prickled. Could Pauline or someone from the wedding have actually called the police on her? For, like, menacing, maybe, or attempted assault?

She had to think.

She had rights, didn't she?

What were her rights, what were her rights, what were her rights?

THUMP THUMP THUMP.

Why hadn't she paid attention in criminal procedure?!

She decided to get more information.

"What is this regarding?" she asked.

A second, gentler voice said, "We need you to open the door. Your sister called. She's worried about you."

My sister? What the fuck?

Things were veering left. She said, in her most authoritative voice, "I don't have a sister, and I'm fine in my apartment, you can leave."

The first voice told Vivian, "Look miss. If you don't open the door we will have to break it down."

Vivian rocked back and closed her eyes, disappearing momentarily into the burning orange at the back of her eyelids.

"Can you please clarify who called? I don't have a sister." she begged. "Can I give you some names, and you let me know who it was? I don't have a sister!"

She imagined Pauline calling the cops, posing as her sister. Or was it Cristina? She'd thoroughly apologized to Cristina when she got back from her honeymoon. In a drunken and tear-filled monologue, she'd blamed her fixation on Pauline and her nutso behavior on her bad childhood and, like, intersectional oppression. Pauline "triggered" her. It was mostly true. And it always worked on *Real Housewives*. Maybe Cristina hadn't bought it.

The man outside said, "I don't have that information on me and I'm not getting cell service up here. Just a family member who is worried about you. Open up."

A family member. Now she understood.

Vivian leaned against the wall, a quaking entity gripping a kettle corn bag, unable to form sentences. After some time, she walked to the peephole and saw two cops, both in their twenties. *Fucking zygotes,* she thought.

The cop on the left was white and had the deep voice and uncaring tone. The gentler voice had come from the South Asian cop on the right. Her eyes couldn't focus long enough to get their names and badge numbers.

Vivian explained that she'd cut off contact with her family and now they were getting back at her by calling the cops.

The white cop insisted again that this was standard protocol.

"A family member calls and says they are worried, you aren't acting like yourself, we have to check on you," he said. "And we aren't leaving until you open the door. You don't want to open it, we'll do it for you."

She started to cry. "I can't open the door to strange men," she heard herself say. Surely, this honesty, this disarming vulnerability might help her out of this situation.

"You can't open the door to strange men, what does that mean?"

She looked out of the peephole to see the white cop laughing. Then a look flashed across his face. She recognized that look. It was the same look she'd seen on Nurse Jackson's face when the patient on the ward had asked her a question and she'd smelled his odor. It was on John's and Judge Mitchell's faces when a client had an outburst, and Dr. Creslin's when he testified against someone unassimilable. It was a look of disgust.

She started to realize that she had to open the door, but her body would not allow it. It resisted. It shook. Her trembling hands had turned white and were freezing. Fugitive pain returned to her lower back. There it was: what she had been trying to describe in the snatched seconds of the day, in the Notes app on her phone. She knew it now, realized it as the central fear at the core of her personality, the fear that it would happen again, the inability to control her body, the inability to control whether she lived or died. How could she trust the boy-soldiers at the door, how could she trust anyone anymore?

There was only one person she could call.

Jane picked up after the third ring.

"Oh my god I love you for not screening," Vivian cried into the phone. "You should screen, though! Why are you answering an unknown number like it's 1985?"

"Vivian? Girl, I thought you were my breakfast tacos. What's wrong?"

"There are cops here. I cut off my family last month and now they called the cops on me and the cops are saying I have to open the door. *I'm fucking high, dude,*" she whispered. "I'm freaked out and can't open the door, I think I have like low-key PTSD or something."

Jane went into action. First, she requested the number of one of the cops so that she could speak to him directly. The cop gave Vivian a number that she relayed to Jane, who dialed from her computer while staying on the phone with Vivian.

Jane spoke to the white officer and explained to him that she was Vivian's best friend, and that Vivian had told her over the phone that she was safe, and that they could leave.

This didn't work, so Jane shifted tactics, telling them that Vivian had post-traumatic stress disorder, and that she was currently being activated.

"Activated, what the hell is that?" he asked.

"Vivian's mind knows, Officers, what she needs to do. Her mind knows that she should just open the door because you are performing a wellness check that you're required to perform because of liability, or whatever. Under normal circumstances, Vivian's fear would be overridden by her rational understanding that the cost of opening the door would be nothing compared to the monetary cost of replacing her door, not to mention the further traumatization of having men with guns forcibly enter her home, and the humiliation of that entire scene, played out for her neighbors, super, and landlord. But Vivian is unable to access this rationality now, because she is in the grips of trauma."

That, and I reek of weed, Vivian thought.

"Look, Miss, this is our protocol," the white officer told Jane. "How do we know there isn't someone in there with a knife to her throat? Her throat gets slit in there by some maniac, it's on us. We just need to see that she's okay, then we'll leave."

Jane hung up with the cop and advised Vivian to open the door.

"Put me on FaceTime," she said sweetly. "So I can be there."

It was the greatest idea of all time, and Vivian did as she was told. Jane appeared through her phone in a burgundy headwrap and a white linen button-down shirt, sitting on the navy-blue couch where they'd watched so many movies together.

"I'm so fucking sorry, dude, about what I said before and what I did to Beyoncé," Vivian said, in a new torrent of tears and laughter at the absurdity of the sentence.

Jane laughed too, and softened. "It's good to see your face," she said back.

Out in the hall, a neighbor was leaving her apartment. The officers called her over. Vivian looked through the peephole and saw Roseydi carrying a dozen bags. She could kiss her.

Vivian explained to her in broken Spanish what was going on.

"It's okay, mama," Roseydi said through the peephole, her wig slightly askew. "It's okay to come out."

Slowly, Vivian opened the door.

She must have been a sight. Hair frizzing in a million directions. Puffy eyes. White face and hands. Armed with the kettle corn. She showed the officers that she was safe and went to close the door, but they insisted that she step out so they could see both sides of her body, "to make sure no one's got you in there."

"No one has 'got me,'" Vivian said, with just enough irritation as to not be tackled.

They said again that they couldn't offer any further information as to why they were there. They didn't apologize. They simply turned and left, sighing and shaking their heads.

Vivian turned to Roseydi, who held out her arms. Vivian stepped into them and let herself be held.

"You're safe, mama, you're safe," Roseydi repeated, patting her back. "Just let it out. Let it all out."

Vivian's feet were planted on the carpeted hallway in the building she had lived in for years. She had shoulders. She heard Jane ask, "Are you okay?"

Startled, Vivian laughed. "I forgot you were on the phone." Roseydi gave Vivian one last squeeze, patted her shoulders, and said goodbye.

"Come over later if you want, mama," she said. "They had a sale at Foodtown for chicken thighs! I'm making chicken soup tonight."

Back inside her apartment Vivian looked down into Jane's face.

"I missed you so much," she said to Jane. "Anytime anything misogynistic happens I always want to text you about it."

"So you're saying you wanted to text me like every five minutes?"

"Basically," Vivian said.

"I missed you, too. Collier's been driving me crazy. She's obsessed with documenting the opioid crisis in the Hudson Valley. I just wanted weekends upstate, but I'm starting to feel trapped inside an issue of *National Geographic*."

"Thank God," Vivian said laughing. "I thought she was replacing me in your heart and soul."

"That's impossible," Jane said. "No one is like you, you know?"

"No one is like you, either," Vivian said.

Later Vivian called her local precinct to make a complaint, planning a whole statement about how her rights had been violated, but when she dialed the number no one answered and the call went to voice mail.

Next she tried the precinct's domestic violence coordinator. A man picked up. Vivian explained the estrangement situation and said that if anyone called these gun-wielding morons again, no one should be dispatched because she didn't need a wellness check.

"My family is more of a danger to me than I am to them," Vivian said.

The coordinator laughed. "How old are your parents, in their sixties? How are they a danger to you, sweetheart?"

Vivian's eyes filled with tears for the tenth time. *These motherfuckers.*

"Besides, this is just the first time they've done this," he said. "Wait to see if it happens again, then call us back and see if we can do anything."

He indicated that he would make a "note" in the "system" and send it upstairs to the precinct, "but I can't make any guarantees," he said.

———◆———

Vivian waited for Jane outside the precinct. According to her research, she didn't have any cause of action against the police. They hadn't actually broken her door down yesterday.

"Thanks for coming, dude," Vivian said as Jane took the stairs to the precinct two at a time. She wasn't sure what else to do or say.

"Of course." Jane hugged her. "Channeling Maxine Shaw today, I see."

Vivian laughed with relief. She'd made sure to dress like a lawyer, it was true—black skirt suit, heels, and red lipstick.

A female officer, Durba, greeted them in the precinct lobby entrance. As Vivian spoke, Durba's face lit up in recognition. She was the officer who had fielded the calls.

Durba said that yesterday a man had called the precinct many times, that he'd said he was Vivian's brother, and that the calls were from another state. The man had said that someone claiming to be his sister had texted him from a strange number.

"He kept calling, so worried about your messages."

"Well, I was cutting them off."

Durba shrugged. "He said the texts didn't sound like you."

Vivian's chest tightened. Michael didn't know at all what she sounded like.

"That's it?" Jane asked. "That's all he said, and you sent someone running over there?"

Durba nodded.

"So there was no allegation that I was a harm to myself or that I was in imminent danger?" Vivian said. "That's right, I know the standard."

"She's a lawyer," Jane added.

"Still," Vivian continued, "a decision was made, based on phone calls from someone in another state with no evidence of danger, to dispatch two male police officers to the home of a public servant, and when I verbally assured them that I was safe, they refused to leave, threatening to break down the door, forcing me to have a panic attack, and now leaving me unsafe in my own home? That's what you're saying."

"I see you're upset. And I'm sorry this happened. But we had to dispatch someone. It is protocol in these situations."

"What if I die?" Vivian asked. Jane rubbed her back.

"Calm down, ma'am, please."

"What if I'm murdered in my own home by a trigger-happy legacy cop from Staten Island because you needlessly dispatch someone to my home?" Vivian banged her hand on the table, sending a loud echo through the precinct lobby. People with guns turned toward her and Jane.

"I'm sorry," she said, putting her hands up automatically, her voice breaking as she turned back to Durba.

"Can you please help her?" Jane asked. "Is there anything that can be done so that this doesn't happen again?"

Durba's brown eyes registered Vivian's pain. Either that, or she was afraid of a formal complaint being filed, an assemblyperson called. Durba spoke quickly to assure them that this would not happen again.

"I can place a note next to your address for the operator to see."

Vivian relaxed a little.

"If anyone calls again, dispatch will not be sent."

"I have your word?"

"My word, yes."

At the diner from a window booth, Jane ordered tea for them. Vivian's face was all wet and she felt raw, flayed open. For a while all she could do was tear her napkin into shreds of equal length, carefully arranging them in a line in front of her. When she tore the last piece, Jane handed her another napkin and she did it again. She looked out the window for long periods, gripping the little teacup with both hands, calmed somehow by the ritual of holding the cup, sipping from it, and setting it down.

"Anything that would make you feel better?" Jane asked. She was pointing at the menus, hesitantly optimistic.

Normally there was such a barrier between Vivian and comfort, but now she instantly knew the answer. "Pancakes."

"Cool." Jane smiled at her reassuringly. "Pancakes."

They were buttery and golden brown. She cut them in half and then into quarters before smothering them in glugs of syrup. She ate them all, savoring the crisp edges, cleaning the plate with her finger.

Jane insisted on taking her home and staying awhile. She made more tea for them, then proposed a singer-actress marathon. *Carmen Jones, Pillow Talk, Where the Boys Are.*

"I used to hate being forced to watch *Carmen Jones* when I was a kid. Now I'm singing along to all the songs," Jane said.

"Who made you watch it?"

"My mom. She needed something on for hair-washing day. She'd sit us down and comb and braid our hair after. What little we had." Jane laughed. "But somehow she made it last the whole two hours." Jane seemed to glow then, briefly giving herself over to reverie. "Anyway, sorry to—"

"It's fine, you're good," Vivian said.

As Dorothy Dandridge ordered Harry Belafonte to blow on her freshly painted toenails ("Makes 'em dry faster") Vivian said, "Is this the movie that got me into foot worship?"

"Seriously. She's so hot in this."

"They both are."

Pillow Talk heralded a whole other world of male beauty. "Where have I been?" Vivian squealed. "Rock Hudson is a beautiful man. He's too tall to fit into the car? I'm a mere mortal, this is too much to handle."

"They were best friends, him and Doris Day. She was like one of the only people who knew he was gay."

"Did Tony Randall just slap her? Jesus. You should make a supercut of men hitting women to end their hysteria."

"Totally. Screen it at my dissertation defense."

Then, in *Where the Boys Are,* a surprise assault in the third act. "I thought this was a spring break romp. You mean this whole time, the Connie Francis song was, like, a warning?"

"Pretty much. It turns out that *Where the Boys Are...* there's rape."

The films were each about sixty years old, but relatively speaking, that wasn't so long ago. It was a world Vivian recognized. There were cars and a black woman with some rights, singing in a mixed club. And then men hit women in public without warning, to control their behavior. It was important, after all, to document this.

"I can't wait to read your book," she told Jane. Jane said she couldn't wait to read Vivian's, either.

When Jane left, Vivian got scared again. What if someone else called from a different number? What if the operator didn't see the note? What if the note was overridden by someone with more authority and a different opinion of the situation?

Minutes passed in worry, and then Reginald jumped up onto the couch next to her. She watched him, cautiously gauging his desires. He looked at her solicitously and began to purr, so she reached out a hand, gently rubbing his chin and neck. Then, in a hypnotic daze, he kneaded the area beside her with his front paws while drooling, before slowly curling into a ball and drifting off. She petted him as he slept, watching his spotted belly rise and fall.

CHANGES (PART ONE)

NOW THAT VIVIAN finally had time to herself, she intended to use it better than anyone else had ever used time, in the history of time users. She would write a phenomenal book of undeniable genius. But other tasks clamored for her attention. She simply had to rid her email inbox of all that spam, Reginald must be played with for a full hour, and she had waited long enough to deep-clean the refrigerator using a homemade paste of baking soda and white vinegar.

Fuck it, she thought one day while rolling a spliff, intending to lower her inhibitions and ride some thought-waves all the way to literary fame. The inhibitions were lowered, all right. Two exhales later and she was launched into a terror-fueled daydream of the police coming back to assassinate her. They'd come at night while she was asleep and she wouldn't be able to hear them banging at the door. They would have no choice but to break the door down like they had threatened before and they'd enter the apartment and they'd shoot her and she would die. The shooting would happen in slow motion, of course, since, even at her most disordered, Vivian was still susceptible to the influence of cinema, or at least, like, the Wachowskis. The shot would be slow-motiony enough that she could hear the crack of the bullet followed by the thump of the round leaving the chamber, then the lump of searing metal burrowing its way inside her. The daydream ran on a loop, killed a hundred times in a single afternoon.

But even when she wasn't spellbound by marijuana, there was too much noise in the hall. Piercing voices, rolling carts, heavy gaits with bomblike steps, locks clicking and the doors, always doors opening and closing and slamming and creaking. *Who the fuck wants to leave the house,* Vivian wondered. She startled at every movement or voice out there. Was that high-pitched yawp a woman laughing or a woman screaming? Is a child playing or is a child being hit? Is the super passing by, or are those *footfalls coming toward me*? Increasingly, her tendency was to assume danger rather than benevolence, so that, for instance, she knew the man coughing just outside her door was doing so to lure her out, and once she stepped into the hall he would grab her, force her back into the apartment, assault her, and then strangle her with a computer cord, an extension cord, or his own leather belt. While hiding all the cordlike materials in the apartment she heard the elevator bell ring, and the coughing man, presumably, got into it.

It took hours to go anywhere. She started making calculations like *How many streets do I have to cross in order to get to the grocery store, and of those streets, how many involve the risk of being hit by a left-turning car, left-turning cars being the most dangerous to a pedestrian, and of those, the majority being sport utility vehicles driven by men.* She was back to staying indoors and using paper towels to wipe herself again. It was a mess.

One day she managed to write, *I'm becoming my mother.* She thought of Anita, trembling in Midtown, and her heart broke for her maker while she judged her own mind. She knew she had to speak to someone.

Jane was full of opinions about this and said she could only ever have a black therapist. "I'm not telling white people my secrets," she said.

Vivian thought having a white therapist might actually be easier. "Less pressure? To be some kind of black, you know," she said. "I'd be so busy thinking they were going to judge me for listening to the Carpenters or whatever that I wouldn't be able to *get well*."

"Or maybe," Jane said, peering down over her in a pair of oversized glasses worn for show, "you just grew up around a bunch of white people and are more comfortable with them."

"You're not wrong. But seriously, it's really comforting being around white people! If they ever challenge you, you can just accuse them of being racist."

Jane laughed. "You know what, Vivian? Don't overthink it, just do you."

———

Lisa was a social worker with double Ivy credentials. Her bare-bones website seemed self-designed, and on it she wrote that we all develop defense mechanisms to help us to survive our childhoods. In therapy, she went on, we can decide which of those defenses we'd like to keep, and which ones aren't serving us anymore. Vivian liked this approach, as well as Lisa's glancing mention of feminism, and scheduled an appointment.

Knowing that Lisa would be evaluating her, Vivian spent

some time before the first session lining her lips and model-
ing outfits. She exclusively wore a minimizer bra these days,
not wanting to be reminded of her expansion or her sex.
She chose a long black tunic over black skinny jeans to
further confound a judgmental eye. On the way there, Vivian
Googled Lisa and scrolled through her personal social media.
She was married and had three children that she seemed to
be raising without violence in New Jersey.

When Vivian arrived at the ritzy co-op building that housed
Lisa's office suite, she was suddenly very thirsty. The waiting
room was painted a dreamlike blue, with innocuous close-up
photos of plants, trees, and flowers on the walls, and white
noise machines outside each of the three therapy offices. She
gulped down two paper cups of water courtesy of the cooler
and walked through the small space, straining to overhear
one of the sessions, but she couldn't discern anything.

The *Psychology Today* selection on the wall was a cultural
critic's playground: a white woman trapped inside a box
was meant to depict depression, a white woman sitting
in an Oscar-the-Grouch-looking trash can demonstrated the
pain of being rejected, and a white woman painted like
a devil showed that we all have dark thoughts. *Have the
models even consumed enough calories to have complex emotions,
though,* Vivian thought, while bracing for one of the doors
to open.

Minutes later, Lisa came out into the waiting room, where
Vivian sat posed in an armchair, fingering the rim of her third
cup of water.

"Vivian?"

Lisa had stringy deep-brown hair, looked late forties-ish,
and was wearing an oversized camel-colored poncho sweater

over boot-cut denim jeans and brown clogs. She seemed friendly and guileless, like an American dog.

Vivian followed Lisa into a snug, lamplit room with an oak desk, a bookshelf filled with psychology classics, a red Persian rug, a leather couch overrun with throw pillows, and a low dark brown leather armchair that matched Lisa's hair.

"What is it about a Persian rug that makes me want to open up emotionally?" Vivian began, kicking at it with her foot.

Lisa laughed and closed the door. She smiled warmly at Vivian and gestured for her to sit on the couch across from the armchair, which Lisa now sank into.

While looking at the bookshelf, and not Lisa, Vivian slowly pulled out the notebook she'd packed and opened it to a blank page, uncapping a blue pen with her teeth.

"I love Karen Horney," she said, causing Lisa to look over at the bookshelf. When Lisa turned, Vivian spied a tiny desk clock that she could look at to gauge the time and noted that Lisa drank Starbucks, even in the evenings.

"Oh yeah?" Lisa said, amused. "What do you like about her?"

"She's a good writer. And her theory of neurotic types is my favorite. I love the phrase 'morbid dependency,'" Vivian said in a Mid-Atlantic accent.

"Yeah, I always felt like her concept of 'womb envy' should've taken off more." Lisa waited a beat. "Too bad we live in a patriarchy!" she said. Her smile was so warm and pure that Vivian couldn't help but smile too, though the joke was a bit on the nose.

Before Lisa could say anything else, Vivian said, "Anyway. I guess I'll start."

She moved up to the front of the couch, shifted her legs

in Lisa's direction, sat up straight, and stared at Lisa while she spoke.

"I just cut off my family because they are all insane and I don't like them. No, you know what, *I hate my family*. Fuck families *in general*. I need a T-shirt that says *I survived the nuclear family and all I got was post-traumatic stress disorder* and then on the back it'll say *and this lousy T-shirt*. But seriously. I don't know what it means to 'have' post-traumatic stress disorder and I don't want to be limited by it, so I'll say I'm experiencing those symptoms. My family is trash, they let me get treated like shit in front of them, beaten in front of them, raped, all the stuff little girls go through, and then when I tried to declare my freedom they called the cops to my apartment and I had a bit of an extreme reaction in that I couldn't open the door to the cops and I was convinced they were going to attack me, ha ha. This was completely irrational, I feel scared for myself, and worried about the stuff that is happening now, which I'll get to in a second."

Vivian took a drink of water without taking her eyes off Lisa. She continued:

"But I also feel in touch with myself and with the pain I am experiencing. I feel clear on that point—that I am in pain. I'm suffering, man. And it seems like something worth exploring through art, you know, a particular kind of female suffering. I quit my job! I was a lawyer at a psychiatric hospital, so I know a lot about your field, Horney and stuff, I'm like an amateur psychologist, I could've been a therapist if only I had more empathy, I'm very *judgmental*, you know, I don't like it when people *fail*, mistakes embarrass me. I am still haunted by the fact that, if I'd had a chain lock on the door when the cops showed up, it wouldn't have been such a big deal, I probably could've opened the door faster, so it feels like it's all my fault. Also I got dumped by this musician who I thought was my soul mate (*turns out he just activated my attachment system*). My friend Max got me a new gig reviewing documents for corporate lawsuits, and I can do it from home in my spare time because, well, the plan was to write a novel but the thing is I sit there and I don't write anything because I'm too afraid, the things I hear out in the hall are very scary and I start spinning out, imagining my own murder. I mean, I've gone insane. Not *insane* insane, because I'm not even capable of that, but insane for me. I'm basically being killed every day. If not by the police then random men. I had to stop running in the park because I was convinced that a perpetrator was gonna hit me in the head with a tire iron and drag me off into a wooded area, where he'd rape, choke, and dump me. Lots of choke-and-dump fantasies. So then I tried to run in the neighborhood, but I was convinced I was gonna get hit by a left-turning car. So if it's not, like, literal traumatized-feminist-type scenarios then it's a more Freudian situation where the car is the *symbol* of the male violence I'm ultimately, completely incapacitated by. So then I can't run, and I'm just blowing up, you know, I keep getting bigger, and then I wrote it here, in my notebook, see, *I'm becoming my mother*, aka, an overweight agoraphobe who will never amount to anything. And I'm here, I guess, because there is nothing I can do about it."

Vivian stopped talking, finally, and began to pick at the lint on her black jeans while watching Lisa intensely. Before Lisa could say anything, she added, "So, that was a lot. What are you thinking?"

"Honestly?" Lisa said.

"Please," Vivian said, making a "be my guest" gesture.

"You sound really *prepared*," Lisa said in a nonjudgmental way. "It kind of felt like you were making a speech just now or, delivering a monologue in some play."

Vivian laughed.

"That's good," she said. "It's true."

And then, in a split second, as if to demonstrate her skill, Lisa turned serious. "But I am hearing that you've just had a very traumatic event, with the police banging on the door and threatening to break it down. That sounds really *scary*. And it sounds like you had significant trauma before this event, and are going through profound changes."

Vivian knew that Lisa had been trained to say these things, to reiterate and to affirm. Normally she'd be turned off by all this sympathy, looking at it through a filter of irony and criticism. But Lisa seemed genuine.

"And I want you to know that what you are experiencing right now makes sense. Based on what's just happened to you, it's understandable that you're afraid. It's understandable that you have bizarre thoughts and that you're suspicious. Your adrenaline must be through the roof."

"You know that I shower with the door open and my back against the wall? So that I can see everything," Vivian said suddenly.

"That sounds really hard. Your home is supposed to feel safe," Lisa said.

Lisa said it didn't matter, to her, whether Vivian endorsed a PTSD diagnosis or not. The label wasn't important to her, but it was important to address Vivian's very real, very valid, physiological disturbances first, because if those were overloading her system they would interfere with Vivian's ability to do any of the higher-order thinking and functioning she needed to be creative.

"I'm wondering if there's anything that would make you feel safer in your apartment. Maybe if you got a chain lock, because then, if the police come again, you could open the door with the chain still on, so you'd have that extra sense of safety. What if you got one of those?"

Vivian nodded slowly, like a child, and scrawled it in her notebook as a to-do.

"If you start to feel a little safer, maybe then we can get you to that point where you can feel comfortable enough to start writing," Lisa said.

They decided to see each other a couple of times a week, and Lisa offered a discounted rate. She also suggested that Vivian join a support group for adults estranged from their families. She would send along some referrals. Vivian agreed to this and left feeling temporarily reassured, but later remembered her distrust of traumatized people in groups. Though she wished to be the type of woman who could "heal" in a support group, she knew, from her work at the hospital, that such groups were likely to reproduce abusive dynamics, so she read about familial estrangement on the internet instead.

First, she read an essay by a woman who had estranged herself when she was in her late twenties. The woman had been physically abused by her father as a child, and once by her brother when she was an adult in the bathroom and wearing only a towel. When she confronted her mother and father about the abuse, the father blamed her, saying she was a difficult child, and the mother made economic excuses ("Where would we have gone?"). They fought for hours. Soon after, she cut them off. Years later, her father called and said he was in the town where she lived and wanted to see her. Vivian frantically read as the woman described the sense of danger she felt that day, how she instinctively fled to a hotel and called her therapist, how her partner stayed home and dealt with the father. The day did not end in a meeting or a violent episode or reconciliation. The woman had a support system in place and she knew, now, how to keep herself safe.

Vivian closed her computer and cried, then called a nearby Polish locksmith, a compact and balding man who sang a ballad from his country to himself as he efficiently worked to install the "beautiful, bright brass" chain lock that he assured her could withstand over two hundred pounds of pressure. She tipped him fifty percent because he was fast and didn't objectify her, and when he left she practiced sliding the chain into the lock over and over until she was satisfied.

Vivian read another essay by a young white woman whose father had repeatedly called her and emailed her after she cut off contact with him. He would have his toddler leave the woman voice mails. He had his wife call the woman to try to talk her out of the estrangement. When the woman blocked his email address, he invented new email addresses. In one email, he threatened to "hunt her down." She spent some time considering getting a restraining order against her father but ultimately did not; it felt stupid to do so, and somehow not appropriate.

Before reading this essay, Vivian had thought she would not like the writing of the young white woman writer. She had believed that the young white woman writer's work would be characterized by the disaffected irony of a white person who has not experienced anything traumatic, yet still suffers. But in the end Vivian was grateful for the woman's bravery in articulating her experience. Vivian felt less ashamed and grateful for the ability to change her mind about someone.

Later she joined an online forum for estranged adults, reading with frenzied interest the members' stories of abuse, chaos, and neglect. Some of the members had worse childhoods than hers. They had had injuries requiring hospitalization. They had not been believed when they had told, or they had been blamed. Others had better childhoods than hers. The worst thing that had happened to them was a cruel divorce, or watching their mother break the china dishes. But they had all decided to walk away from a family system that seemed to promote harm. Sometimes a final act of betrayal led them to estrangement, but more often than not it was a seemingly banal incident that felt, to the estranger, indicative of the larger problem within the relationship, which often had to do with a lack of acknowledgment of past abuse, being misunderstood or not heard, or the estrangee violating clearly established boundaries.

One night Vivian made an impulsive post about what had happened that day with the police. *Has this happened to anyone before?* she wrote. It had.

One after the other, the forum members told their stories, explaining that this was a normal part of the estrangement process. In the days immediately following cutoff, they said, the estrangee would often behave in ways that seemed hysterical and violating. They might show up at the estranger's workplace, leave massive amounts of voice mails featuring a roller coaster of tonalities from anger to contrition, or send dozens of unwanted emails or letters or packages to the house or workplace of the estranger. Sometimes, as in Vivian's case, they called the police to do a wellness check. The forum members referred to these acts collectively as an "extinction burst," a behavioral psychology term referring to a blast of defiance when the brain is denied a familiar reward. Often, as part of the extinction burst, the estrangee would send other family members to the estranger's house or have them call the estranger to try to talk her out of what she had done. The people on the forum referred to these family members as "flying monkeys" because they serve at the command of the estrangee. Members encouraged Vivian to stay strong. *You did the right thing*, one of them wrote. *And I know that you will get through this.*

Some days Vivian was convinced that as long as her family knew her address she was in mortal danger. They would show up at her apartment, demanding that she open the door, making a scene, embarrassing her in front of her neighbors, ruining her life. But then Lisa reminded her that, like the woman in the estrangement book, like the woman in the essay, and like all of the adult children estrangers, Vivian knew how to keep herself safe and that in a way, though Vivian strained to imagine the worst thing possible, her family had already done the worst thing possible, by calling the police, because the police were the only people she could not say no to.

———◆———

"I'm so angry at Anita today!" Vivian said to Lisa one day.

"What has she done, to make you angry?" Lisa asked.

The night before, Vivian had woken up from a nightmare, though she didn't remember what it was about. She explained, "I just lay there after, cycling through bad memories. It's like channel flipping. On this channel I'm saying a bad word and being shoved into a wall by her boyfriend, on this channel I'm blowing bubbles outside and then I talk back and he makes me drink the bubbles, and then I'm choking on the bubbles. And I became very angry at Anita, for leaving me alone with a sadist."

But the channel she ultimately landed on was the one years later, after the violent man, when Anita and Julio had thrown her blind cat out on the street. Noodles, an orange-and-white tabby, developed cataracts at fifteen and started peeing on everything: the floor, clothes, towels, area rugs. It was driving Anita and Julio crazy. Vivian was thirteen when she came home from school and found Noodles in the driveway.

"I thought it was an accident at first, you know, so I brought him into the house. Anita leapt off the couch, screaming, and ordered me to take him back outside. He'd peed on the new curtains, apparently, and that was the last straw. Julio had been the one to throw him out. He was the decision maker, you know. Anita's yelling was a bit over-the-top, to be honest, a little *too loud*, like she needed *him* to hear that she was on board with his decision. But I also think she was trying in her stupid way to protect me from *him* yelling at me? And again, he never hit or anything—yelling is the furthest he would go. But she would often do that, anticipatory yelling. In addition to the regular yelling. That's like the only intervention she could come up with, to preemptively side with him. It was bizarre and made a cruel kind of sense, but it only made me hate her more."

"What did you feel in that moment?" Lisa asked.

Vivian shrugged. "I don't remember."

"Did you cry, do you think?"

"Hell no. Fuck them. I wouldn't let them see me cry. I got yelled at, took the cat back outside, and petted him a few times, saying my goodbyes. And then I went back inside and didn't think about it for several years."

"I'm so sorry that happened to you."

"He was blind! I mean who does that?" Vivian wiped the couple of tears that were skimming down her cheeks. She was surprised to see Lisa's eyes welling up too. That hadn't happened before.

"But anyway," Vivian said. She didn't actually want to talk about this anymore, for some reason.

"It's such a cruel thing to do to a child," Lisa said softly.

"They just didn't care about animals, you know," Vivian said quickly. "It's a different culture."

"They also didn't care about *you*," Lisa said.

"But I must not have cared that much myself, because I went inside my room and started fantasizing about some guy from my high school who I was *obsessed* with at the time, and then I called him! I used the thrown-out-cat thing as a way to get sympathy from the boy I liked. See, that was always my priority in life anyway."

"Do you think those things were related? The boy you liked and the cat, the way you went inside and thought about him and then called him?"

Vivian looked blank for a second. "I don't know. I hadn't ever thought about it."

"I wonder, you know. I wonder if male attention was a comfort for you in that moment, and maybe at other moments."

"Probably. I guess," Vivian said, and stared out into space in silence.

CHANGES (PART TWO)

A LATE-SPRING DATE with a filmmaker who had just returned to the city after weeks on the festival circuit began with what she perceived to be an omen: she was early, and he was late. This made her feel that she had less power in the situation automatically and she resented it, but she need not have felt this; the filmmaker would later explain that his ride was late picking him up because she was having her own emotional problems following a rough breakup.

Eventually, she saw a sweaty red figure in a suit standing at the door, looking at her, assessing whether she was the woman he was looking for or not, or perhaps assessing whether, based on what she looked like, he should go through with the date at all. The figure moved closer, said her name with a question mark at the end, and apologized for being late. They hugged hello. The man looked enticing in a way she had experienced before, but also "mildly mentally ill," she thought, likely due to creative isolation.

In order to get a table, she was told that she would have to settle her drink tab at the bar, so they had to sit there, awkwardly, while she settled it, which gave him time to make her describe the book she was reading, but because she was nervous about being on display and hadn't even finished her drink, she couldn't describe it well. She called the writer a *wunderkind* and the filmmaker's face lit up when she said the novel took place in Northern France. He suggested its setting, maybe Lyons, and she said, "No, Picardy? I don't know where that is," to make herself sound meek and vulnerable.

The filmmaker said, "I love books but I never know what to read on my own. I have to hear about them from a friend. Or like I'll be in a bookstore and then just stumble upon something and be like, 'What is this weird book?'"

By this point she was signing her check and said, "Oh, that happens to me too. Like when I go on vacation, when I travel, I have to have, like, my travel book. I will experience great anxiety if I don't find the right book to travel with. I also experience great anxiety about having too many choices. So what I do is I go to my local library, which is a small library, and I just wander the stacks until I find the book, you know, but it's very loaded, like, *What if I don't find the right book?* Once I went on vacation to Miami and I didn't have a book with me and I still experience regret about it. Like, the vacation would have been so much better if I had had a book to read, I still can't believe I didn't bring a book with me."

She stood up to reveal her outfit, which had been carefully chosen to evoke timelessness: black pilgrim sack dress, black platform sandals, gold hoops, and a gold cuff bracelet.

Once they got their table, the filmmaker took the seat against the wall, which was typically her preference but she allowed it. He said he'd been in meetings all day. She replied that she hated meetings and smiled. The filmmaker then said that he was in meetings with "like, the Safdie brothers" and she said, "Oh, so you're in interesting meetings then." He told her that, according to various producers and executives, the only two kinds of films that could be financed these days were sequels and adaptations.

"Fascinating," she said, and he asked her which films she liked. She listed white faves: Robert Altman, Whit Stillman, David Lynch. The filmmaker said he believed it was very possible that *Twin Peaks* involved something true that happened in his hometown. A fisherman had found the body of a teen-aged girl stuffed into a large trunk, and she looked just like Laura Palmer.

"That would make a great podcast," she said.

The filmmaker tried to impress her by saying he was raised in a matriarchy but "not like—" and then she completed his sentence, "not like in a cult." He laughed and said no, his mother and grandmother just "ran the show" and the women he grew up around "were like tomboys." She wondered whether the platform sandals had been a mistake.

There were moments when he made lingering eye contact and looked at her hands as if to touch them and he expressed spontaneous gaiety at the quality of her monologues. She felt blissed out then, and thought he was falling for her.

When they left the restaurant, he hugged her and said, "Well, I'm going to meet a friend, so." She was crushed, but then he added that he was "in town until Wednesday." She stumbled over her words, saying she was maybe free on Sunday and definitely free on Monday. He told her to text him and they both kind of ran away. The next day they made a date for Monday, which he then canceled, and she never saw him again.

In the days following the encounter, Vivian obsessed over the filmmaker. In her mind, they traveled together throughout the Pacific Northwest and the high desert of New Mexico. They worked on projects and exchanged ideas. He recommended poetry and Taoist texts, and she shared her favorite novels and the great classics of psychology. They took turns sharing their favorite films, at one point cuddled up together in a tent wearing rain slickers. Vivian accompanied the filmmaker to award ceremonies; other women wanted to be her. Due to his modest fame, they were photographed regularly, always laughing with all the force of life and love.

"It's completely absurd!" Vivian said to Lisa in therapy one day, after describing the fantasies.

Lisa laughed. "What's absurd about it?"

"We had one date and I'm obsessed! I know he's just the Guy of the Month and I don't *want* to be thinking about him, I want to be over him. And I don't want to have these fantasies anymore. They're embarrassing," Vivian said, making a face.

"Getting over feelings of interest and caring isn't easy. It takes time. Those feelings hang around for a while, you know, they don't just get banished," Lisa said.

"I know. But I don't like it," Vivian said, mock-pouting.

"None of us do!" Lisa said. "What about what we talked about before, with your childhood cat getting thrown out and about how these fantasies play a role for you, does that feel right?"

"I think so. I think I use the fantasies to feel better about stuff. In this case—rejection. And honestly? I feel like I need them to get to sleep."

"These fantasies are kind of genius, in a way."

"Do go on," Vivian said, hand on chin.

Lisa believed Vivian's developing brain contrived her romantic fantasies to form connections with people and to stir up amorous feelings that might make her feel better when she was anxious, depressed, or bored. The fantasies were testaments to Vivian's resourcefulness.

"But now that you're an adult and moving deeper into your recovery, maybe these fantasies aren't feeling so useful anymore? Maybe you're feeling turned off by them a little because you're outgrowing them."

Vivian felt a wave of triumph as Lisa spoke.

"And I think they will start to ease off a bit with time. Until then, don't be so hard on yourself in your thoughts. I think you expect purity from your thoughts. Let me tell you, it's not possible!"

Vivian laughed. "I wanted you to tell me that if I worked really hard, I could make the fantasies go away."

"Well, what you resist persists."

"I also think I fixated on the filmmaker because he leads this creative life. I just thought it would be so inspiring to be with someone like that."

Lisa ventured that Vivian had historically ceded her own creativity to the Guy of the Month, imagining that his creativity would osmotically possess her, without her having to actually do anything. So no wonder ruptures with these men were so catastrophic; proximity to the man held the key to her own creative powers, and when he left, he was taking her creative potential with him.

"But we know that's not true," Lisa said. "You are writing steadily now, whether you're dating someone or not."

"I'm so jealous of him too, though. He's had years to be free and create. I'm just starting in my thirties. I wasted my young years helping people, working in a high-stress environment and for what?"

"Were those years a waste, though? I think you had some very strong political and social commitments that it was important for you to act upon," Lisa said reassuringly.

"I guess," Vivian said, reluctant to be so comforted.

⚬—◆—⚬

Soon after talking to Lisa about the filmmaker, Vivian decided to stop dating altogether. She had clawed her way toward some semblance of a regular writing schedule; cutting out the enormous time suck of romantic entanglement seemed like a natural next step, at least temporarily. So now she had much more free time, but she also found herself without what Lisa called her "primary defense mechanism." She had to take care of herself. It was terrifying.

Vivian wrote all summer in her living room, facing the windows. Most writing sessions were embarrassment-filled terror pits loud with rude voices, hurling accusations. The thing about writing is that you are faced with your entire life. Every subterranean fear, every overwhelming event, and all unspoken desires will come to a writer, unbidden, when she is finally alone with herself. So while writing might seem, to an outside observer, to be the pinnacle of leisure, it is actually, for someone with a highly compromised consciousness, someone like Vivian, a most dangerous occupation.

Oh look at you, a voice would say, *assuming your life is interesting. It's embarrassing to write about yourself, can't you imagine something?* But she discovered a trick. She could argue back. *I love when artists use themselves as the basis for their fiction. Doesn't everyone do that to an extent? There's nothing to be embarrassed about.* And on and on.

Or, she would sit down to write and would become afraid of becoming famous. It didn't matter how far-fetched the notion was, she was hijacked by the terror of being recognized on the street, doxxed and threatened with death online for espousing feminist views or having the wrong opinion about something that didn't matter. So then instead of writing, Vivian was back to shaking with fear and imagining being attacked by strangers.

Often, she thought of her mother. Her feet were cold one rainy day and the only clean socks in the apartment were a purple pair of Halloween booties, covered with black bats and cats, that Anita had gifted her years ago, when she was home for the holidays. "Aren't they cute?" Anita had said. "They were five ninety-nine!" Vivian wept, with automatic and evolutionary affection, while squeezing the socks into a tight ball. Then she slipped into them and got on with the task of writing about it.

That summer, liberals and the media were very concerned with families, threatened as they were by the current administration at the border. Irony seemed insufficient to describe it, but it was curious that just as Vivian was exiting both the family structure and the field of public service, her intellectual and political peers were, for the first time it seemed, looking outside themselves and toward disenfranchised others through the lens of family. It was what she called *a new activism.* She would come to associate that time with a regular, painful interaction with certain loaded phrases like "families being separated" and "children ripped from their mothers." Each encounter with these words provoked a reminder of her own transgression, but it also made her angry that so many people were out there defending family through signs and raised voices, through petitions and phone calls. She knew she would be shunned were she to venture even a minor critique of the covert assumptions of the new activism, so she defensively self-aggrandized, telling herself that the world was not ready for her take on The Family. She was ahead of her time, and maybe this was what it felt like to have antiracist sentiments before a like-minded collective had arisen or to have been against sexism before the First Wave. But then she decided that it was a bit stupid to question the new activism, because even if the women and children that Vivian cared about were trapped *not in a country, but in families,* she wanted to say but didn't, forcible separation by the state was its own horror, likely to produce new traumas and abuses, and besides, child-Vivian wouldn't have wanted to be forcibly separated from her family because it was, at the time, hers.

"If the people suffering at the border weren't in families," she said to Lisa one day, "would anyone care about them? Is that what's being implied there, your suffering is of value *only if* you belong to a family? And this concern about brown families is new, by the way. Families being ripped apart was literally how white people made money and paid off debts, for a century in this country. I'm just tired of this pro-family propaganda, we should be talking about abolishing the family!" she said with a breathless flourish.

Lisa laughed, dutifully, and then put on her empathic face.

"It makes sense," she said. "It makes sense that you would be questioning the family structure. After all, that structure didn't exactly work out for you."

Vivian recoiled at this. She was making an important argument, and what she was saying was true. *So typical for Lisa to deflate my intellectualism, therapists always have to bring everything back to the realm of the autobiographical—*

"What's going on for you right now?" Lisa asked.

"I wasn't actually talking about *my* family just then. I was making a statement with broad applicability and I feel like your comment is, like, taking the air out of what I'm saying," Vivian said.

"I didn't mean to do that," Lisa said. "Is there anything else you'd like to say on the topic?"

"I just don't want to be reminded of them all the time," Vivian said.

"Are you reminded of them all the time?"

"Of course. Families are everywhere. A mother and a daughter in an elevator can set me back for hours," Vivian said, laughing to herself.

"What do you mean by 'set me back'?" Lisa asked.

"I don't know, man," Vivian said, putting her head down. "I cry if I see an adult being affectionate with a child, I cry if I see an adult scolding a child. The whole *relationship* overwhelms me."

"What do you think is going on for you when you see a child getting affection?"

"I'm jealous."

"Anything else?"

Vivian was quiet for a moment.

"Just ... sad."

"What does that feel like?"

"I'm not sure."

"Anything going on in your body?"

"Tightness. In my throat. And stomach."

"Let's just sit here together and breathe, maybe," Lisa said.

"Sure. But I'm not going to cry," Vivian insisted, head still down.

"That's fine."

They sat quietly for a while. Vivian remained with her head between her knees, breathing into the knots, lumps, and resistances. She didn't look at Lisa at all, but she knew she was there. Eventually, beyond the hum of the air conditioner, Vivian started to hear the early-evening traffic outside. It was innocuous, even pleasant.

—◆—

Sometimes she would start reading a book that was so alive, original, wise, or sensuous that she would have to put it down. It was like she couldn't take how good it was. There was the book about a lonely woman who tries to change her life and form a connection with a single mother and her small child, but fails; the book about a man who attempts to turn a transactional relationship with a male sex worker into a non-transactional relationship, but fails; the book about a brilliant woman's unrequited obsession with a man whose brilliance she fears; the book about a man who does a lot of drugs.

The best writing was like a good friend, in the way that it gave you permission to be yourself. If she could do for others what these writers had done for her, these tiny moments of removing shame, she thought, then these months, then years, of doubt and struggle would be worth it.

In desperate need of company, she went to a comedy club with Cristina one night and watched a guy bomb.

"Is there anything worse than a comedian bombing in a room full of strangers?"

Cristina shrugged, digging into an overpriced nacho bowl. "It's information, you know. Nobody laughs, you just go home and make it funnier."

"You're so deep sometimes."

So Vivian went home and made it funnier.

She wrote about a character walking down the street trying to be a subject but being treated like an object. Then the character imagined herself turning into a literal object— in this case, a spoon—and laughed loudly on the street while picturing a giant man picking her up and hurtling her toward his mouth. She wrote a scene about the pain of being home alone without a low-calorie snack. She wrote pages and pages about some violent incident from her childhood that revealed the truth about the abuse of power and how we are all implicated in it, and then she deleted it and wrote jokes instead.

She wrote through the fall and the winter.

It wasn't easy. Negativity and criticism hovered, poised to take over. Sometimes she gave in to the perverse pleasure in being mean, bleak, and angrily ranting. Sometimes she dissociated for hours at a time. Mostly, though, she stayed on track and felt occasionally like a genius. Eventually the sentences started to add up to something resembling a story.

She often felt overwhelming surges of compassion for her former clients. She imagined that if she ever really lost it, if she were ever publicly experiencing what she was now privately experiencing, she would want someone to treat her with kindness rather than hold her down, shackle her, and forcibly inject her with heavy medications that might further traumatize her. Though she couldn't bear a return to public service, she would never forget her clients, survivors all.

One February day, Vivian said to Lisa, "Now that I'm not spending all my energy preparing for future attacks and trying to seduce white dudes, I can write for hours at a time." She laughed. "It's so cool!"

Lisa smiled and looked at Vivian admiringly. "So cool," she said back.

———❖———

Come spring, the human race's collective spirit regenerated, bare shoulders celebrated the shucking off of heavy coats, and eyes feasted on tuliped walkways. The wind was intermittent and when it came, all the leaves gently brushed against one another. Unseen birds chirped everywhere and streams of tourists took pictures of Carrie Bradshaw's apartment.

Then Vivian saw Matthew walking out of a jazz bar in the West Village. There he was, someone who had lived in her mind for a year, standing right across the street from her with his saxophone case on the ground resting against him. She stopped mid-stride and watched him. He was looking down at his phone, as if trying to figure out where to go next. As he tucked a strand of hair behind his ear and bit his lip she felt a surge of affection.

She chewed the inside of her mouth, considering. In less than five steps she could be in front of him.

Apprehension would flash across his face as he saw her beaming up at him, but he would return quickly to that boundless confidence that had simultaneously attracted and frightened her.

She'd say hey and ask him how he was doing and they'd go back and forth a bit. He'd tell her he'd finished a gig—he played this club a couple of times a month—and then he'd ask her how her writing was going.

Vivian would say that when they had known each other, she'd talked about her book at a rate inversely proportional to how often she worked on it.

They would laugh together and break eye contact.

Now, she'd say, it was the reverse. She was almost done with a novel about "the long-lasting cognitive effects of traumatic overwhelm," she'd say. "It's a comedy." But now that she was actually writing, she felt that she almost couldn't talk about it; she was too much implicated in it and if she didn't get it right she didn't know what she would do with herself.

She'd say that in addition to the novel, she was writing casually about her relationship to music. Jazz, particularly bebop, connected her to the history of black brilliance and innovation and it inspired her to call that up within herself. Also, she liked to analyze the faces of the musicians as they played, their little tics. A bassist might bite his lip (ideally, Matthew would understand that this was a reference to his own behavior); a drummer's eyes might roll up into his head. She felt like they were existing both inside and beyond their bodies, as close to something like ecstasy as she had ever seen, and that, she'd say, was what she felt sometimes, when singing or dancing. But it was never like that with writing, which was painful but in the most productive possible way. She would tell Matthew that she sang in a choir now and was really loving it. That winter they performed a multipart Christmas cantata in a packed church with brass and organ and accompaniment.

"I got to sing right up against the horns!" she'd tell him. Some old childlike part of her had returned.

Matthew's face would soften as it had on one of their dates.

"Well, you should come see me play sometime," he'd say. "You can tell me what my tic is."

"I'd love that," she'd respond, unable to stop smiling, unable to maintain eye contact.

A bus barreled by and a cloud of exhaust snapped Vivian out of her reverie.

Matthew looked up from his phone, and Vivian reflexively bounded up the block before he could see her. She sought refuge behind a tree and, feeling like a rom-com heroine and rooting for herself, she laughed.

"No fucking way," she said.

Before heading to Jane's, Vivian decided to treat herself to a late lunch at a small café. On the way there, she heard a man's footsteps behind her, heavy and rapid. No way to tell whether he was a harasser or a man in a hurry. The fact of daylight did nothing to assuage her fear. She jogged ahead automatically and then, when she felt safe, she turned around. The man was hurrying to catch up with his dog, which had become fixated on the hidden treasures in a smoke bush. *My paranoia makes sense,* she reminded herself.

Inside the café, while she was standing at the counter to place her order, the barista asked Vivian if she wanted something from the pastry shelf that she had apparently been staring at.

"I don't know," Vivian said, inhaling the aroma of sweet carbohydrates.

It was a simple question, but she could not answer. Did she "want"? What did it mean to want something? How did you know if you should act on an urge? Would future Vivian regret this decision?

Lisa said the rules and restrictions of diet and exercise were a way to organize the chaotic world she'd grown up in, and to avoid being shamed. Vivian said she just liked being skinny. Either way, her thoughts and habits regarding body image and weight were still deeply entrenched and wouldn't dislodge anytime soon.

She didn't order any pastries, and frowned while pouring half-and-half into her iced Americano until it turned the right color. After this, she selected a straw with a feeling of unreality and slowly put the lid on and, still feeling unreal, inserted the straw through the X-shaped hole in the lid, then sat on a stool to eat her salad next to a woman who seemed to be flaunting her ability to wear white pants.

The woman in white pants had tiny calves, but whatever, she'd probably been born that way. Vivian looked out the window as she ate. A man wearing his long hair in a half-hearted ponytail stood against a parked car. He was talking to an older, balder man. The ponytailed man's hands were in his pockets, his head was tilted as if flirting, and his hip jutted out seductively. It was marvelously womanly. Vivian loved these gestures and memorialized them in a note on her phone. When she looked up again, the ponytailed man had changed his posture. His upper body was fully raised and his legs were spread widely as he spoke, taking up more space while maintaining eye contact with the bald man. Each time she looked back at the ponytailed man he was in a different position, either folding into himself or expanding out, so that finally his stances ceased to be gendered at all, and Vivian was thoroughly contented.

On the subway ride to Jane's there was no drama. The car she was in smelled like salami at first, but then a man sitting across from her sprayed the air with cologne, and when Vivian smiled at him, he smiled back without desire. The old woman next to her was grooving to what sounded like Russian pop, and a mother put her baby on the floor. He was a big baby, a real heavyweight. He just sat there, assessing the world with large unblinking eyes, alert and curious.

The topic at Jane's that night was yo' mama jokes.

"Mmm, yo' mama jokes, so cozy!" Vivian said, rubbing her hands together mischievously.

"Yeah, they reek of the nineties," Jane said, laughing.

"Would they even work today?" Vivian asked. "Like, what if a little kid tells a yo' mama joke and then the other little kid is like, in a little-kid voice, *I don't believe in the nuclear family, so this joke has no effect on me.*"

Jane joined in: "Or the little kid is like, *But I have two moms, so which one are you talking about?*"

"Or the little kid is like, *Because of the toxic dynamics in my family, I'm actually parenting them, so is it really me that you're insulting?*"

"*And why are we spending so much time on our mothers, when we both know that Daddy is the real enemy!*"

When they recovered from their laughter, Jane asked Vivian to help repot her plants. "They do this growth spurt thing in the spring. So you'll have to earn your weed today," Jane said, standing and beginning to arrange some plants on the tarp-covered floor and coffee table.

"Speaking of...," Vivian started. "You should know that at some point during The Fight I kind of...took some of your weed?" She went into an accentuated shrug, palms and eyebrows up. "The Comfort Killer…"

"It was you! You bitch. I thought I was losing my damn mind," Jane said, with a mystified smile.

"I am so sorry, dude. I realize I broke all kinds of codes. But if it makes you feel any better, I paid a major karmic debt for it? As I'm pretty sure it contributed to the events leading to my breakdown."

Jane shook her head and handed Vivian a bag of dirt. "You're working that off, believe me."

Vivian raised up her hands. "At your service!" She rolled up the sleeves of her denim work shirt and got into cross-legged position.

"How do you know when you have to put them in new pots?"

"See this one?" Jane said, picking up the *Calathea ornata* and showing Vivian the holes at the bottom. "The roots are coming out here." The leaves were large with striking white pinstripes on the top, tinged with red underneath. They rustled as Jane touched them.

"And Nicki, my *monstera,* she's tilted. These stems are so heavy," Jane said. "You want the plant to grow up straight."

Jane handed Vivian a money tree.

"I just got this one a few weeks ago and I haven't named her yet. She's already grown to eight inches!"

Vivian watched as Jane got to work on the *Calathea ornata.*

"So first we're going to loosen the plant to get it out of the pot," Jane said. "You can try squeezing the pot and sliding the plant out."

Vivian tilted the money tree to its side and then, cradling the braided trunks between two fingers, carefully squeezed the pot. The soil separated from the side of the pot. She looked inside and marveled at the domed tangle of roots and dirt.

"Wow!" she said. "The roots take the shape of the pot!"

"Yeah! Okay, so now you can kinda jiggle it out."

Vivian slowly lifted what Jane told her was called a "root ball" out of the pot and massaged it per Jane's instructions. The roots were tightly bound at the bottom, but Vivian gently rubbed them loose. Once freed, they revealed themselves to be tan, succulent, and numerous.

"Great job. Now I think with those we might want to gently cut them? To give them some direction."

Jane passed Vivian a pair of scissors and Vivian began to separate the roots slowly and carefully. "There we go, that's better," she said to the plant as she cut.

"Did I do it right?" Vivian asked Jane, showing her the newly freed roots.

"Yeah you did it! Now you can pack some soil into the new pot like I'm doing here," Jane said.

Vivian watched as Jane used a small spade to dump dirt into a larger terra-cotta pot and transferred the *monstera* into it. She tilted her head this way and that as she packed the dirt in.

"It needs to sit in the new pot at the same level as the old pot, see? So we put some new soil in to raise it," Jane said.

"How much soil do I put in?" Vivian asked.

"You can just estimate—here," Jane said, offering Vivian the spade.

"I'll just use my hands," Vivian said. She gripped the trunk in her left hand and, with her right one, dug out handfuls of dirt, which she packed all around the grassy-smelling plant, smoothing out the air pockets with her fingers. The dirt was cool to the touch and she loved how it blackened her nails. She gingerly settled the plant into its new home, taking care to spread out the roots so they'd have room to grow out and looking over at Jane every once in a while to make sure she was on the right track. She scooped a little more soil into the pot, patting and pressing until the plant stood up straight on its own. Once she was satisfied, she rotated the pot, examining the plant. The oval leaves tapered to a point at each end. The older, more fully grown leaves were dark green, shiny and strong to the touch. At the top, lighter-green leaves were slowly unfurling. All over, the tiniest buds had started their ascent. For a short time, Vivian had no thoughts at all.

ACKNOWLEDGMENTS

A writer is lucky to have one good agent; for my debut, I was blessed with two. Thank you to Mariah Stovall for your early belief in this novel, and to Stacy Testa for helping it over the finish line.

Thank you to my editorial soulmate, Jean Garnett, as well as Mike Noon, Barbara Perris, and the entire team at Little, Brown. Thank you to Sharmaine Lovegrove and Maisie Lawrence for giving this novel a home in the U.K.

Thank you to everyone at the Center for Fiction for your early support: my 2018 fellowship there gave me the confidence to finish this book.

Thank you to Anne Horowitz for reading early drafts with such enthusiasm, rigor, and care. Thanks to friends who read portions at pivotal stages: Jess, Christian, and especially Zoe, a rare jewel of a human.

Thank you to Tommy Pico for helping me discover that I wanted to be a writer, and for all the songs.

Thank you to Josh O., for our conversations about writing and life, and to Justin, for our conversations about music and life. Thank you to Jeremy, for keeping my creativity alive in law school.

Thank you to my work friends who have become real friends: Andrea, Brett, Josh E., Maura, and Thomas.

Thank you to Stefanie and Alyson for discussing books with me for five years; you are brilliant readers and incomparable friends.

Thank you to Kelly, for your boundless empathy.

Thank you to Noah, for your unwavering belief in me and my work; thanks too, for laughing with me every day.

Finally, to the survivors of violence that I've known over the years: I'm indebted to your stories, your humor, your resilience, and to the protected environments that we have created. There's no group of people I respect more, and I could not have done this without you.

CHANTAL V. JOHNSON is a lawyer and writer. A graduate of Stanford Law School and a 2018 Center for Fiction Emerging Writers Fellow, she lives in New York.